Cover Design © 2017 Louisa Maggio
Interior Format The Killion Group, Inc.

# TRUTHS

## An ART OF EROS Novel

### Book 1

## KENZIE MACALLAN

Steel Butterfly Press

*To anyone who believes that light can come from darkness with love, this is for you*

# CHAPTER 1

*Marabella was certain* tragedy couldn't strike again. She rubbed her hands up and down on her black knit pants then curled them over the cold, grey armrest. Her knuckles turned white. There were many fears that clouded her life. God, when would she ever get over this one?

The seat next to her shifted as someone sat down. She looked up to see a large man trying to get comfortable in an average-sized seat. He glanced at her sideways without a smile. His bloodshot eyes lacked warmth.

Something curled up inside her but she needed to warn him. "I'm going to apologize now before we take off. I don't like to fly. Turbulence is the worst for me. Just ignore my heavy breathing." Her body stiffened as she suddenly looked down again.

Air rushed out of his nose. "You know flying is the safest way to travel, right?" His Scottish brogue was laced with irritation.

Her head snapped up. "Oh, God, like I haven't been told that a million times!" Her shoulders rounded inward. "I'm so sorry. I didn't mean to snap. I've even studied the mechanics behind it all. I can't get my head around it." She drew her lips tight to prevent her from making more of an ass of herself.

Hanging her head, she started her breathing exercises. Breathe in through the nose and out through the mouth. Lamaze technique 101. She tried to block out a plane packed with Spring Breakers making their way out of the Big Apple to their island location. Excitement crackled in the air and laughter travelled in waves.

He turned to her. "Are you okay? You're not going to pass out on me, are you? Then I would have to hold you for the rest of the flight." His lips curled at the edges.

She tilted her head up as her cheeks warmed in time to see his cocky grin. "No. Oddly enough, I'm okay with the takeoffs and landings. It's the in-between parts that freak me out. I always anticipate the worst." His grin faded as annoyance registered on his face.

A young college guy popped up from the seat in front of her. "Hey baby. Whatcha doin'? Scared to fly? Come to papa. I'll make it all better for you." His words slurred.

Before she could say anything, the man next to her leaned over and grabbed him by his t-shirt. "Hey mate. Why don't you sit down and shut your mouth?"

The drunk's two friends stood up to defend him until the Scotsman stood up to his full height.

"Really?" The look in his eyes warned them he wasn't in the mood to play as they slowly took their seats. He plopped down in his seat and turned to her. "I don't think you'll be hearing from them for the rest of the trip to Cancun."

Life had been a roller coaster ride for her. Her emotions resembled something that had been sent through a shredder. His eyes tried to penetrate her. Could he see the cracks in her wall?

The plane leveled off and was flying smoothly. She calmed herself enough to take a closer look at him. His appearance didn't scream runway model. Thank God. Her late husband wore that curse. It wasn't all it was cracked up to be. His ego outweighed his looks. This man had rugged good looks. Charm came through the dimples in his cheeks. His strong jawline with a slight curve in his nose was accented by a very small cleft in his chin. His full lips were sensuous. The scar above his right eyebrow only added to his appeal, giving him an air of danger. She could only imagine that combination attracted the ladies. She wanted to run her hand through his messy, dark brown head of hair that curled slightly at the ends. Her eyes perused downward. He had the build of a warrior. Given his attitude and presence she should have been intimidated but she wasn't.

Taking him in visually did things to her. She caught her breath at the thought of touching him, creating a jumbled mess of excitement and curiosity with a hint of fear.

Her gaze came back up to see his eyes hadn't left her. She got lost in a pair of deep moss-green eyes with flecks of amber. Her lips parted as she gave a small, almost inaudible gasp. Yep, she got caught ogling. Time paused as they stared into each other's eyes as something unique traveled between them. Her reaction unsettled her making her heart race. She dared to be delighted by the encounter.

"See something you like, sweetheart? What's your name?" He turned on the charm.

Yes, she did see something—or rather some-one—she liked, but she wouldn't let him know that right away. Fear niggled at her edges.

"Marabella Luccenzo. Everyone calls me Mara. And you would be?" Her eyes continued to lock on to his, holding her own as she extended her hand.

"Marabella. That's a beautiful name. MacGregor Creighton. I go by Mac. Are you headed to Mexico for business or pleasure?" Warmth traveled from his hand as lust flickered in his eyes. He grinned like a dog about to chase a ball.

"My sisters kidnapped me for a last-minute forced vacation. Unfortunately, we couldn't get seats together. Otherwise, I would be breathing next to them. Sorry." Any relaxation left her demeanor as her body tightened up and she released his hand.

"Don't apologize. But if I kidnapped you, you wouldn't be sitting alone. You have a death grip on something in your other hand." His eyes zeroed in on her closed hand as his smile faded.

"You're going to think I have the maturity of a twelve-year-old," she sighed. "It's a porcelain dragon. I made him when I was a child. He's light green with yellow spots and used to have gold wings. His name is Eros."

She opened her hand to show him her minute token of security. He smiled at the friendly big eyes and lopsided smile on the dragon's face. As he tried to reach for Eros, she drew her hand away and closed her fist.

He spoke to her as if she were a hurt child. "When I was little, I had a keen interest in drag-ons, their color meaning, symbolism, and origins. Green is a symbol of growth, awakenings, and rebirth. Gold is a color of wealth and strength. He has some fascinating heritage."

"That's interesting given what has happened recently." Sorrow crept between her words. "I'm sorry. I don't want anyone else handling him. His wings are already broken and the ends are sharp. I know it's silly, but I feel more secure when I have him with me. I made all kinds of little creatures when I was little. But his silly grin is the one that got to my heart. I named him Eros before I knew what Eros meant."

"Love. He's been loved a lot. How did the wings break?" His brows furrowed.

He had struck her where it hurt most as her body recoiled. "It's a long story and not worth getting into right now."

She looked away from him and out the window.

———◆———

*Mac came on* this flight expecting to sleep after a long night of partying, ending with a brunette between his legs. Instead, he got a seat next to a woman with a light blue button up shirt and gray sweater, the uniform of a straight-laced gal.

A curtain of chestnut brown hair covered her face as she breathed into her lap. Hyperventilation and vomiting weren't on his agenda. He let out a deep sigh. This wasn't going to make his bloody day. There were plenty of young women with tight bodies as he thought about joining the mile high club with one of them.

Her curtain parted revealing amazing steel blue eyes. She drew him in with those eyes as if she recognized a kindred spirit in him. Grabbing him on the inside, she poked an unfamiliar place. Her classic beauty mixed with innocence and honesty was refreshing. His hand twitched to touch her because she wore it so naturally.

His body tensed. He wanted to take her worry away as her anguish over the dragon made him curious. He would save the dive into that depth for later. What made her tick? She needed to be unwound a bit. Damn it! What was wrong with him? This wasn't his style. His usual MO wasn't to rescue damsels in distress. He had always been attracted to strong, detached women. The woman next to him was quite the opposite. He sensed her strength, but she wasn't detached in any way.

Never taking the time to get to know someone, he was usually a bump-and-run kind of guy. The less he knew, the better, but not this time. Something grabbed a hold of him at his core and wouldn't let go. Fear continued to creep inside him. His mixed reactions sparked an interest in the beautiful, strong creature next to him.

The plane jumped and bumped with some light turbulence. She bounced up as Eros got dumped into her lap. Gripping the armrests as if they were somehow attached to Earth, little beads of sweat formed on her brow. He wanted to put his arm around her inflexible body. But he sensed some-how he shouldn't touch her. Not yet.

Her steel reinforcements were firmly in place. Her hands held and released the armrests several times. He watched her battle with keen interest. She put her head down and breathed through her anxiety. Then gave him a triumphant smile that didn't reach her eyes. Her false sense of bravado got to him. The vulnerability made her the per-fect mess. Insecurities hiding behind her smile made him want her more. He didn't just want her physically. He wanted what she held inside her. A good game of chase seemed to be in order.

He opened and closed his left hand. He was try-ing to make a decision. As if asking for a dance, he held out his hand for her to take. This simple act of relinquishing control went against every fiber in his body.

"I won't bite. I promise." He waited for her response as his heart sped up.

She hesitated at first, struggling with the deci-sion. Carefully, she slid her petite hand into his larger, protective one. His hand dominated hers almost completely enveloping it. Her eyebrows rose as he held her eyes with his own. Energy flowed through his veins, awakening a part of him he thought had died. Warmth came from her like a force that reached down inside him. The tingle made its way through his body. Her breath-ing instantly settled into an even rhythm.

"Your hand…it's surprisingly strong yet deli-cate." His thumb rubbed the top of her hand. The buzz between them had begun.

"Your hand is huge," she said in a soft voice

with a smile. His hand curled around hers as protection.

He sat close enough that the honeysuckle scent of her hair drifted to him bringing him back to his childhood. The Creighton family farm had rows of honeysuckle bushes that bloomed twice a year as the smell permeated the air. A lump formed in his throat at the memory. A bolt of lightning went through him. Her scent transported him to a place of laughter and peace. He could almost feel his sister tapping him on the shoulder. The power of those memories signaled that he needed to proceed with caution. Things inside his heart started to pay close attention pushing away some of the fear.

Looking at her made him stop and take note of what he was missing in his manic life. He wasn't going to survive the flight without falling a little for this *leannan*. Taken by surprise, he hadn't thought of that word in years, the Gaelic word for sweetheart that held so much meaning for him. He was headed for disaster and in some foreign territory.

The plane made another jolt as she sucked in a breath, her body tensed. "I'm sorry. It scares me to death. I always have the sensation of falling from the sky." She gripped the armrests even tighter, trying to slow her breathing into a relaxed rhythm again. She glanced up at him, smiling sheepishly. "I hear a Scottish brogue, or do you just put that on for the ladies?"

At least there was a little fire in kitten's belly. He wondered what else was hidden under there. So much to explore, so little time. He leaned into her space. "Do you really think I need to put on an accent to get the ladies? I'm offended. How did you pick up on the fact I'm a Scotsman? Most Americans confuse my accent with Irish." He waited for her reaction.

"I studied at Edinburgh College of Art years ago in an exchange program. I loved it there. It felt like coming home. There's something very cozy and homey about Edinburgh. Listening to the natives speak Gaelic sounded like a song. Whenever I took the train to London, I got lost in the lavender fields of thistle." She had a faraway look from the memory that brought a sweet smile. Her face lit up from her smile. He wanted to make sure he had her smiling as often as possible during his short time with her.

He leaned back in his seat and looked up. She had captured the ambiance of his homeland. "Scotland tends to have that effect on people. I grew up not far from Edinburgh. Played rugby and lived there most of my life, but I've done a lot of traveling for work. In fact, I just interviewed for a job in New York City and needed a vacation. Decided to head to Mexico."

He revealed more than he wanted to about himself, but it seemed to come easily with this angel. The lock between their eyes tugged at him. He sensed something stronger under her outer layers. When was the last time he took a real interest in a woman? Warning bells went off, caught between wanting to run and wanting to stay. His scattered emotions made him restless. His mission in life: to avoid all feelings or any deep connections to any woman. This woman pulled the breath out of him by simply holding his hand. Given his line of work, he had to be in control, physically, emotionally, and psychologically. Not when it came to Marabella though. She already had him second-guessing himself.

———◆———

*This aura of* being safe and protected with him was something Mara hadn't experienced in many years—maybe not ever.

Fear gripped her as a perfect stranger conjured up so much emotion with one touch. Once the turbulence stopped, he held her hand again, looking at her with understanding eyes. Was he just trying to distract her? Her mind jumped everywhere. She didn't want to seem like a freak in front of him. Her senses reeled, not sure if her anxiety was from fear of flying or fear of being seduced by the Scotsman. He invaded her on every level, the way he smelled, looked and sounded. There were many years of experience to draw on when it came to escaping from other people who were too close to her. Getting up away from the safety of the seat belt wasn't one of them.

The voice of her late husband came back to her like nails on a chalkboard. A cold sweat broke out on her forehead. 'Stupid girl! Do you seriously think he's attracted to you? I was barely attracted to you. Pretty face but not much else. You're broken, remember? No good for any man.' She remembered why she built the steel wall with rivets welded solidly in place, retreating to that place of safety. Protection from the fear.

Time flew by as the crew handed out drinks. The flight attendant gave her attention to the Highlander. "And what can I get you to drink, sir?" The blonde batted her eyes with a smile that said, 'Come get it'.

He gave her a faint smile. "I think I'll stick with water. It was a rough night." He winked at her.

"Will you be in Cancun long?" Her voice oozed sex as she poured his water.

"Not long enough." He took the water with her business card tucked underneath it.

He left the card under the cup of water as she got her ginger ale. As the flight attendant made her way up the aisle, he took the card, ripped it up and stuffed it in the seat pocket in front of him. "I don't much care for blondes." He smiled as he took a sip of water.

She covered her mouth and laughed. During the short flight, the light conversation eased some of the intensity of their connection, which never seemed to waver. Comfort and warmth ebbed and flowed between them with each glimpse and laugh. He seemed restless in his seat, fidgeting every so often. During a couple more turbulent times, she gripped the armrests, praying for the flight to be over.

The plane landed in Cancun. Their journey had come to an end. He stood to give her room to move into the aisle. As she waited, her sisters shoved their way toward her. They asked if she was okay and if the flight went well. When she turned around to introduce Mac, she only caught a glimpse of the back of his head. A strange feeling of loss came over her, missing a man she barely knew but who had made his presence known.

———•———

*Mac needed to* get the fuck off the plane before he did something stupid, like ask the name of her resort. She had affected him on every level, in every way, from her words to her smile. He'd learned early on that woman were unpredictable and not terribly dependable creatures. Eventually, they would leave you.

He couldn't stay still, torn between keeping his distance and wanting to show her exactly how he wanted her. He didn't do dating. No strings attached. Friends with benefits was his safest bet. He could tell that Marabella wasn't that type of woman. His pull toward her scared the hell out of him. She rose above every woman he had ever met. If he stuck around, all bets were off.

Heartbreak avoided. Score one for the Scotsman.

# CHAPTER 2

*The pebble stone* pool deck massaged Mara's feet as she walked to the lounger on the ocean side of the pool. The sunlight danced on the clear blue water. A soft breeze came off the ocean teasing her as it caressed her skin and ruffled her hair. The sun warmed her body just enough to be comfortable. As seductive as the tropical surroundings were, she was too lost in thought to pay much attention. Plopping into the poolside lounge chair, she still hadn't accepted her new reality at only twenty-seven.

Warm thoughts of Mac wove into her mind, causing her body to respond. She rapidly pushed those thoughts aside as other things needed her attention. This latest chapter in her life hadn't been an easy road and not one she totally understood yet. Thank God for her sisters, Raquelle and Leigha. They were her rocks. Without them, she would have completely fallen apart. She snapped out of her retrospection as her sisters strolled across the deck of the infinity pool.

"Hey, what are you up to under your big-ass hat?" Raquelle yelled from across the pool. She loved drawing attention to herself.

She waited to respond until Raquelle was in front of her. "I'm thinking about how I got to this point in my life. My husband is dead and I'm sucking on an umbrella drink in Mexico," she responded contritely.

Leigha shook her head. "That's a lot to take in considering it's only your first day of our getaway. Give yourself some time. It's only been three months." Leigha was always the one in control and so well put-together with a level head.

Raquelle chimed in with her anthem, "But we're here to parrrr-teee! You need to snap out of it."

"Yeah, well, I need to figure out what's happened in my life. How did I become a widow? I need to make some real changes before I start celebrating." She looked down at her drink, swirling the umbrella in the pink liquid. How many she would need to consume before it would kill the pain?

Leigha frowned. "What happened was your husband died in a grisly car accident under suspicious circumstances. Then you find out about a life insurance policy he took out on himself with you as the beneficiary. What was Brock up to? Or should I say into?" Shooting high-end fashion, Leigha had a unique perspective on life, taking things in from many different angles. She took refuge behind the camera after a career in front of it. Mara always welcomed her views, whether she agreed with them or not.

"Doesn't that say it all? I, for one, think he was into some pretty shady shit. He was always about money and keeping up with the Joneses. Everything was never enough for him. You were never enough for him, that bastard." Raquelle cut right to the chase.

"Raquelle!" Leigha raised her voice. "Was that necessary!?"

"Mara needs to know. Brock is dead, for God's sake." Raquelle turned to Leigha, hands on her hips.

"What do I need to know?" She asked hesitantly, regarding her protectors.

Leigha sighed deeply, sitting down on the side of the lounger facing her. "Honey, Brock was cheating on you. I know you don't want to hear this, but it's true. Raquelle and I saw him out being very cozy with some Kardashian wannabe. We didn't want to tell you. You were busy with your openings and so happy with your success despite Papa's critiques." She finished on an exasperated breath.

"Well, if it makes you feel any better, I had my suspicions about his infidelity. A lot of it was my fault. I don't blame him," she sighed heavily.

A rivet wiggled, ready to pop out of its steel cage. Rivets held together the shield she built to protect the image of her marriage and her broken soul. Anger about events in her life scorched her barricade like a dragon's breath to steel. Her wall needed to come loose and set her free. She had been hiding in the darkness for too long.

Raquelle's eyes flashed angrily at Leigha. "There's no excuse for that cheating asshole. And what do you mean it was your fault?" She snapped her head in Mara's direction.

"I don't think I'm exactly wonderful in bed.

Brock never seemed satisfied." She tightened her fists at the thought of how things went when it came to sex between her and her late husband. The act of sex had grown more unpleasant as time lagged on in an unfulfilled and unhappy marriage. She wiggled around in her lounger hoping they would stop asking questions.

Another 'aha' moment brought to the conversation by her two lovingly overprotective sisters. Despite their company, sadness, emptiness and loneliness filled her. The information about Brock's infidelity didn't surprise her, but still hit her hard, confirming what she didn't want to believe. Her marriage had been an illusion on so many levels.

Taking a deep, cleansing breath, she had grown accustom to latching on to despair. Weighing her down, it grounded her in insecurity and inadequacy. She needed to find a way to push past the wall to find some freedom.

"How do you know it wasn't his fault?" Raquelle demanded with her hands up in the air. She took no prisoners in the sex department...or maybe she did, tying them up and beating them for good measure as a dominatrix.

"I don't know. I don't want to talk about this anymore today. What are you two up to?" She sipped her drink waiting for it to coat her nerves.

"Raquelle decided we should go deep-sea fishing. She saw some cute guys signing up for the trip in the lobby. You know how she is, free spirit and all." Leigha rolled her eyes. "Do you want to come with us?"

"No, you go ahead and catch dinner. I'm going

to stay here and get some drawings done for some upcoming shows. I'll see you later." Her words came out on a strangled choke. The combination of being a failure as an artist in her father's eyes and a failure in marriage weighed on her chest.

Leigha leaned over, brushing away a wavy strand of hair from Mara's forehead, pushing it behind her ear.

"I don't want you to spend too much time thinking about the past because that's where it needs to stay. Focus on the future and where you're going. Brock isn't worth another minute's thought." Leigha could be so tender and understanding, knowing just what to say.

"Well, I always thought he was a total pig. You never should have put up with his bullshit." Raquelle announced as if it were all so clear.

God help the man who ends up with that woman. Let him be strong. If Raquelle only knew how much of a pig Brock really was, she'd probably go non-linear. But Mara's response was well rehearsed. "Can we talk about this later? You two need to go catch something." She shooed them away with the wave of her hand.

Her thoughts traveled back to the wonderful Scotsman. The only bright light in her life lately had been Mac. He'd sparked something in her she didn't quite understand. Her hand had the physical memory of their connection. He made her feel alive. Her body remembered the tingling sensation at his touch and the loss of comfort and safety when he left. Disappointment lingered because she never had a chance to thank him. She was curious about his quick departure. Would she always be the woman men turned away from?

She searched through her beach bag for her form of solace. When her feelings were conflicted, she reverted back to her childhood love of a medium called air-dry clay. Over the years, she had made many little figurines out of clay that dried without the heat of a kiln. Eros, her first creation, marked a significant time in her life when she knew she would be a sculptor. He served as her dragon muse, sparking her creativity.

The time had come to create another little animal to get her through her current rough patch. Examining her small bags of clay, she chose red. Her hands did the work, as her mind became the blank slate. She began turning the clay into the shape of another dragon. She took it as a sign of bigger and better things to come. Contentment settled over her body, becoming lost in the cool touch of the clay. By the end of the day she would have her next wonderful muse. She wanted to be open to all life's possibilities as her thoughts kept wandering back to Mac. He stirred something in her that she couldn't shake.

# CHAPTER 3

*Mac staggered down* to the pool of his all-in-clusive resort and flopped into the closest lounger. Beyond exhausted and head pounding, he laid back on the lounger. His first night in Cancun had him 'get his drink on' with a couple of ladies in attempt to forget about the enticing Marabella.

The five-star resort boasted spectacular surroundings but he couldn't get into it. He would have to take it all in later when his mind wasn't so muddled. This trip to Mexico had been his only vacation in five long years. His never-ending marathon had him burned out and running hard. The scattered pieces of life's disappointments needed to be put back together. Even on vacation, the agency managed to give him one more assignment.

Pushing himself up into a sitting position at the edge of the lounger, he hung his head in his hands. A tiny prickle on the back of his neck caught his attention. He scanned the area across the pool. Squinting to sharpen his focus, he wanted to make sure he was seeing things correctly. He scrubbed his face with his hands. Yep, that was her. Marabella. The beauty he couldn't forget about no matter how hard he tried. His hands balled into fists. She was his first thought that morning even after a night of tits and tequila. How could he ever forget how she affected him? Releasing his hands, he folded them in prayer over his nose and mouth. He breathed out heavily, trying to figure out his next move. The pull to her was automatic and without rationale.

Two women stood next to her. He assumed they were her sisters. They had pushed their way toward her on the plane as he made his escape. But neither one of them moved him the way Marbella did. The mystery woman piqued his curiosity. She rolled over him like a warm ocean wave that lulled you to a peaceful place down to your soul. Stirring his emotions, she took him off-balance. The gods of torture had placed her right in front of him. He preferred friends with benefits for a reason. No one got hurt. But he couldn't turn away from her. This was either going to be one hell of a train wreck or the most beautiful sunrise ever.

He studied her from across the pool. Her sisters walked away, leaving her to play with something in her lap. She wore a black one-piece bathing suit with a short pink sarong exposing her well-toned legs and generous cleavage. She focused on her hands but the sadness never left her face. It traveled across the pool in waves, punching him in the chest. An empty umbrella drink sat next to her. He wanted to disprove the hold she had on him. As he grabbed the pink drink from the outdoor bar, his hand shook slightly. Since when did he get nervous about getting a woman a drink?

She was unfamiliar territory.

Wandering over, he glanced at the pool, imagining what it would be like to get her wet. He set the fruity drink down next to her and waited for her response.

She glanced over as recognition hit. Her eyes followed his big forearm with a smattering of dark hair upward to be confronted by his huge shoulders under a black t-shirt, messy brown hair. Goosebumps formed on her skin, as her breathing picked up. He hadn't even touched her.

"Is that drink for me, Mac?" Her soft tone held reserve.

"Aye, I'm not much of an umbrella drink kind of chap. I thought I would keep your appetite wet." He wanted to push her little, trying to gauge her reaction to his double entendre. Years with the company taught him that you needed to be able to read people well or suffer the consequences—which, in this case, may end with his shattered heart. His body tensed, aware of the tug between fight or flight. He wanted to walk away but staying seemed to be winning this war.

She peeked up at him from under her hat, her eyes soft and sincere. "I took you for more of a whiskey guy. Like the whole bottle, from the looks of it." She gave him half a smile. "I want to thank you for putting up with me on the flight. You're a real gentleman. There aren't many of those left in the world." Picking up her drink, she stirred it with the umbrella.

God, if she only knew, she would probably run for the hills. The dark side of him wanted to take her to edge to find out if he could bring out her wild side. He wanted to possess her until she screamed out his name, begging for release. Reel it in, mate.

"You don't need to thank me. It was my pleasure. By the way, are you trying to tell me I look like shit after a night of drinking?" He chuckled. "I guess it's a small world. How long are you here for?" His fingers dug into his hips. Those eyes with that body had him forgetting about any other woman on the planet. Dangerous territory. The dance between staying or fleeing continued.

"My sisters and I are here for ten days. I needed this getaway to rethink and recharge." Sadness pulled at her face.

"Do you mind if I sit down?" She nodded. He moved around her, pulling the lounger over so he was right next to her.

She gazed down at her piece of clay that started to take shape. He regarded the blob, wondering why she would bring clay to a pool. Then he remembered Eros, her safety net.

"I hope Eros had a safe landing. Do you take clay wherever you go?" he said with a serious tone.

Her chin came up. "For your information, I'm a sculptor and yes, I take clay wherever I go. It helps me think and unwind. My hands and head work together. They always have." Her gaze returned to the clay in her lap.

"Do you make anything else?" He leaned in to get a closer look.

Her head popped up and her smile made an appearance. "I've created other pieces like small pigs, lamb and fish. My collection grew over the years." Her fingers feathered over the red clay. "I donated one of my bigger free-spirit pieces to the hospital. Then they asked me to make something for the children's wing. I thought it would be a great opportunity to hand them out to the sick kids. Their smiles lit up their faces. They loved to touch the little sculptures." Her smile reached her eyes making them sparkle.

"I volunteer once a month to help the kids make their own creatures. I hope having their own muse would help them get through their illness. Making their own little creature is unique and colorful experience for them." Her smile slipped. "The two things that seemed to be missing in my life."

The knife struck his heart at the mention of sick kids. "So you're an artist?" His fascination continued as he waded into deeper water.

"Yes. I create dancers in motion and free-spirited creatures. Then I caste them in bronze putting them in permanent motion." She gave him a weak smile as if she didn't quite believe it herself. "So what do you do to relieve stress?" she said prickly.

He took off his sunglasses. Leaning in to her, he hoped to take in her scent again. She gasped as his breath lightly brushed along her neck. Unlike on the plane, he wanted her full attention. She closed her eyes for a moment and when she opened them, he scrutinized her intently. "My head and hands work together, too. I could show you how I relieve stress. However, it usually includes someone of the female persuasion." He used his artillery of charm, pushing her to see what she would do with it.

Blush tinted her cheeks. The women he kept

company with wouldn't have batted an eyelash at his retort. Seeing her blush had him craving more. His cock started to come to life, which amazed him considering his intake of tequila the night before. He wanted this woman underneath him. His reaction to her was visceral. He would dive in and never come up. Those thoughts and emotions clouded his judgment and his control started to slip. God, when was the last time just talking to a woman had his body on full alert?

"Well, how do you know I want you to show me? Look around you. There are plenty of females for you to persuade." She came right back at him, challenging him with those intense blue eyes and sharp words.

He moved around uncomfortably as he tried to manage his full salute. Kitten has sass, too. Her mouth would get her into trouble, in more ways than one. This was going to get interesting. He had the devil on his shoulder. He loved a good challenge. Mystified by her response, she was a contradiction in so many ways, from her coyness to her innocent blush. He let his gaze follow down to her gorgeous, toned legs and back up to her large, supple breasts, resting on her beautifully flawless face.

He responded, "Oh, I think you want me to show you. I can tell by the shine in your eyes, the blush in your cheeks, and the way your breath makes your luscious cleavage go up and down. You're a dead giveaway. By the way, there's only one woman here I'm interested in persuading." Let the sparring begin.

Her nipples stood at attention. As her hands

came up to cover them, the clay dragon slipped onto the pool deck.

He caught her hands and gently forced them in her lap. "Don't hide. I like you like this." He squeezed her hands. She sucked in her breath, which puzzled him. Why would she be surprised that he would want to look at her? He adored exquisite women. She never ceased to surprise him. The wheel of questions began to turn in his head. He'd let her off the hook this time. Glancing at her pert nipples, he picked up the dragon and examined it. "Seems like the beginnings of a dragon. Is this one to keep Eros company?" His eyebrows furrowed together. He found her fascination with dragons adorable strengthening that invisible silken cord between them. "Red dragons can represent some dark stuff, like death, anger, aggression, and danger. It can even be a warning." His tone held no amusement.

"Well, that would make sense considering what's happened lately in my life. You might say I'm at a crossroads. It's time for a new muse to help me sort through it. Maybe the danger has already passed." Her eyes were weary.

"What crossroads are you at? It sounds interesting. You like to keep me guessing." He stayed focused on her, wanting her to reveal a little more of her broken parts. What kind of danger was she in? His body went on alert, hazards of the job.

She took a deep breath. "I lost my husband about three months ago. Some things are starting to come to light that I would have liked to stay in the dark." A flash of anger crossed her face.

Leaning back, he shut his eyes briefly trying

to hide his painful memory. "Saying sorry isn't enough. I know what it's like to lose someone you're close to. I lost someone, too. It was a living hell to watch, not being able to do anything about it. Sometimes, people leave behind holes." He hadn't spoken to anyone about her. Those words were long overdue. Sharing this fragment scared the shit out of him. Her death bled him like an open wound, leaving a gaping hole. Loved ones could be gone in an instant. Life could turn on a dime. He teetered between wanting to tell Marabella everything to not wanting her to see the man he had become. The one who was closed off · and alone.

As she spoke her next words, he was certain he would be sharing all of it with her. He would fight through his pain to get to the other side.

"I can tell by the pain in your eyes that the person was very special to you. You're right. Sometimes, sorry isn't enough. My husband died in a suspicious car accident. No one can figure out what he was doing in Brighton Beach that time of night. As some things have come to light, I'm not sure I knew him at all." She shut her lips firmly.

Her words hit him hard. She really believed she didn't know the man she called her husband. He couldn't think of a worse betrayal. He stared at her flawless face, made up to perfection. Every lash was in place with enough blush to appear natural. The foundation and eyeliner were exact to enhance her features. He wanted to peel away the mask to reveal her. Why did she need it? He itched to know more about the workings of her.

Reaching out his hand, just like on the plane,

he opened his palm to her. He wouldn't feel her energy again. That was a fluke at best. Given the current revelations about her past, he wondered if she was rolling in waves of the emotions he was so familiar with.

"What are you smiling about?" She tilted her head to peek up at him.

"I'm wondering how lightning strikes twice. What are the chances that you and I would be staying in the same place?" His eyes devoured her enticingly. The wolf to her kitten. He was one-step away from crossing the abyss into dangerous territory. He had never entertained the thought of fate. She had him questioning everything.

———◆———

*Mara turned her* body toward him. He smelled heavenly as the combination of clean, citrus and spice filled her senses. The way a real man should smell after a shower, not the heavy musk of her late husband's expensive cologne. Dragon wings fluttered in her stomach as a lump caught in her throat. This man made her heart race and her palms sweat.

She couldn't help but feel like she knew him from somewhere. When she opened her eyes, they connected with his. Just the two of them as the world seemed to fall away.

She chanced putting her hand in his as a hot tingle flowed to her toes. He was the eye of her storm. Her body relaxed as her safety net returned. Another rivet holding the steel tightly shut started to come out, letting a sliver of light weave between the sheets of metal. The warming light made her think that she might not have to protect the image of her marriage. She wanted to share things with him but feared he might use it against her in the end. Her lack of trust in men reared its ugly head again. But he affected her, his voice and—God help her—that accent. She hoped he wouldn't judge her. She wouldn't have to protect herself in her fortress of steel. With each thing she revealed, there seemed to be more freedom from her confines. What the hell was it about this man that made her burn when he touched her? Craving his touch, she needed to get inside him.

She volleyed back with a smart retort. "Well, I think you followed me here so I could hold your hand." Oh, she felt a little cocky. Why not? She needed a distraction and wanted to bring his 'charming self' down a notch.

"Are you sure it's not the other way around? I remember someone grabbing my hand during the plane ride here. I bet there are a lot of things you can do with those talented hands. I think you might be a little smitten." He gave her a cheeky grin, his eyes full of wonderment, daring her to come out and play with him.

"Smitten! I think someone is a little high on himself right now." She leaned back in her lounger, keeping her eyes locked on him, never letting go of his hand. She caught the questions swimming in his eyes.

"Really? Well, I think someone needs to cool off in the pool before she gets so turned on by me she starts to break a sweat." With that said, he let go of her hand, stood up, and peeled off his t-shirt.

Holy Heaven, he was cut to perfection. Nice pecs and ripped abs, a sculptor's dream.

Leaning down, he placed his hands on each side of her hips and whispered in her ear, "You have three seconds to take off your clothes before I get you wet." His voice was laden with that mesmerizing Scottish accent suggesting an image of hot sex.

She barely had a chance to rip off the sarong and throw her hat to the side before he grabbed her hand. He stalked toward the pool with her in tow. She squealed, trying to keep up with him, down the stairs and into the water.

He submerged them in the warm water together. The water surrounded her as she started to float away. His arm wrapped around her, anchoring her to him, her back to his front. She loved the way his arm gripped her, unwilling to let her go. His warmth spread through her. She felt safe from head to toe. There was a foreign feeling of excitement as the soft whisper of wings fluttered in her stomach once again. His fingers slid across her stomach as she flinched. Her ass bumped against his tight stomach. She could feel his excitement building.

"And where do you think you're going?" He whispered in her ear before turning her around to face him. Their noses were inches away from each other. Her breath became shallow as he touched her jawline with his wet thumb. "I hope you put sunscreen on that beautiful face. I wouldn't want you to turn into a cooked lobster out here. However, there are other parts of your body that I would like to make hot." He gave her a crooked smile.

Startled, it took the air out of her lungs as she moved away from him. He could be so tender with her, yet possessive and sexy. He cared about a little thing like if she got burned or not, but had sex on the brain. She never had that kind of attention from a man in...well...when was the last time anyone called her beautiful?

"Let's play a game. Hmm? You know 'Simon Says', right? Well, this is 'Mac Says'." Mischief played his eyes. She caught on right away.

"Well, Mara says you have to catch me first!" With that, she spun out of his arms and dove into the clear blue water. She knew he'd let her go so he could catch her again.

She hadn't swum out far before he gripped her ankle just before she reached the other side of the pool. Shooting up out of the water, she laughed out loud. She turned, coming face to face with him. He wore a huge shit-eating grin. His hair slicked back with wide eyes written with the intent and curiosity of a panther ready to strike at his prey. Pinning her with her back to the side of the pool, he put his arms underneath hers. Her heart pounded in her chest. She was giddy with a mix of fear. Her body tensed like it always did with a man in such close proximity.

---

*Hearing her laugh* speared through the middle of

Mac's chest. Her laugh reminded him of his sister when she was young. The little girl inside the woman who liked the game of chase fascinated him. He visualized what she must have been like as a child. Her hair flowed behind her, running through a meadow being chased by her father.

As soon as he caught her, she went rigid. The light left her eyes. What would make her react like that after such playfulness? What was he going to do with the woman in his arms? He decided to push her a little to see her reaction. He leaned closer to her ear, "Now that I've caught you, you need to give me my reward—a kiss." Floating back, he allowed her to make a move. He waited to see if his kitten would continue to play.

Her cheeks turned red. Her eyes gazed at his lips as she gently bit her lower one, calculating her next move. She had the look of a pinball bouncing off confused emotions. Slowly, she leaned in for a first kiss, lingering a breath away before she whispered, "You forgot to say 'Mac says'." Without warning, she dropped underneath the water, arms over her head, and swam away. He had given her a way out. Smart girl.

He dove in after her, not to chase but to watch her body slice through the water. She swam with the swiftness and grace of a dolphin. Her body moved fluidly as she broke through the sun-sparkled surface. His eyes followed her long, lean and athletic as she walked up the stairs and out of the pool. He was definitely a leg man, wondering how they would feel wrapped around his waist, as he was snug inside her.

When they reached the loungers, she turned

around and threw her shoulders back in confidence and defiance. She bumped into his hard chest, startled by his closeness. "Are you hungry?"

He put her chin between his finger and thumb, lifting her face up to him. "You may have won this round, but I don't give up easily. So yes, I am definitely hungry." He leaned in closer so only she could hear his words. "I will have you, guaranteed."

---

*A shiver ran* through her. Mara was at a loss for words. He had hit every nerve in her body. He didn't mince words, letting her know, without a doubt, she was in his crosshairs. There was an ache between her legs she didn't want to acknowledge. No one had ever made her desire so much. She leaned into his grip, letting the words wrap around her. His handsome hands captivated her. She wondered about how they would feel as they skimmed her face and body.

Fear and worry seemed to fall away. All these new sensations were alien to her, tilting her off her axis. She shouldn't be thinking about this after just losing her husband.

Could she be the delicious woman he hungered for? Would he destroy her from the inside out, the way Brock had destroyed her? Was he a player looking for a quick lay? There were so many questions that ran through her head. She felt dizzy.

"Then let's order some lunch and talk. You're a very interesting man and full of...energy." She glared at him with one eyebrow cocked. If he could read her mind, she would challenge him to reveal some of his secrets any way necessary.

# CHAPTER 4

*Mac ordered a* light lunch of fruit, cheese and small-assorted sandwiches. He sat close enough for their legs to touch, flirting with future possibilities. His gaze skimmed her legs and torso. He met her eyes and spoke firmly. "Eat up. You could use some weight. I like my women with a little meat on them."

He winked at her as he fed her a strawberry from the fruit plate. His eyes focused on her lips as they wrapped around the strawberry while he held his breath. Her mouth appeared tentative one minute and confident the next, devouring the strawberry to the stem. The dichotomy added to her sensuality. He ran his thumb along her plump lower lip, wiping away a drop of strawberry juice and licking it. Her gaze locked onto his thumb as his tongue captured the sweetness. Her eyes became hooded from his touch and seductive play, but her body withdrew from him.

Feeding her strawberries was alluring, but he needed her less skittish and more trusting. She reminded him of a deer waiting for the gunshot in the forest. He read her well enough to know she would try to bolt at the first sign of danger.

All aspects of her were fascinating, from spirited to fearful. He would need to dig a little deeper to find out the source her fear.

He appreciated her lack of seduction. She was strong yet flirty, a dangerous combination for any man. Her appeal was that she was herself, unaware of how much of true self she revealed to him. He had made a living out of reading people by watching them carefully. Most times, it was a matter of life or death.

———◆———

*Mara jerked back* from him. His face tightened as if he were trying to hold it together. The strawberry tasting triggered her body as it clung to her past. The hair on the nape of her neck stood on end as goose bumps formed down her arms. She stiffened at the sensation of being watched. She didn't want to swivel around and seem obvious so she remained focused on the plate in front of her. Chalking it up to being paranoid, it set her on edge.

He drew her attention back to him but seemed to miss her brief discomfort. "So, tell me about how and where you grew up."

"I grew up in Greenwich, Connecticut. My father, Antonio Luccenzo, is a world-renowned sculptor and my sisters, mother, and I are very well taken care of because of it." His face remained impassive. She continued on, "My mother, Guil-ianna, was an actress when she met and married my father. She gave up her career when she got pregnant with me. Mama taught her girls to be very independent and, as it turns out, we are all artists in our own right. We've had no choice but to stand on our own." The safety pin opened pricking her heart. "Papa travels a lot for his international gallery openings."

His soft eyes were focused on her. The undivided attention made her self-conscious. When Papa was home it was all about him and his world of art. Her late husband showed no interest in anything she had to say. She continued her story in a quiet voice. "When I was little, I was a dancer. I loved to dance; jazz, ballet, modern, or any movement I could express with my body. Mama took me to all my rehearsals and recitals. Then I grew into a woman's body full of curves. Curves and dancing don't exactly go together. I couldn't stay as thin as I needed to continue on that path and be successful. My dancing career ended and I headed full-on into sculpting, my second passion."

She buried her nails in the palm of her hand to ward off the familiar pain of loneliness, regret and the echo of Papa's criticisms that boiled to the surface. She didn't want to reveal her weaknesses hidden behind the steel-riveted impediment. Trembling on the inside, she wasn't sure why she wanted to share this piece of herself. She exposed more than she wanted to fighting to hold back the tears as they threatened to spill over. That simple shift from dance to sculpting served as a catalyst to the domino effect in her life.

He held out his hand as she slipped hers in. "I think we all give up childhood dreams at some point. Mine was to become a dragon trainer." He winked at her and she laughed, a relief to a tense moment. She appreciated how well he had read her and tried to comfort her with humor.

"So, it sounds like your father wasn't around much. Are you very close with him?"

She wiggled in her chair. Damn, this man was perceptive. How could she get around that? She didn't want him to see the real her, the damaged one. Wouldn't being attracted to a stupid man be easier? Nope, that would just irritate her. "He isn't around much. Papa is either in the city at his studio or traveling to the next big opening. How close can you get to someone who is never there?" She swallowed her bitter tone. "But my sisters and I have the best of everything, from cooks, to chauffeurs, to security guards. And we are all very good girls...well, with the exception of Raquelle, the wild child." Her sister was the exact opposite of her in so many ways, always managing to stoke Mara's embers.

"Why are you smiling? I bet there is a story or two there. Do you wish you were more like her?" He tilted his head interested in her answer.

"Raquelle is more than any one person should handle. That's why it takes three of us—Mama, Leigha and me. We orbit around her, so to speak. She always has something going on. She goes through men like water. Out of the three of us, she had the least amount of boundaries growing up. The portrait artist in her reads people very well. She's always had an instinct for telling if someone is on the up-and-up or if they're a dog." Her words held a warning that said, 'wait until you meet her; then I'll know all about you'. "Raquelle never did like my late husband. She made her distaste for him known early on, even to him. Let's say they weren't the best of friends. A little later in our marriage, Brock seemed to change. He was one thing in public but something else behind closed doors."

Stopping abruptly, she wrapped her arms around herself. She wanted to be rid of the chains that weighed her down. Not wanting to be veiled by darkness, she clawed at her steel cage. She craved the light. Like all abused creatures, she wanted to be free of the bonds that held her but scared to death of freedom.

She averted her eyes, focusing on the food that became droopy in the afternoon heat. A shiver ran through her. Without a word, he reached out to hold her hand, lightly stroking her fingers. Even in the warmth of Cancun, she couldn't escape the coldness her memories still held of Brock. She began to wonder if the Brock behind closed doors was normal. The comfort of Mac's hand calmed her.

She needed to switch gears before she imploded from the painful memories. "Mac, I talked on and on while you've said very little about yourself. What's your story? I'm sure it's very interesting." She let out an exhausted breath. Her shoulders sagged relieved to be focusing on something besides her tortured past.

———◆———

*Surmising that her* husband wasn't of great caliber, it wasn't the time to push her into telling him more. Mac felt compelled to share part of his story, just not too much, considering how affected she had been opening up about her life.

He didn't share himself with the women in his life, but he couldn't stay camouflaged behind his pain forever. "I grew up in Musselburgh, Scotland. My family owns a farm and we mostly raise sheep. We don't live the high life, but it's a good life full of hard work. I grew up with two older brothers and a younger sister." Where the bloody hell did that come from? He cut himself off from continuing the part of his story that hit a nerve, his sister.

The pain in his heart clawed to get out. He hesitated then decided to continue by redirecting his tale. "I followed my brothers into the military, RAF, after my schooling and got trained in security. The military has been the better part of my life, traveling around the world and such. Now, I'm aiming to get out, venture into the private sector and stay in one place for a while." He couldn't reveal that he went on to become MI6 on highly classified missions. Bambi would have bolted for the hills given that information.

She slid her hand out from under his, removing herself from him, both physically and emotionally. He was unsure what caused it.

He avoided talking about his sister Kendall at all costs. Her death was barbed wire wrapped around his heart, tight enough to grip but not bleed. He spent years losing himself in women, avoiding any real closeness or anything with any depth. Avoiding any more loss. The pain was too much. No talking necessary, nothing to share.

The sympathy of the woman before him made him want to give her this piece of him. She didn't seem to want anything from him except who he was as a man. Tired of running, tired of hiding and sick of superficial women, she, of all people, would understand the loss and grief after just losing her husband. He understood the hollowness in her eyes, but fear held him back. The fear of loving someone too much, then losing them in the blink of an eye. He'd had his fair share of loss, from his sister to his colleagues. He wasn't ready to open up quite yet.

A lump stuck in the middle of his throat. He shifted gears asking about her artwork. He loved watching her eyes light up as she talked about her creations. She had a passion in her he didn't think she often showed people. Her laugher...well, that did things to him he didn't even want to think about.

She beamed. "I am the third-generation sculptor in my family, a double-edged sword. I'm the firstborn and not a boy. Not good in an Italian family of artists. I studied at RISD, Rhode Island School of Design, earning a Master's degree from Yale, but those credentials weren't good enough for my father. He is a classically trained artist from Italy. There's no match for that." A flash of anger and regret skimmed across her face.

She held her chin up. "Despite my father's low opinion of my creations, people like my work. I actually make money as a sculptor, which is almost unheard of. Business is booming. I have to keep up with the demands of my clientele who want busts done of themselves." She rolled her eyes. Pausing, her eyes became focused and clear. "My sisters and I never really fought when we were kids, but there was a distance between us. The recent events in my life have brought us closer together than ever."

He wanted to hold her, make it better. There would be time for that later. She required space.

The sun began to make long shadows in the late afternoon, bringing their day to a close. He wanted to be with her again as soon as possible to unravel more of her. "So, have you ever been scuba diving before?" He already knew her response.

"No. But I think I would like to try it. A new beginning means trying new things." Her false bravado came to the forefront again as she pushed herself out of her comfort zone.

———◆———

*Mara would agree* to go scuba diving if only to find out his secret loss. Something niggled at her. She recognized the subtle changes of deceit that quickly scrolled across his face when he talked about his job. Brock used to get that look when telling half-truths. He thought he was hiding it, but she had years of experience reading Brock's lying face. He would cast a hard stare into her eyes when she questioned him as if to say, 'Go ahead and challenge me.' That's how she knew he was cheating.

Had she been wrong about Mac? Was there a

liar inside him? Her attraction to him might be nothing more than pheromones in action, a puff of chemistry, lust at best. They had barely touched skin to skin. Suspicion and regret started to snake their way into her head, having her take a small step back from the edge. One steel rivet drilled back into place.

She wanted to probe underneath the rogue man finding the cracks in his fortress. He seemed a master at the art of seduction, using it to deflect from what truly lied beneath. It struck her as odd that he didn't he have a family at this point.

"Well, there's a class early tomorrow morning for resort certification, and then an open water dive in the afternoon. How does that sound?" Determination came barreling through his words.

Agreeing to the unexpected new adventure was a big one for her. She never would have entertained the idea of scuba diving. Her heart skipped a beat with the notion of spending more time with him. Thinking about him moving in the water half-naked did things to her. This would be his test.

# CHAPTER 5

*Mara came back* to the suite and col lapsed on the bed, praying sleep would take her away from reality. In her dreams, Mac would be trust-worthy. Confusion set in about the events of the day. She ping-ponged between her strong connection to him and distrust. Longing for him to accept her with all her broken bits, she couldn't gauge how he would react once he found out the truth.

He seemed genuine and protective, even giving her a glimpse of the man behind his created facade. But that one blip on the radar she recognized instantly as a cover-up. Was it all a ruse? It couldn't have been just to get her in bed.

Waking up from a restless nap, she looked around her luxurious bedroom. A cream and beige palette accented the dark wood floors with pops of coral. The ceiling fan whirled above her as the soft light streamed in from the slider, coaxing in the ocean breeze.

Her body warmed with thoughts of him. He exuded masculinity from his body, mind, and smell. She couldn't have been that wrong about him. Although her track record wasn't great when it came to men.

He gave her a snippet of his heartache, losing someone close to him. She related to the pain that twisted in her chest wishing he would share more with her. Shaking her head to rid the thoughts of him, her sisters barreled through the front door.

"Hey, Mara, are you here? What you are up to?" Raquelle sang from the living room.

"I'm here trying to take a nap but was interrupted by two loud females." She laughed. "How was fishing?" She knew the double meaning would get Raquelle talking.

"Well, since you asked, I reeled in a big one and will be seeing him later. Leigha entertained one of his friends, but you know how faithful she is to Tom, the yawner." Raquelle coyly smiled at Leigha.

"I wondered if you caught any actual fish. You always catch men; that's a given." She deflected, inwardly wishing she were more like Raquelle in the 'free spirit with men' department.

"No, we didn't catch any fish." Leigha rolled her eyes and turned to Raquelle. "And what's with the comment about Tom? I thought you liked him?"

"I do, if you want someone to crunch numbers and do your taxes. He's just kind of boring, that's all." Raquelle put on a little pout as if to say, 'Don't hate me because I like 'em rough and ready'.

"Well, you know what, Raquelle? We can't all have Tarzan, now can we." Leigha raised her voice. Spinning on her heels, she headed for her bedroom.

"What the hell was that about?" Awkward silent filled the room as they were a stunned by Leigha's outburst. "Something must be going on that she hasn't told us about. She'll come around when she's ready," Raquelle stated with confidence at her latest evaluation of her sister's situation.

"Are we going to dinner? I have some things I'd like to talk to you about. I need some input on my life at the moment," Mara said quietly, rubbing her hands together.

"What kind of soul-searching did you do at the pool, anyway?" Raquelle had a worried look on her face.

"I'll tell you over dinner. Do you think you can make up with Leigha in the meantime?" She gave her the 'fix it now' look.

In their social circles, one was taught to always dress well for dinner. She wore her standard Armani little black dress, perfect for any occasion. Leigha wore a long, draped gown by Donna Karen in navy blue satin with a crisscrossed back. The way it hung on her made her appear even more statuesque. Raquelle out shined both her sisters with her Alexander McQueen black and red stained glass knit sheath dress, snug in all the right places and fit like couture. The final accent was the shoes, ranging from Stuart Weitzman Sail Crystal-satin pumps to Jimmy Choos to Louboutin.

With her chin up, Raquelle said, "Don't we resemble Charlie's Angels, sans the guns?" She strutted like a runway model, working it more than Leigha and Mara. They were the spotlights to her center stage. But the three of them drew attention from men and women alike.

They entered the restaurant and came to a stop.

Parchment paper sconces casted a soft light on the cherry-wood walls to create the warm ambiance. The tables donned a sea of color, from burgundy to sage greens resembling a warm, cozy quilt. Each table had its own touches of decoration, accented by a big ornate bouquet of flowers from orchids to dahlias. The oversized doors opened wide to a deck that seemed to spread out over the ocean. They let their artistic souls take it all in.

The evening started with appetizers as they chitchatted about the day. The air filled with the quiet tension of a musical instrument strung too tight and could give way at any minute.

When Mara couldn't deal with her own fidgeting anymore, she rapidly blurted out, "I met a man on the plane ride down here. We spent the afternoon together. We're going scuba diving tomorrow morning." She had hit them with the one-two punch. Sitting stone still, she waited for their response.

"Would you care to elaborate on this encounter? I didn't even know about a man on the plane ride. And since when do you scuba dive?" Raquelle sat up straight.

"He sat next to me on the plane. His name is Mac. He's from Scotland. He seemed nice enough at the time and even held my hand to keep me from freaking out. We all know how anxious I am about flying." She laced and unlaced her fingers, glancing up briefly up to see if she still had their attention. You could lose Raquelle in the middle of a story due to boredom.

"What I didn't know on the plane is that he's staying here at the resort. We met up again at the pool today after you left. We went for a swim and talked about some personal stuff. There were some things that seemed a little off, though. At least I've been trained well in the telltale signs of a man lying or telling a half-truth. After dealing with Brock, I don't need his lying shit." Her hands balled into fists.

Her sisters grew quiet as they stared at Mara. A rivet popped out as a wisp of light snuck in. Her bravery began to build, making her stronger and bolder. The truth was about to unfold like a black napkin with an intricate interior design. The threat of Brock ceased to exist, no image to protect. She could let him go for good.

Raquelle started off, "Whoa, whoa, whoa. Okay, you need to slow down. What lying shit are you talking about? You did say you shared some intimate information with him, right?"

"He talked about his job but the deceit was in his eyes. It was there and gone. I don't know. Maybe I'm wrong. He seemed so interested in me. It's the way he looks at me, like I'm the only woman in the world. He makes me feel special. Maybe it's part of his charm to get women into bed. I feel like we have a connection, one I've never had with a man before. Then he shared some personal stuff, but I guess that's all part of his game. Right? He's playing me." She sputtered her words in self-doubt.

Leigha delved a little deeper. "What did you talk about, exactly?"

"We discussed Brock's death, our different upbringings and the death of someone close to him. I got the sense he doesn't like to talk about the person he lost. I was surprised when he shared it with me. He seems genuinely affected by their death, as if they were very close. When we were in the pool, he asked me to kiss him, which I didn't do. I guess that was a good idea, considering he's a player." Her words rushed out. She always second-guessed herself compliments of Brock.

The conversation lulled as Leigha and Raquelle reviewed the revelation of the day's events. The waiter interrupted their contemplative moment to take their order. Little did they realize she was about to drop an even more horrific bomb.

Dinner came with two bottles of wine, compliments of Raquelle. Mara started to move her food around the plate. Anxiety took over, as she planned out what she really wanted to talk to them about.

Raquelle moaned and purred over her food. One would think she was making love to it. She ate food like she lived life, to the fullest.

Leigha, the neat eater, ate each food group separately in small bites, ever the lady, always in control. "What happened to this person?" Leigha asked clinically.

Before she had a chance to answer, the feeling of being watched came back again. The hair rose on her arms. She glanced around the restaurant, looking to identify the source. Nothing appeared out of the ordinary or familiar.

Leigha noticed her discomfort. "What's wrong, Mara? You look spooked and you have goose bumps on your arms. What's going on?" Leigha reached for her arm to soothe away the fear.

"At the pool today, I could feel someone watching me. I had the same reaction as now, goose bumps and hair standing on end. I guess my mind is playing tricks on me." She tried to shake off her paranoia to continue their discussion. "So, where were we?"

Raquelle honed right in on the kiss. "So far, I'm not hearing 'player'. Tell me about the kiss that didn't happen. Why didn't you kiss him? Kissing is the first clue to any real chemistry." She played a young version of Dr. Ruth. Any sex problem that needed to be solved, Raquelle was your go to sex therapist.

Mara dug deep, balling her fists under the table and willed herself to move forward with her story. Everything started with this conversation, one revelation at a time. "I didn't kiss him because I was scared I wouldn't be enough for him, like I wasn't enough for Brock. My body tensed up like it always does. Why do you think Brock cheated on me? It wasn't because I was so wonderful in the bedroom. He couldn't stand to touch me and we always had sex in the dark." Her fists started to shake as anger took over her body. Rage had opened a door. She wanted to shove it open to see what was behind it.

Raquelle leaned in and spoke softly, "What do you mean, he could barely stand to touch you? In public, he always seemed attentive and you two presented as the 'perfect couple'." She used her fingers for air quotes.

"What happened in public and in front of family was not what happened behind closed doors. He acted differently when we were alone. He wasn't very nice most of the time. I thought it was the natural progression of things, like that's what happened after years of marriage." Tears of shame started to well up behind her eyes. This tidbit was only the tip of the iceberg. The information hung like dead air, making it hard to breathe.

Even in her warring emotional state, her body became aware of him before she laid eyes on him. She peeked up sideways through wisps of hair. Mac stalked toward their table like he owned the place. He looked at her sisters with interest as he stopped at their table.

"Ladies, how are you this evening? I'm Mac. Mara and I met on the plane ride down here." He reached out his hand to greet Raquelle and Leigha as they introduced themselves to him.

She gave him the once-over while he tried to win over her sisters. The green polo shirt hugged his chest and accented his eyes. Khaki pants matched the sports jacket that hung on him perfectly. Her heart beat wildly, wanting nothing more than to reach out and touch him, to seek out the comfort that only he seemed to be able to give her.

He turned to her. "Mara, I... Are you okay?" He fell quiet. His brow creased as he tried to assess the situation.

Her hand shook as she covered her mouth. "Yes, I'll be fine. Thank you for asking." She shook her head to stop the tears from falling, horrified that he might be able to really see her.

He hesitated for a moment as if contemplating to stay or go. "I'll be on my way then." He turned to her sisters. "It was nice to meet you. Have a nice evening." Standing in front of her, he blocked her view of the restaurant. "Mara, I'll see you tomorrow morning. We can talk then." His gaze never left hers, leaving no room for negotiation.

She had to give him credit. He was good at the game and definitely in control. A few tears weren't going to deter him.

Raquelle leaned over. "Really, Mar? You left out the part where he's tall, dark, and ruggedly handsome. The way his eyes locked on to you tells me he's into you. It seems to me you two made a serious connection. I would have to be around him more to tell you if he's a player but my gut says, not where you are concerned."

She couldn't think about Mac. Standing at the precipice she needed to take the leap. "Can we get back to what I was talking about? I'll deal with him tomorrow, or maybe he won't show up." There was a pang in her chest. She was convincing herself she was never going to be the woman he needed or, in the end, wanted. Imagining being intimate with him seemed too much. Her emotions shook under her skin. What a disaster.

"Oh, honey, I don't think Mac is anywhere near done with you yet. Nice try, though. You better buckle yourself in. It's going to be a bumpy ride." Raquelle spoke into her glass of pinot while swirling it around. Her smile said, 'been there, done that'.

"Go back to what you were talking about with Brock," Leigha spoke with caution.

She became self-conscious. "Can we continue this back at the room? There's more to all of this, but not here." She managed to choke out her request, catching her tears before they fell.

Leigha and Raquelle exchanged several curious glances with one another as they continued to finish dinner.

She ate very little food. Her alcohol consumption had given her the courage she needed to continue the talk and face the music.

———◆———

*Earlier in the* day, as she sauntered away from him with that goddamn gorgeous ass of hers, Mac had already decided to go after her come hell or high water. This wouldn't be the proverbial roll in the hay. Driven by some internal mechanism, it seemed more important than ever he have this woman. One soul in search of another. His soul was marred from all the things life had thrown him. Wasn't everyone's to some extent?

After the day's intimacy, not being near her lacked the comfort he craved from her and only her. He had grown tired of cold, empty romps that never led to anything. She brought out all angles of the man he really was—caring, kind, protective, possessive and, God help him, loving. Those characteristics had slipped underneath the surface.

He had built a wall that wasn't working for him anymore, sharing more with her in one afternoon than he had ever shared with any woman besides Kendall. There was an ease talking to her about the things that cut the deepest because she understood the place where you teeter on the edge, afraid to look down. You cocoon yourself from the world, anchoring to a familiar yet dying tree, terrified it might break out from under you. You hold on to what's comfortable in order to survive. But sometimes, you need to let go of those safe things so you can fly again. He wanted to fly with her.

When he approached her table, his chest tightened to see her so upset. He got the feeling her emotional state had nothing to do with him. She had mentioned her late husband and some revelations about her life with him.

He seated himself with his back to the wall, putting them in his line of vision. It never ceased to amaze him how much his job affected how he functioned on a day-to-day basis. His newfound case, Marabella Luccenzo. If he went all in for this woman, he needed to uncover everything about her.

He surveyed their table, as their discussion seemed to intensify. She pushed the food around on her plate. Her emotions seemed heavily tied to her appetite.

They stood to leave. She appeared dazed as her sisters led her out of the restaurant. Their close interactions told the story of a tight-knit unit. They had each other's backs, Marabella being their sole focus.

His appetite seemed to wane after seeing her so shattered. In his heart, he hoped somehow her late husband hadn't hurt her, but his head told him he left behind invisible scars. He couldn't imagine anyone hurting her. He suspected she put everything into her marriage. She exhibited beauty, humor and kindness, with an unexpected innocence. He was sure all her sculptures reflected the elements of her character. Finishing a light dinner, he needed to sleep. The last forty-eight hours had been eventful. Tomorrow might bring some clarity to his murky situation.

# CHAPTER 6

*M*ara's sisters escorted her back up to their suite cloaked in silence. They sat in the living room made to comfort the soul after a long day at the beach. French doors opened to a large balcony with a view of the ocean. A gentle breeze came off the ocean, making the tissue-thin curtains billow and twirl. Dark wood floors gave way to various hues of green, from the couch to the overstuffed chairs, strewed with embroidered pillows with beach scenes.

If only her life had some of that gentleness and comfort. She sat on the couch as her sisters sank in the big oversized chairs on either side of her. The furniture seemed to hug them in, waiting for the next storm surge.

Raquelle ordered another bottle of wine. "I think it's going be a long night." She typed out a text to the 'the fish' she caught earlier, canceling his naughty night out with the sex goddess. One of her beloved sisters was in trouble, needing some serious TLC. Nothing would get in the way. "So, let's go back to asshole Brock behind closed doors." She voice was firm. "What do you mean, he barely touched you and only in the dark?"

The tears rushed back to the edges of her eyes. As her toes curled over the edge, she was ready to take the jump. She gathered a courageous breath, ready to paint a picture of her decayed intimate life. "In the beginning of our relationship, sex was quick and only slightly painful. He never kissed me, only a quick peck and then he would close his eyes and proceed. He would always turn off the lights, telling me I may have a beautiful face but the other parts of me weren't so pretty and he didn't want to look at it." Taking a moment to gather herself, she clenched her hands. "Sex is not enjoyable for me. In fact, over the years, it had become quite painful. He preferred blowjobs to sex."

Tears streamed down her face. She was unable to hold back the deluge. His comments were so shocking and hurtful that at the time, she wasn't sure what to do. That's when the building began. Clean on the outside with its brushed-steel finish, made to appear strong and high-end, but sealed shut with rusty iron rivets, keeping in her darkest secrets. She thought it was unbreakable. No one would witness the darkness and loneliness. Her self-imposed prison separated her from the pain.

Things had changed since his death. She was able to breathe, wanting to break out. Her trans-formation began with this confession, her truth to breaking free.

Their eyes grew wide stunned by her revelation about what went on behind closed doors. The perfect picture shattered.

Leigha moved to sit next to her and held her hand. "What other parts was he talking about?"

"You know, south of the border. God, this is so embarrassing. I don't know who else to talk to about this." She covered her mouth with her shaking hand. Leigha had confusion and anguish written on her face.

Raquelle stood up from her chair and sat on the other side of Mara. She took her face in her hands, brushing away her tears and stated, "Since I'm obviously the sexaholic in the family, I'm going to need some details to figure this out. What you're saying is he didn't like your womanly parts. Was he a closet gay?"

She took a deep breath. "I think we have established he wasn't gay. Did you ever stop to think I might not be pretty from head to toe? Well, I have. I did some research online and apparently, some women have painful sex. I accepted it to some degree. I went to the doctor not too long ago, but she said physically there's nothing wrong with me. What I need to know is how normal was my sex life with him?" She saw doubt and pain in Raquelle's eyes. She also knew there would be more questions coming her way.

"Is it possible he just wasn't tender and loving in his approach?" Leigha reached for another explanation.

"I have no idea. I've only been with one other man before him. You remember Robert, my freshman year? Well, he was quick and to the point. I think he was embarrassed because I never saw him again. I met Brock soon after and he thought I was a virgin. Sometimes it was better than others, but it has never really been comfortable for me. I always seem to tense up." She gripped the edge of the couch.

Raquelle resembled a pit bull, protective, tenacious, and tender all wrapped into one. She blew out a breath. "Let's start from the beginning. How did sex happen between the two of you?"

Oh, she didn't want to go there. She couldn't tell them everything. Some of the things he said to her she couldn't repeat. She figured he was trying to do some kind of role-playing she wasn't familiar with because it came across so cruel.

"We would come home from being out, strip down, get into bed and do it."

There, that should do it. She would have to be satisfied with her rendition of the events.

"What did you 'do' exactly? Was there foreplay?" Raquelle determined to make this about him and not Mara. She gave her credit.

Exasperated, she began to describe her sex life in greater detail. "He would roll on top of me, pinch my nipple really hard until I made noise and then plunged into me. It hurt so bad it burned. Sometimes I bled. When he would take me from behind, it ended with the same results, and that was with condoms, too. Sometimes, I gave him a blowjob or he forced me, to avoid the whole experience. I got good at those to avoid the pain of sex." Her tears made dark spots on her dress as she let them fall into her lap. "It got to the point where I would fake being asleep when he came home so he wouldn't even try to have sex with me." She huffed out a breath. "But in the last year or so, he didn't seem interested anymore. Of course, by then, I suspected he was doing it with someone else. So, you see, it wasn't his fault. This is the way I'm designed." She was relieved to be done with the recounting of her horrible sex life.

Raquelle stood up and yelled, "Holy. Fucking. Shit! Are you kidding me? Mara, he didn't do anything to get you ready for him. What a fucking psycho pig! And he forced you to give him a blowjob? I would have bitten the damn thing off! I should have killed him while I had the chance. What you experienced with him was not normal. It was abusive and inconceivable, to say the least. What was he thinking? And you're right, the reason he wasn't interested anymore because he was fucking around on you." Raquelle turned away and started cursing in Italian with hands flailing in the air. Their parents had brought them up bilingual, which had its advantages, sometimes.

She blankly stared at Raquelle, as if she had snakes coming from her head. What the hell was she talking about? Get her ready? He certainly wasn't going 'down there.' He referred to her sex as ugly. She understood why he cheated. It didn't take a psychologist to figure it out. Watching Raquelle angrily stomp around had her dumbfounded.

Leigha's eyes grew wide and horrified. "Okay, first, Raquelle, you need to calm down because this isn't helping Mara. Two, thank God you used condoms because that man got around. Third..." She hesitated for a moment, as her eyebrows furrowed. "It sounds like he was punishing you for something. He had to have known he was hurting you. I don't think he was an inexperienced man when it came to the bedroom."

Her perspective seemed out of left field.

"Punish? But why would he punish me? I didn't do anything to him or even embarrass him. In fact, I tried to stay out of his way most of the time. I was always trying to be the good wife." She held her head in her hands as it reeled, leaving her perplexed. Her life fell apart before her eyes. A piece of yarn from her imagined beautifully knitted marriage had come unraveled until there was nothing left but an ugly muddy pile of gnarled string. Tilting again, she was completely off-balance. She had that uneasy feeling before and knew it was coming. This was different, something unexpected, as dizziness took over.

Raquelle had come back to the conversation and stared at Leigha as if she held all the answers to this mystery.

Leigha went on to explain her theory. "He was doing something right with someone, because the woman we saw him with was definitely experienced. There's no way a woman like that was going to put up with abuse in the bedroom."

Raquelle stood with hands on her hips. "You know, you're right. I didn't think of that. So, why was he so cruel and abusive to you, Mar? God knows he married you for the trust fund money."

Their father had set them up with a trust funds to make sure they were well taken care of, but with the understanding they would also stand on their own someday. Each of them quickly learned how to manage money and was gaining success in their artistic fields.

Mara turned to Raquelle, noticing grief in her eyes she hadn't seen before. She started to cry. She hung her head in her hands and sobbed. Taking in huge gulps of air, her body shook. Her mind and emotions on overload as her head spun at this newfound information.

She mumbled, "How could I have been so stupid and naive?" Her sisters held her trying to reassure her that Brock was the problem. "I guess life can teach some hard lessons." She laughed through her tears. "Things aren't always as they seem." She cursed the pair of naive glasses she wore, making the world seem safer.

Leigha spoke away from them as if she were talking to herself. "We all experience sex differently. Mama never sat us down to talk us through it so how were you supposed to know what was normal or abnormal?"

In the back of her mind, she sensed something was off about her relationship with Brock. Her experience with men was almost non-existent before him. She repressed it, not wanting to bring it out into the light and face it. The things he said to her during sex would never come to light. She wasn't about to add to the disfigured picture.

They hung on to her for dear life, creating a circle around her in a veil of protection. She clung to her life rafts and couldn't imagine life without them. Leigha rubbed her back, telling her over and over again it would be all right and she could get therapy back home. There was nothing left in her tank. Exhaustion had set in.

"I think I want to go to bed now. We can talk more tomorrow. I'm overwhelmed with all of this and need to process it. If I thought I was broken before, I'm really broken now." Her sisters were two of the strongest, most intelligent and caring women she had ever known. She hoped some of their strength would rub off on her.

Her emotions were raw and burned, as if exposed to the sun for too long. Abuse? Punishment? Was that what her marriage had been? He was never particularly affectionate, more cold and distant. But why? Did he ever love her? She'd thought so in the beginning. Did he just want the money? He did spend a good amount of it, until he started making a lot of his own with the investment firm. That was when he began to distance himself from her. Opening Pandora's box gave way to more questions than answers. She was exasperated knowing she would never get answers. The only light at the end of the tunnel suggested he might be the problem instead of her.

She knew for sure she never had the connection to Brock that she already had with Mac. Her feelings for her husband lacked those fluttering wings of excitement and the sensuality that coursed through her body at the sight of him.

Raquelle leaned her head against Mara. "You better get some sleep, because you have a hot date with a handsome guy. I think it's the perfect distraction for you, Mar." Raquelle lived for the next conquest. The time had come for her to take her sister's cue and live a little. She was curious to find out about Mac and expunge the ghost of Brock.

# CHAPTER 7

*Mara's head pounded* like a jackhammer. She didn't have much to drink, but the emotional semi had run her over and left its mark. Even dead, he managed to reach out and beat her down emotionally.

During her meltdown, she realized she'd lost her husband long before he died. Their marriage had been a facade to seem normal and happy for the sake of their social circle, masking what really happened behind closed doors. God forbid she didn't appear to be perfect in a world full of imperfections.

The blanket of shame lifted off her shoulders as she finally shared her 'behind closed doors' story with her sisters. They gave her love, support and non-judgment. The therapy session helped to break down her confines and build herself back up again to prove she was stronger than he gave her credit for. Being six feet under he could do a lot less damage. He deserved his new bed.

God, how could she be thinking like this? Had she snapped, or was this what it feels like when you've had enough?

Her body and mind were drained. She sat on

the edge of the bed listening to her sisters' muffled voices behind the closed door. Her core was an empty vessel, floating on the rough sea of life. She craved peace, quiet and a hot shower.

Her body moved as if walking underwater toward the bathroom. The floor was done in white marble with salmon-colored veins. Clear, shell-shaped washbasins perched atop white wood cabinet under brushed nickel faucets. Her artist eye took in all the details. She should have been impressed, but her head was in a fog. She wasn't processing anything.

Her compass focused inward, consuming her. She turned on the rain shower, pulling the hem of her nightshirt over her head before she pulled her panties down her legs. Her nakedness startled her as she took in a ragged breath. For the first time, she really looked at herself.

Leigha's comment came back to her. Maybe she *did* look like everyone else. She flirted with the idea that maybe unfulfilled sex wasn't all her fault. Would she be able to have sex without excruciating pain?

Wanting to get in touch with her body, she closed her eyes, aware of the fullness of her breasts under her hands as they traveled down to the unwanted area. Self-satisfaction was never one of her favorite activities. Anything sexual reminded her of Brock's scalding words, making her embarrassed and ashamed. She avoided touching herself as much as possible, almost never examining her naked body in the mirror. Why look at something that caused her so much pain?

She concentrated on her face, crafting the perfect mask to hide behind. Her reflection showed pink swollen eyes as her fingers skimmed sunken cheeks. She needed to start eating more.

Stepping back from the mirror, her body came into view. She wanted to rediscover herself to find out what she missed. The word 'normal' popped into her head. If she dared to be brave enough, she could break those barriers that held her captive for so long.

The idea of a spa day entered her mind, then shopping. She wanted the works—massage, facial, and yes, waxing. Raquelle always talked about a Brazilian wax. Needless to say, she didn't even know what the hell it was. As painful as it sounded, she wanted the full treatment. She felt empowered, as if a new chapter in her life was being written, opening her up to other possibilities.

Entering the shower, she wanted to wash away her past. Her hands ran over her body as the steam from the shower enveloped and warmed her skin. She took the fresh-scented shower gel in her hands and couldn't help but think of Mac. Had she misjudged him? He embedded himself in her head and heart. His eyes spoke volumes as they searched her deep down. She imagined the places he would put his hands. Would he be turned-off by her inexperience? The thought deflated her as she palmed her chest over the pain.

She needed to start with her. With new resolve, she wanted to discover what her body liked because it had already been forced to do what it didn't like. There was an irrepressible need to take the journey to find out what she had missed out on. She wouldn't let Brock, the asshole, leave her broken. In Raquelle's words 'Oh, hell-to-the-no'. She wanted to infuse some of Raquelle's take-no-prisoners attitude.

Starting with her fingers on her nipples, she carefully played with them ever so gently, a stark contrast to the brutality of Brock's touch. Her touch was kind and gentle. Warmth laced its way all over her body. Mac. She couldn't get him out of her head, wanting his hands on her body. Imagining how his hands would skim down over her stomach, she found the place between her legs. Determination made her want to bust out of the place keeping her from happiness, pleasure, and intimacy.

Closing her eyes, she breathed deeply in through her nose and out of her mouth to gain some calm. Her mind drifted to Mac, making him her safe anchor. He would know what to do and how to do it. Would he want hair or no hair there? She decided to go with no hair, wanting to be able to react to and see everything. She wanted to strip herself of everything that came before Mac. Her fantasy continued with him sliding his finger between her legs, playing there for a while, sliding up and down. Her touch amazed her. Her other hand lightly stroked the inside of her thigh and over her lower abdomen. She opened her eyes as her heart sped up and her skin started to flush.

Her breath caught as her finger slid over her clit, reacting with sensitivity and electricity, waiting for her to rediscover it. Circling around several times, the pressure began to build, unable to remember the last time it felt this good. She paid close attention to all the sensations traveling through her. The tingle spread through her body and hummed with satisfaction.

Her other hand traveled back up to her breast. She played, squeezed and softly pinching the nipple, lathering it up with shower gel. Wanting the next move to be sliding her fingers inside herself, she stopped cold. Fear gripped her as her body remembered the pain. Refocusing, she continued to swirl around her clit as pressure continued to build.

Her body wanted and craved this attention, like a gentle wave rolling over her. This wasn't the destructive storm of Brock left behind after tortuous sex. The thought of Mac fed her fire. Her breath caught as an orgasm hit her like a tsunami, rolling over her body. She heard herself moan. The release felt so good as her body continued to respond to her hands.

Breathing heavily, she braced herself on the wall of the shower. The warm water flowed down her body, taking some of the fear and shame with it. The ghost of Brock began to shred. She felt victorious and more alive in that moment than she ever did in her five-year marriage. The winds of change surrounded her. She completed the first step of many yet to come.

She got herself ready for the day in a pair of shorts and a t-shirt, two things she rarely wore. But comfort was key. She stepped into the living room as her sisters looked up with guarded expressions on their faces.

Leigha spoke first. "How are you this morning?"

She could've sworn they were holding their breath. "I'm fine. I'm a fighter. I'm not going to let Brock rule my life from the grave. I don't know what will happen with Mac, but I'm willing to keep an open mind." She walked tall with conviction, sitting down as if she held a secret.

Leigha and Raquelle gave each other a sideways glance of bewilderment.

Leigha said, "You always seemed so fragile and timid, especially around Brock. I almost forgot how much stronger you used to be before you met him. He tried to break you."

Raquelle grabbed Mara's hand. "I'm certainly glad you're not going to let that bastard keep you down. I always knew you were strong. You can't keep a good Italian woman down for long."

The epiphany made them laugh until tears ran down their faces.

She needed to be strong enough for Mac. He wouldn't want someone as broken as she was on the inside. She still teetered between her resolve to stay strong and self-doubt.

# CHAPTER 8

*M*ac *stood with* tightness gripping his chest as Leigha opened the door. His motor seemed to be running on excitement and trepidation.

Mara smiled as she tightly clasped her hands in front of her. Her cheeks had a soft glow to them. This was an about face compared to the previous night. He wasn't sure how to read her.

Leaning in, he gave her a soft kiss on the cheek. "You look beautiful. Did you sleep well last night?" He watched her carefully, waiting for her brave front.

She looked down at her hands. "As well as can be expected." Her shoulders sagged slightly.

He nodded to her sisters and said, "Let's all exchange cell phone numbers so we can be in touch if need be." He covered all his bases, wanting her to feel safe with him. After seeing her so vulnerable talking about her recent loss, he needed them to know he could be trusted with her. They exchanged numbers and confirmed the events of the day.

He held her hand in the elevator, rubbing his thumb back and forth across her knuckles. The softness of her skin created sparks. He tried to relax but his nerves were on fire. His will power was working overtime not to grab her and kiss those lips. He felt her stare.

"What's going through that beautiful head of yours? Hmm?" He gave her one of his interrogative looks.

"You have a handsome profile. I think I want to do a bust of it someday." A stranger look came over her face as if she recognized something.

Glancing over her perfectly made-up face, he assumed it to be waterproof makeup. He questioned why she felt the need to hide. What skated beneath her surface?

Wild thoughts ran through his head. Visions of her naked body, and what his body pulsed for, kept him tossing and turning all night long. He wanted her, all of her, just the way she was. He had plenty of experience with lust. This was something more. He couldn't explain it. She felt familiar to him, like he had always known her. He never cared enough to get this serious about a woman in years.

His encounters started with an initial spark, then, without formalities, the sex party began. But he wanted to take his time with her. They had connected on a different level, making her a game-changer. He wanted to delve into her depths and really understand someone for once. What he couldn't figure out was why his protective side came out around her.

He meant to keep her, but he didn't know for how long. Short-term seemed to be the only option. She seemed clueless on how she affected him, flipping his switch from solitary bachelor to possessive male. He never imagined there was a woman out there who could make him react with such conviction. Even as his emotions ripped through him, tearing away his past, he hid behind his walled existence. He was trapped by fear, the fear of losing her. His emotions warred within him. In an effort to calm down, he let out a heavy breath.

A comfortable silence wrapped them like a fuzzy blanket. When they reached the pool, they grabbed their gear. As he helped her get her gear on, her body stiffened. The more he tried to help her, the more unyielding her body became. "Marabella, are you okay? You seem tense. Is it about last night?" He wanted a resolution to this before they started their training. Her head needed to be clear.

She looked away, avoiding his question. "I'm a little nervous. I've never done this before and I know it can be dangerous." She swept her fingers through her hair, standing with a rigid posture.

He took both her hands in his and lowered himself even with her eyes. "Marabella, you're safe with me. I'm not going to let anything happen to you. I've done a lot of diving. I have experience, and I know all the dangers. I'll check your equipment and mine before we go out this afternoon. I promise." He needed her to understand how important it was to completely trust him. They would be working on the buddy system and trust was key.

She breathed out, as if she had been holding it in. "I'm going to try to trust you, Mac."

He understood her trepidation. This was a start.

He never thought the word 'trust' could mean so much to him. Cupping her face with both hands, he kissed her on the cheek. His gut twisted at the thought of her late husband being behind her total lack of trust.

Her brows furrowed as a soft breeze carried away her, "Thank you." Darkening eyes exposed her fear of the feelings between them more than what was about to happen in the water. Her gaze traveled down his body. A lusty smile graced her lips as if she couldn't get enough of him. She closely examined his round scar under his ribcage with a six-inch scar under it. Running her fingers over the scars, she peered up at him with concerned eyes. He flinched at her touch filled with so much worry for him.

He moved his hand over hers. "Hazards of the job. It's nothing." He brushed off the six-inch scar. If he thought about the dangers of his job, he never would have survived his assignments. He moved her fingers over the round scar. "But this one has my sister's name written all over it." A curious frown crossed her face. "Growing up we had some pigmy goats. We were in the barn when one of the younger, aggressive males decided to charge my younger sister, Kendall, from behind. She abruptly turned around in his path. I lunged in front of him grabbing his horns. He twisted and gouged me under the rib. It took everything I had not to break his neck. That's how angry I was that anything would hurt her. But Kendall would have been beside herself. She loved all animals, including insects. Needless to say, the goat lived to see another day. In the end, something hurt

Kendall that even I couldn't protect her from."
He turned away as feelings of anger and despair
bubbled to the surface with thoughts of losing his
sister.

Until recently, he never spent so much time
thinking about Kendall. He would have to deal
with all the feelings that came with the memories.
Marabella felt safe as he shared pieces of Kendall
with her.

Looking down at the hand that covered her
fingers, he lingered on his scars. He was caught
between needing her tender, healing touch and
wanting to bury himself inside her to make it all
go away. That was his 'go to' for dealing with the
pain. He couldn't lose what he wasn't invested in,
but he was already invested in her.

She gave him a knowing smile and said, "Sometimes the scars on the inside hurt more than the
scars on the outside."

In that moment, they forged another bond
between them. A rope of warmth came from her
heart through her hand. He was wading into a
riptide with this sensual woman.

He shook his head to snap out of his emotions.
"Now, let's get you geared up and hope I don't
have a scar with your name on it after this dive."
He winked at her as she laughed.

They followed directions from the instructor
and swam around the pool. This was all second
nature for him as he gave her some helpful hints.
They even practiced buddy breathing should they
ever need to share air under water.

Fascinated by her, he never stopped touching her, making her aware he was always right

there. His hands caressed her shoulders, her legs, and held her hand. He needed to tread carefully. Not getting aroused around her was becoming increasingly difficult.

———————

*Warmth wrapped around* Mara's body with every touch as she tried to stay focused on the instructions. He made her body pulse, growing more and more comfortable with herself. Her need became stronger as if it had been in a long winter's slumber, finally waking up to warm spring sunshine. He provided her the peace of mind she had missed for a very long time. The thoughts of being normal floated around in her head again.

After a couple of hours of instruction and practice, they emerged from the water rather hungry. She was excited, knowing she tried and conquered something new. Her life had been in such flux with the discovery of Brock's indiscretions that trusting a stranger didn't seem like a wise decision. But, he never felt like a stranger. Time spent with him seemed so natural and comfortable. She prayed she wasn't wrong about him.

# CHAPTER 9

*Mac led her* to a table tucked away in a corner surrounded by colorful tropical shrubbery. She nibbled on bruschetta accompanying a wedge salad with chicken a far cry from the night before when she pushed her food around her plate. He devoured a hamburger and fries.

They continued to share stories, emphasizing the differences in their backgrounds but it didn't seem to hinder their connection. He sat back, scrubbing his hands over his face and let out a breath. The moment had come. He pushed his plate away. "I want to tell you about my sister, Kendall. She was very special to me. Unfortunately, I know all too well what it's like to lose someone close to you." He had her undivided attention. Her blue eyes turned darker with interest and concern. His chest tightened. "She was diagnosed with advanced ovarian cancer in her early twenties. Being diagnosed at a young age is never a good sign, as I found out later. I came home right away and was with her through her treatments. Her illness was the most brutal thing I've ever seen anyone go through." The claws of pain scraped at him. "I stayed with her until she died. I felt like a piece of me died that day too. I've tried to shut it away. But I don't think you ever shut something like that away. Because of our experience with my sister, my brothers and I do charity events to raise money for ovarian cancer survivors." He stopped himself as it all rushed to the surface.

The sword cut both ways. The painful side cut as he relived the events of Kendall's death. The other side gave him some relief to let go and share it with Marabella.

She covered his hand with hers without breaking eye contact, a silent understanding of his need for restraint. "I'm sorry you went through that. No one should have to watch their loved one die. I can't imagine what life would be like without one of my sisters." Changing the course of their conversation, she asked, "What was it like growing up with brothers?" She tilted her head.

His shoulders relaxed. His body was starting to sag under the weight of his emotions, needing a reprieve from the topic of Kendall. "It had its ups and downs. Declan is the oldest, and Campbell is next in line. They're both in the military but in totally different fields." He hesitated and watched her closely. "Declan works for British Intelligence and Campbell works as a cryptanalyst."

Her eyes grew wide with wonder. "That sounds secretive and dangerous." Removing her hand from his, she rubbed her arms. She looked around and behind her.

He noticed her discomfort. "Are you okay?"

She turned back to him. "Yea, I'm fine. You were telling me about your brothers."

He continued on not sure what just happened with her. "We're very close now, mostly because we went through so much with Kendall's treatments and death. I guess losing a loved one can go one way or the other, bringing you closer or tearing you apart. Lucky for us, we became closer. We fought when we were younger, like boys do, but once the fight was over. It was done. Women tend to hold a grudge a little longer." He winked at her not wanting the conversation to feel like lead.

She quipped, "Oh, really? Well, I'm glad you're so versed in the ways of women. I'm amazed you're not married by now, Prince Charming." She gave him a sly smile. He loved when she bantered with him, pushing his buttons a little.

Provoked by her comment, he would set her straight. "You might say I've been waiting for the right woman to come along. When I was younger, I was in a relationship but was always traveling. My job's very demanding that way. As hard as I tried, the relationship eventually fell apart. I thought it wouldn't be fair to jump into another one with someone when I was away so much. Things have changed lately, though, and I want different things than I did before." He easily covered his real reason for staying single, keeping his heart intact.

She laced her fingers together. "Tell me more about the happier times with Kendall." She was an expert at avoiding anything remotely directed at her.

He let out a breath. "Kendall was the baby of the family. She was the apple of everyone's eye. Her energy and spirit seemed to have no bounds.

My brothers and I protected her fiercely. Sometimes, when she was younger, I would see her out in the fields. She looked like one of those forest nymphs with her strawberry blonde hair flying in the wind. I'm the youngest boy, so she and I were very close." He tapped his fingertips together to steady his bearings. "As children, we played together a lot. Hide and seek was always a fun game on a farm with lots of places to hide. She would hide and I would always find her, mostly because I could hear her delirious giggle. No one can take those memories from me. That's how I will always remember her."

He put his sunglasses on. Shedding tears in front of her wasn't what he had in mind. Secretly in awe of her for her insight, she got him to talk about his happy memories of Kendall. Those happy memories were a beacon in a dark and turbulent place for him. Being so emotionally overwhelmed wasn't a good place for him to be. Feelings about Kendall made him want to drink to forget it all, but with Marabella he didn't want to anesthetize the pain anymore.

———◆———

*Mara wished she* could take that all away from him, but she questioned if it was a way to loop her in. No. His grief was genuine. No one could lie about losing a sister—well, except for Brock. He could probably lie about anything.

Mac hid away his hurt. Sympathy wasn't his trump card to convince her to sleep with him.

He showed her his fractured parts and the man behind the protective barrier, afraid to love and lose.

She imagined what he must have looked like as a little boy, with his ruffled brown hair and big, bright green eyes, following the sound of the giggles. He gave her a glimpse of his a soft side underneath all the male dominance, but it was obvious where his protectiveness came from.

He continued as if a faucet had been turned on. "My parents have never been the same since her death. My mother became more distant. I needed to leave again for a job. I couldn't take the emptiness of not having Kendall in the world anymore. I would often catch myself picking up the phone to call her or suddenly wake up realizing, again, that she was gone forever. When I would come home she would always be there. It's been hard for me to go back." He swallowed the lump in his throat.

She took off his glasses and he let her. The hurt in his eyes shown through as he went back to a place he didn't visit often. His eyes glassed over, but he turned away before any tears could fall. Guilt clutched her for asking about something so personal in his life, but it seemed to be the one common denominator between them, the death of a loved one and a distant parent.

She squeezed his hand in a gesture of comfort and he squeezed back. Their silent moments spoke louder than words. "I'm glad you shared a little piece of your sister with me. She sounds like a very special woman who was very loved and protected."

Two things she sure wouldn't know anything about.

His eyes never left hers as he interlaced their fingers without saying a word.

She gave him a moment then asked, "Your mother became more distant? Were you not close with her?" She wanted more of his pieces.

"No. I could never connect with her. When I was younger, there were moments when she was fun and happy. But as I got older, she became more sad, distant, and unpredictable. I never understood why. When Kendall was sick, my father confided in us that our mother suffered from a bipolar disorder. They had trouble regulating her meds. It explained her highs and lows. She's better now with new medications, but it was an abandonment of sorts. It was one of the reasons Kendall and I were so close. Kendall grounded me." His lips formed a tight line. His fortress was starting to crumble. Moving a French fry around on his plate, he grew quiet.

Her words wrapped it up. "When Kendall died, you lost your soul connection, the bond that kept you grounded." Her eyes never left his face. She survived as an abandoned child as well. "It must have been hard growing up with a part-time mother. Thank God for putting Kendall in your life."

He smiled warmly, a smile that said, 'yeah, you get it and you get me.' If they only had a short time together, she already secured herself in his heart.

"Whadda ya say we walk out to the pier and wait for our boat? We have some time yet." He stood up and held out his hand to her.

Holding hands, they walked down to the pier with the warm sand between their toes. She viewed him with a new understanding, sensing there was even more to this man than met the eye. That excited her, but he was definitely still holding something back. She hoped whatever it was wouldn't come back to bite them both in the ass.

The peacefulness between them seemed to be accentuated by the ocean breeze, settling her down to her soul. These were the moments she wanted to capture in a bottle and open on a rainy day. She relished this little piece of heaven but wanted to add a little bit of fun.

Turning in front of him and walking backward, she proclaimed, "Mara says, first one in the water gets to pick what we have for dinner."

She needed to be playful with him after such a serious moment. This had become her favorite part about him, his willingness to play with her. Turning away, she sprinted toward the water, whipping off her soft velour towel, as it fluttered to the sand. She made sure to wear a black and red high-cut designer suit that showed off her legs and tied behind her neck, showing some serious cleavage.

# CHAPTER 10

*Kitten wants to* be chased and caught. Game on. When Mac caught her, he'd teach her who was boss in this game. This girl loved to be chased, and he would be doing all the catching.

He ran after her, snapping the towel off from around his neck. Her body arced up before diving into the water over a small wave. He dove in after her, following her laughter as it rode the breeze back to him. This time he wouldn't let go. He wanted to hear her sigh of satisfaction from the tenderness he could give her.

As she waited in shoulder deep water, he came up from the bottom, skimming his hands along the back of her legs and over her ass. She shrieked and her body quivered. He came face to face with her, resting his hands on her waist.

"So, I take it you like to be chased? This is the second time I've chased you through the water. Mac says you're in big trouble for running away. I want you to run to me, Marabella, not away." Her stomach muscles quivered under his touch as he rubbed his thumbs along the indents.

"I always loved to be chased, from the time I was a little girl. My sisters and I would chase each other around the house. Mama would yell at us to stop and act like young ladies, but it didn't stop us from laughing and screaming in our game of tag." She laughed at her story, wrapping her arms around his neck. She held her chin up and with a cocky grin said, "I get to pick what we have for dinner. I say, Italian."

He leaned in only inches from her lips. "Lucky for you, I love Italian food and women. Will you be doing the cooking tonight? I always wanted to date an Italian girl who knows how to cook." He pulled her hips into his, leading her into deeper water. She had no choice but to cling to him. He continued his story about his love of everything Italian. "When I was younger, I had a friend who was Italian and lived down the street from me. They used to have the traditional Sunday dinner. I went every week. I stuffed myself full of fresh, authentic Italian foods. I fell in love..."

Her eyes grew bigger, waiting to hear about the Italian woman who captured his young heart.

"...with the food." He loved playing with her. She smirked. He had her right where he wanted her.

She moved back and cleared her throat. "First of all, it's Italian woman, as in one. I won't share. And now you assume we're dating and I'm cooking for you? You're moving awfully fast, Mr. Creighton. Before you know it, I'll be barefoot and pregnant, too. You should know I'm a modern woman." Her eyes tightened.

He spoke in a low rasp as he moved his hand behind her neck, pulling her face close to his. There would be no kiss unless she wanted it. She needed to make the next move. "The thought has crossed my mind. You'll be rosy barefoot...and pregnant." His words were reckless, saying them without even thinking. As strange as it sounded in his ears, he could picture it. He never took the time to even think about a wife let alone kids, but right then, inside of a couple of days, he pictured it all with this woman. Peace came over him as Kendall tapped his shoulder.

Flying solo had its perks, but not when he wanted more of a life for himself. At thirty-four, time nipped at his heels to take the next steps. He couldn't help but think what that life would be like with Marabella. Able to peek out over his fortress, he viewed the pasture of honeysuckle on the other side. He never imagined having some-one break through his defenses so effortlessly. His wall didn't seem to have a purpose anymore. She gradually chipped away at it, coaxing him to step into the light. He hoped the walls would crumble down to the last stone.

Taking her with all her imagined flaws, she needed to believe in her beauty, inside and out. After all, beauty is in the eye of the beholder. He would be the only one to behold her, needing her to understand she would only belong to him. He was already hers for the taking.

Her eyes widened at his proclamation. "Mara says, kiss me, Mac." This wasn't a request. Lust floated in her eyes. They begged him to erase her pain.

He leaned in and gingerly kissed her soft, full lips. Her body jolted as she hummed with satis-faction. He urged her lips open as he flicked his tongue across her lower one. She opened just enough to let him in, encouraging him. Tugging gently at her hair, he tilted her head back, giving him more access to that luscious mouth of hers. He pushed his way in and their tongues tangoed, twisted, and swirled around each other. Sucking on her lower lip, he urged her on. She replied by nipping and licking his upper one. Her lips opened again, inviting him in. She deepened the kiss, demanding he feel their connection.

She sucked on his tongue, making it clear the things she could do with his cock. He retreated, but not before giving her a nip on her lower lip, a warning about who had control.

All that sexual tension found an outlet in one kiss. Hungry and hot, it could easily lead to other things, like him burying himself in her for the rest of the day. His body craved her. He wanted to make love to her, but stopping this was necessary before he lost total control. God, he needed to be in this woman but not here, not now. She tested all his limits. She moaned in protest when he broke away to look at her. They panted as their foreheads fell together. He leaned back to search her face.

"Damn, woman, what you do to me." His heart pounded wildly filled with passion.

Her eyes searched his with a strange mixture of passion and trepidation as her body recoiled from his. She distanced herself. Her body tightened.

"You play 'Mara says' very well, Mr. Creighton." She had found the courage to hold on to some control of her own.

"Oh, so now it's 'Mara says'? Where did you

learn how to kiss like that, *leannan*?" He continued to play with her, not letting her answer him. She needed to understand what she was in for when it came to being with him. Leaning in closer, he flicked his tongue over her lower lip before savoring her mouth. He needed to shorten the distance between them. The kiss was needy for both of them as electricity crackled between them. Her body loosened as she grabbed the back of his hair and held on. That pull went straight to his cock. He connected with her emotionally, but he wanted her physically.

He moved his hands down to grip her voluptuous ass, pulling her closer as he lifted her. She wrapped her legs around his waist lining up with his rigid cock. She moaned, the moan he had been waiting for. He read women's bodies like an expert and loved hearing his affect her. Trailing kisses down her cheek, he nipped her ear. He gently bit the tender place where her neck met her shoulder. For the first time, she said his name on a begging, raspy breath. He became even harder, wanting to hear it again and again, preferably every time he made her come.

"*Leannan*, I'm barely hanging on here. If this were a private beach, I would take you here. But now is not the time or place. I want to take my time with you." He panted, waiting for yet another facet of her to surface, the one that lived underneath the skin of a scared fawn. He wondered if his kitten was really the lioness in disguise.

Her hand lowered between them to stroke his cock. "Aye. The lass knows what's she's doing." He closed his eyes. Her touch was firm as she palmed him up and down. Damn, he could lose it right in his swim trunks like some damn teenager. He made a low grunt in the back of his throat. He opened his eyes as those big, blue innocent eyes of hers just about undid him.

"Is this what you're going to do every time I run away? I'm enjoying this torture way too much." She moved her hand up his hard abs and over his firm chest. Her hand trembled.

He gripped her around her ribs and held her away while grazing his thumbs under her breasts, causing her to swallow hard. He murmured, "I've only begun the torture. Let's see how quiet you can be with the beach full of people behind us." No smile accompanied his playful statement. Her arms came up to cover her chest as her head hung down.

His broad back was facing the beach, so she was sheltered from prying eyes. "Trust me, no can see what we're doing out here. I will never do anything to embarrass you. Move your arms and look at me. I want to touch you." She moved her head up as her arms floated away from her. Her smile was unconvincing.

His thumbs came up to rub her pert nipples back and forth through her suit. He wanted to see her reaction to what he was doing to her. Her eyes fell to half-mast with hooded lust as her arms came up to loosely wrap around his neck.

He untied the knot behind her neck. Her body tensed once again as she closed her eyes. He kissed her as he slid the front of the suit down to her waist, exposing her to the warm ocean water.

"Hold onto me." His voice sounded like gravel.

He rolled her nipple between his thumb and finger while kneading the other. Her breasts fit perfectly in his hands, full and round, even more beautiful than he imagined.

———◆———

*Mara opened her* eyes to see his handsome, masculine hands on her breasts, heightening her arousal. The sensation gave her permission to feel free to be half-naked in the water.

She couldn't believe he enjoyed seeing her in broad daylight. Darkness had been her only friend when it came to sex. She wasn't embarrassed or ashamed to be out in the open like this. He made her a little bolder with his kind words. Unlike Brock's caustic comments that always bit at her and dripped with sarcasm to keep her at a distance. The anxiety of being exposed evaporated. If they got to the point where she needed to tell him about her problem, would she be able to let him see her scars? Releasing those thoughts, she made the hum of a satisfied woman. She wanted to be brave. She wanted to feel normal for once.

His lips curled into a devilish smile. "God, you're so sensual like this. They're perfect and fit in my hands nicely."

She bent her head down, gripping his shoulders.

"Hey, what's going on in that head of yours?" He raised her face with his fingers under her chin.

"I was thinking how I missed out on being with a real man all these years." Regret squeezed her heart.

He frowned. "I have to believe things happen for a reason. I'm here now. I'm not going anywhere." His hand came to the back of her head as he pulled her into another heated and possessive kiss. His thumb brushed past her lower lip down her chin, her throat, and settled at its destination. He kept one hand playing with her nipple as the other traveled down the softness of her belly to between her legs. His fingers carefully stroke her up and down. Her body went rigid as she started to back up.

He took a moment to reassure her. "Marabella, relax. Close your eyes and let yourself feel. Just breathe." His voice low and scratchy with that incredibly sexy accent, as curiosity etched across his face.

Closing her eyes, she breathed out, praying her body would relax. This was Mac. She could trust him with her body. She repeated the mantra in her head over and over again.

He continued to stroke her. His touch sent sparks through her body. She had never experienced anything like it. He read her body, adding the right amount of pressure and making her move into him. As his fingers made a downward stroke, the heel of his palm put pressure on her clit. Back and forth, up and down then circled around. He went to slip his finger inside her suit and her hips jerked back on their own.

"I can't..." Dark terror flooded her senses. She moved to get away from him.

"You're okay." He held her firmly to him as her body trembled, telling her she was okay over and over again to calm her down.

"Do you want to talk about it?" He whispered.

Instead of answering, she simply shook her head back and forth.

Regret coated his words. "I'm sorry. I didn't realize I was moving too fast for you. I would never push you."

She pushed back from him. "Don't be sorry. It's me who should be sorry. It's always me. Let's go before we miss our ride." Her vision blurred from tears of shame and embarrassment. She gave him a light kiss as reassurance and tied her suit back up behind her neck. Swimming to shore, he followed behind her.

She couldn't believe what happened. She almost let herself go with him. His tenderness and patience with her allowed her body to relax, if only for a moment. He didn't push her when she said no. She should have been scared and embarrassed, but he put her at ease. It felt natural to be with him. She could almost hear Raquelle, "You go, girl!"

When was the last time she let go? He listened to her body. But will he be able to deal with her if she tells him about her dysfunction?

Fear and anxiety clutched at her. She wanted to be normal, free of the pain and shame that came with trying to be intimate with a man. Anger bubbled up inside her.

———◆———

*Eyes followed her* as she swam to shore. Those eyes knew exactly what happened between her and Mac. It only stoked the fire that burned. Rage grew due to a failed attempt to get to her and the fact that time was running out. The vigilance would continue until the moment presented itself and a move could be made. There would be no remorse, only a means to an end.

# CHAPTER 11

*Mac ached for* her knowing something went terribly wrong. Her shame and embarrassment hinted to more of her story. His gut told him her reaction had everything to do with her late husband. He wanted to make things right for her and needed to earn her trust.

She fit snuggly into his body as he put his arm around her for the ride out to the dive location. He didn't give her a choice, pulling her to him, letting her know he wanted her no matter what, or how slow they had to go. He stroked her leg and waist, reassuring her.

He recognized an almost irrational need to protect this woman. There would be some hurdles to overcome before they could truly be together. Only time would tell if she would really trust him after he pulled back the covers on his little white lie.

When they reached the dive location, the engines shut down as the waves slapped the sides. The boat bobbed up and down keeping rhythm to the music of the waves. He unlocked her from his protective guard to gather their equipment.

They suited up after he did a step-by-step

inspection of all their equipment. A natural syn-
chronicity flowed between them as they helped
each other with the tanks, masks and regulators.
As instructed, they plunged backwards off the side
of the boat into the pristine crystal-blue water.

They sank into another world. She took her time
to acclimate to the breathing apparatus again. He
waited to see how she would do in open waters.
After a couple minutes, she gave the thumbs-up
and they swam off side by side in watery silence.

Floating among the many brightly colored fish
and surreal coral reefs, the underwater world was
more vivid. The two of them seemed like aliens
as various marine animals came in for a closer
inspection. She brought along an underwater
camera to take pictures of her newly discovered
world.

The beauty and tranquility of being underwater always amazed him, but he also knew some
of that came from the woman next to him. The
peacefulness that settled within him had been
long overdue, feeling grateful in the moment.
Most people could go through life and never
experience this kind of serenity. He would always
treasure his moments with her.

They swam underwater for a short time when he
pointed to an eel in a coral cave. He motioned for
her to go ahead of him to take a picture. Turning
back, he caught sight of something in his peripheral vision. A huge sand shark glided toward her,
probably out of curiosity more than anything else.
She must have sensed something too as she turned
around, coming face to face with the shark.

He knew what to do to deter a shark from

advancing further. He glided between her and the shark, punching it square in the nose. The shark turned abruptly away from him as he leaned back to avoid its tail.

In the confusion, she got hit, ripping her regulator and mask off her face. Panic set in as she realized she had no way to breathe. Her arms began flailing around. The water stung her eyes as she opened and closed them. Bubbles surrounded her, increasing her anxiety as she became agitated. At fifty feet down, she wouldn't make it to the top without air.

He shoved his regulator her mouth as he firmly held her upper arms to let her know he was there. Starting buddy breathing with her, he prayed she would calm down long enough to remember her training. She took a couple of breaths, getting her nerves under control. Not being able to see, she had to completely rely on him to help her ascent.

After a couple of breaths, she started to calm down. He began to slowly lead them to the surface. Taking the regulator from her for air, he created a rhythm between them. She blew out air on the way up. They went back and forth until they floated to the surface. He never let go of her. He never panicked. His calmness came through like an extension of his being that reached out to her, reinforcing her trust in him.

Breaking the surface of the water, he was thankful to be breathing earth's air again. They lay out on their backs to calm down and become reoriented.

"Are you okay? Let me see your face." He hadn't let go of her hand.

She turned to him. An angry red welt seared her right cheek.

"Does it hurt badly?" He stopped short of touching her, for fear it would hurt her even more.

"Yeah, I think I need some ice. Thank you for rescuing me." Even dazed by the whole experience, she looked at him in awe. Had anyone ever come to her rescue before?

People yelled from the boat about the sharks and to get back on board. They swam back to the boat without a second incident and bagged some ice for her cheek.

"I guess my new adventure turned out to be a little more than I bargained for." She regarded him with sad, tired eyes, another reminder of how life can change on a dime.

———◆———

*One minute*, you could be enjoying everything life had to offer and the next, you were fighting to survive. Mara twisted her hands in her lap, realizing she really only had moments with him and nothing more. After this vacation, she would never see him again. He would be her string of memories that she would tuck safely away in that bottle.

She wanted to give herself to him but that required her to uncover all of her horrid secrets. She didn't know if he would want her after she exposed her scars.

He smiled. "Make that a minor diving incident, and I will save you as many times as I need to.

That was a freak accident. I think we should get back in the water as soon as possible so you can erase this memory."

Holding her closer, his lips pressed against the top of her head. He checked her cheek several times as she continued to hold the ice on it. His attentiveness made her ache knowing he was everything that she never had in her marriage.

The ride back to shore was silent as the silk cord between them tightened. The incident drew them even closer together, unearthing more of their true selves.

Climbing off the boat, utter exhaustion took hold of her. She just wanted to go back to the suite and lie down for a while. They walked hand in hand to the pool when two women approached them.

"Hey, Mac! What are you up to? We had a blast the other night and hope you're up for us again tonight." The southern twang came from a blonde in a gold bikini with fake boobs up to her ears. She and her friend balanced themselves on sky-high stilettos, wearing huge Jackie O sunglasses that covered their leering eyes. They made it obvious that they had been with him.

She tensed and dropped his hand as if it were on fire. Growing up in Greenwich she was well aware of the McMahon legacy of the WWE and felt a 'Roman Reigns Superman punch' coming on. Its target, Bimbos One and Two. But instead, her inner Diva played her role with class and dignity. Some habits were hard to break.

Slipping her feet into her wedge flip-flops, she reached for her bag as it slipped from her hand and dropped to the sand. She shoved everything haphazardly in her bag. Standing up, she squared her shoulders and spun away from him. "I have to get going. I've got things to do. I'll see you around, Mr. Creighton." She spoke to him over her shoulder without the direct eye contact.

Pivoting on her heels, she walked as fast as her dancer legs could carry her without running. She had *some* dignity, after all. He called her name but she didn't turn around. He was nothing more than a player and she had 'sucker' written all over her forehead. She wouldn't play anyone's fool again. Having lived it with Brock, she refused to let any man in her life who had a revolving door on his dick. This wake-up call hit her over the head. Score: Mara one, Mac zero.

*Icicles hung off* her words stabbing Mac. He stood there stunned by her reaction. The fawn heard the rustle of the leaves in the forest and bolted away. She automatically assumed the worst, even after the afternoon they shared together. He didn't blame her because, quite frankly, it didn't bode well for him.

In an instant, her impenetrable wall was up, acting as if nothing happened between them. What she didn't realize, this was just Round One.

He turned to the two empty vessels standing in front of him. "Sorry, ladies, not tonight. The other night was enough for me. I'll be staying in for the evening. See ya."

The woman in the leopard-print bikini purred, "Aw, come on now Mac. Don't you want to get to know us better, maybe without clothes this time?"

"Oh, I can see plenty from here, and there's just not enough 'real' to whet my appetite."

They scowled as if he would dare state the obvious. He turned away. Already done with them, he almost stepped on a red shape in the sand. He bent down to pick it up, recognizing the dragon she worked on the day before. Stuffing it in his pocket, he continued on to his suite, wanting nothing more than a shower and nap.

Pre-Marabella, he would have gladly entertained the twosome to make it a threesome. But his new woman would be taking up all his free time and energy. A well-planned strategy was key to navigating these new waters. He wondered if kitten had any clue to what she was in for.

If she wanted to play hard to get, then let the games begin. MacGregor Creighton doesn't give up.

# CHAPTER 12

*M**ara rushed to* catch the elevator. Her mind spun as she became furious with herself. Hitting her floor number several times, she was distracted by thoughts of Mac the player. Damn it to hell! She had attracted yet another one. They seemed to have a direct GPS linked to her.

A tall man walked quickly to catch the elevator. His hair hung out from under his dirty baseball cap, the bill of the cap tilted down covering his face. Her skin prickled at the sight of him. Her breath caught in her throat, rendering her immobile. She let the doors close right before he reached them. She sucked in a breath as she heard him banging on the doors.

Her hands started to shake. She blamed her frayed nerves and current dilemma, Mac. She had been so stupid. He was probably having a good laugh at the pool with the Bimbos, making plans with them for later. Playing his game at her expense, her hands balled into fists. She couldn't imagine an end like this after all they shared, allowing herself to feel safe with him. She trusted him. Lesson learned. Thank God she backed off from going further, preventing her from being a total fool. Playtime was over. She needed readjust her sights on a real man or commit to a life of being alone.

Her polished steel defense erected itself, completely intact. Not a crack to be found, not even for a wisp of light. At least she was used to the dark and lonely place. It kept her safe from the pain and offered a lot less heartbreak. She was broken and tired of the confines of her shield. Overwhelmed, she needed to talk it over with her sisters. Carrying a heavy rivet gun was a hell of a lot of work.

She stalked back into her suite and, of course, the minute they saw her face, they flung themselves at her.

"Oh, my God, Mara, what happened?" Leigha went to touch the swollen red welt streaked across her cheek.

She stepped back, surprised, having forgotten about the injury to her flawless mask. "Shark attack. Mac saved me. Too bad he ended up being an asshole player." Her response exposed the weariness of the afternoon. She lifted an ice pack and held it to her swollen face.

"Thank God Mac was there to save you, Mar. Wait. Did you say asshole player?" Raquelle frowned at Mara's choice of words. She led her to the couch to sit down, applying some aloe to the welt.

Leigha joined them and chimed in, "Well, don't stop there. Tell us what happened and why you think he's a player. Start from the beginning." Lately, Leigha seemed more curious than usual about the navigation of relationships.

"Well, we had a little romp in the water before

the shark attack. He made me...um...very happy."
She wasn't sure she wanted to share everything
with her sisters. She steeled herself for her next
confession. "I was ready to take the next steps and
I really wanted to be with him. As patient as he
was with me and didn't push me, my body resisted
him. I stopped before he could go any further."
She sniffled trying to suck the tears back in.

"He sounds like an incredible man, Mara. I hope
you can see this through. Live in the moment
with him and enjoy it all." Leigha looked like she
longed for what Mara might have with Mac.

She couldn't imagine where that came from.
Leigha appeared to be in a satisfying relationship
that seemed to make her happy. Another reminder
that things aren't always what they appear to be.

"It was freeing to just let go. I trusted him with
my body, which is a totally foreign concept for
me. He read me so well. I could feel him study-
ing me, but in a good way. He said he wants to
know everything about me. I don't know if he's
willing to accept me the way I am. He gained my
trust after he rescued me from drowning. That
was beyond scary." Anxiety took over as she hung
her head down, lacing and unlacing her fingers.

"Mara, what's wrong? You should be having
the time of your life with a wonderful man. We
want you to let loose and free yourself from all the
Brock garbage." Leigha hit the nail on the head.

She felt free yet secure with him until his two
hoochie mamas showed up. "We were walking
back to the pool area when two bimbos showed
up and commented on what a great time they had
with Mac the other night. So, in other words,

they all had one big orgy." She puffed out an exasperated breath.

"Whoa, whoa, whoa. Just because they said they had a good time doesn't mean there was a wild sex party. Did you let him explain himself?" Raquelle wore the rational hat for once.

"No," she muttered.

A part of her wanted to believe he was a player so she wouldn't have to unpack any of her baggage. She would never have to tell him her secrets, even though he already suspected something wasn't right about her. Wrestling with the riveted constraint, banging up against the walls at regular intervals, she was torn between its security and wanting it gone for good.

"Mara, you need to live in the moment right now and enjoy every minute. You never know when life will all come to a crashing halt." Sadness came over Leigha's face. She couldn't help but wonder what secrets Leigha held that would make her say such a thing.

"Leigha is right, you know. Don't worry about tomorrow. Do what feels good now. You don't owe anyone anything. Give him the benefit of the doubt. Hear him out. Look how much he watches out for you. That means a lot. Players don't try that hard to pretend to care about someone who may or may not be a quick lay. You need to let yourself go and explore that man from head to toe. That's exactly what the doctor prescribes." Raquelle crossed her arms over her chest. She was a professional in the live freely philosophy.

"You better rest up because tomorrow, we're going on a shopping spree. You are getting an outrageously gorgeous dress and then we're going dancing. We haven't done that in forever." Raquelle's remedy to any shitty situation: shop for something expensive, splendid, and attention getting and show it off.

"Thanks. I don't know what I'd do without the two of you. Who knew this would be such an insightful vacation and I would need a protector, of all things." Her words fell short as if contemplating her next move. "You know, you're right. I can't think about what might or might not have happened with those women. But I sure can make him sweat a little." She felt a little more triumphant as she stood and made her way to the bedroom for a nap before dinner.

By late afternoon and drained from the day's events, it didn't surprise her that she hadn't heard from Mac. He must have figured out that she saw right through his game. Mara says, 'Fuck off, Mac'.

Making her way to the living room, she touched the side of her face. The swelling had gone down. The redness could always be covered with makeup.

The day had worn them all down as they decided to order in and have an early night. Tomorrow would bring some much needed bonding time between them with full relaxation. She wanted Mac out of her system and looked forward to the distraction.

# CHAPTER 13

*The next morning* Mara carried the dagger of the bimbo encounter in her chest. Caught between wanting to be right about Mac and wanting to be wrong, she couldn't escape how he made her want him with every gentle touch and kind word. Questions niggled at the back of her mind. Is he that way with all his women? Is that why they came back for more?

Turmoil gnawed at her but she wanted to shut it out. She needed to keep pushing forward and make changes. It felt like having an out-of-body experience. She hardly recognized this strength, but she embraced it. When life gave you lemons, you made lemonade. When a player crossed your path, you needed to play him.

She made her way to the living room and sat down at the table. "By the way, I'd like us to do a spa day with the works, including that Brazilian wax thing, whatever that is. I refuse to let Brock's abuse keep me down. I'm alive and he isn't. I don't even want to think about Mac. I need things to change. I know I'm the only one who can make those changes." She wasn't as confident as she sounded. The conversation with her sisters seemed to swing wildly from heavy to light.

Leigha and Raquelle glanced at each other and then at her, awestruck. "Well, halle-fucking-lu-jah. I had no idea what condition you would be in today, but I'm glad you've decided to fight. About the Brazilian wax thing...it hurts." Raquelle beamed with excitement. Mara had found some balls, so to speak.

"I want it all gone. I want to get in touch with myself again. I need to see and feel everything from now on. If I ever decide to have sex again, I don't want to hide." Staring down at the table, she wondered where that all came from.

She felt skittish about what she was about to do. If she didn't want to hide, she should rid herself of the make-up. But that seemed drastic. She still needed her mask, protecting the image she always put forth.

Leigha chimed in, "Hey, first of all, you need to slow down. You went from zero to Raquelle inside of twenty-four hours. You need to stop and evaluate what your marriage to Brock was all about. What was going on with him? Why did he want to hurt you? Let's not forget about the DNA tests."

Horror ripped through her chest. "Oh, shit! I forgot all about that. They took those hair samples. What are they looking for?"

Leigha looked up warily. "I think they are trying to figure out if Brock's body was actually in the car. A man without a head or hands is very hard to identify. They're working with what little they have left of him."

Raquelle held her coffee mug and turned to

Leigha. "When did you turn into CSI?"

"Well, I watch a lot of crime shows. There's a lot of information on them about this kind of stuff." Leigha sat stick straight and sipped her morning white tea, not bothering to make eye contact with either of them.

"You know what? I don't want to think about him today. Today is my day with my sisters. Screw him. He was miserable to live with and I probably should have left him, but that would have been another failure in Papa's eyes. Besides, Papa seemed to like him so much." She gave out a long sigh that came from deep within her lungs. "Let's order room service and indulge in a wonderful brunch, go to the spa and shop. What do you say?"

They both nodded and ordered a huge brunch, complete with French toast, Eggs Benedict, bacon, and fruit. They spent time chatting about what they wanted done at the spa.

Raquelle gave her some advice on the Brazilian wax procedure. "Smaller strips are better for first timers. Are you sure you want the Hollywood leaving you completely bare?"

She answered with a resounding, "Yes."

The pain couldn't be any worse than sex. Determined to know what Brock saw or didn't see, she would be the final judge and jury on her body. Score another one for her. Pollyanna has left the building.

Their spa day included manis, pedis, massages, facials and of course the wax. She would meet up with her sisters after the scheduled body primping. Wanting to put her best forward, she wore her perfect mask. They were going to hit the club and dance their asses off. Screw Mac and his harem. She'd find someone else.

A storm was beginning to form in her. She wanted to cut loose a little and partake in some mixed beverages, following Raquelle's prescription for partying. The girl knew how to party, always the star attraction, knowing how to work a room and bring in the guys.

Throughout the day, she reflected further on her relationship with her sisters. As close as she was with them, they each were so individual, adding different dimensions to their sisterly unit. Their closeness came out of necessity because of an absentee father and they needed to be there for Mama. They depended on each other for everything, especially day-to-day activities. Mama seemed to be submersed in a quiet despair, missing Papa with no way of getting to him. He seemed detached from his family for various reasons, including being married to his career and passionate about his artwork.

Her lack of knowledge about men came from her distant, if not non-existent, relationship with her father. Evidently, she knew nothing about men. Otherwise, she never would have dated, much less married, Brock. Sadness weighed her down and then her angry rose. She wasted all those years with him. But like Leigha pointed out, things happen for a reason.

She would persevere to figure out the reason for marrying Brock, the cheater and abuser. But once was not enough for her. No, she needed to be attracted to Mac, another liar. With his job in security, protecting people came naturally, giving them a sense of safety. He certainly used it to his advantage to get laid. But her intuition nagged at her that something was different about him. He could have anyone he wanted, so why hang out a woman with cracked parts? Her tears pushed behind her eyes as she analyzed her own insecurities.

Sitting in the tranquility area waiting for her sisters, she hoped the pain between her legs would soon go away. God, the wax hurt! Determination led her to want to see herself. What she saw didn't seem to be that out of the ordinary. She appeared to be like everyone else. The only other naked women she had seen were her sisters, but she hadn't exactly examined and compared.

Satisfied with the results, she'd find someone who loved all of her, head to toe. She wondered what Mac would think. Would he like all of her like this?

Her sisters sauntered around the corner like two very lazy cats in need of a sunny window. "Well, girls, how did everything go? Did you enjoy your spa day?" She fought back the tears so they wouldn't start asking questions again.

Their skin was rosy and buffed, with satisfaction and good health written all over them. "Oh, yes. This hit the spot. I'm ready to go shopping, take a nap and be ready to dance my ass off tonight. However, you might not see me until tomorrow morning." Raquelle wiggled her eyebrows, plopping herself down in the oversized, cognac-colored, soft leather chair.

"Let me tell you, if Tom could give me a rub

down the way Pablo did, I would have sex with him every day." Leigha smiled contentedly but it didn't reach her eyes.

"You mean you aren't having sex every day? What's that about?" Raquelle laughed as she teased Leigha.

Leigha smacked Raquelle on the shoulder as they all started laughing. Only Raquelle, the one not in a relationship, would want sex every day. she hoped Raquelle's future husband had a strong libido.

They got dressed and headed out for some shopping. The resort property boosted high-end boutiques with all the designer names like Celine, Armani, and Donna Karen. They frequently bought from those designers shopping in New York City. But the unique French boutiques like Bebe carried some sexy sassy clothing, in case they wanted to show off their wild sides. Raquelle made a beeline for the sass-on-a-rack stores.

"This is the perfect store. Look at all the cool, funky, sexy dresses that can attract all the right attention." She was as gleeful as a guy at a strip joint. Funky sexy trumped designer.

Leigha and Mara sighed reading each other's minds. Oh, here we go again. She's in the zone.

"Oh, Mara, I spot lots of dresses that will look sexy hot on you. Here, come and try a couple on for me." Raquelle went into her singsong voice. They were doomed to end up with revealing out-fits, hopefully with a little class.

After trying on close to twenty dresses each, they all picked their favorites with shoes to go with each outfit. You couldn't have one without the other, a traditional girls–out–shopping rule. They took their treasures back to the room, hung them up, and headed to their rooms for long-awaited naps after a relaxing day.

She lay in bed, wondering what Mac was up to. Did he go out partying after the dive? Did he get together with the bimbo twins again? Better yet, why did she think about him at all? She knew why. He wormed his way into her head, knocking on the welded door to her heart. He found a way to sneak behind her shield. The hold he had on her couldn't be ignored. Her internal compass always seemed to point in his direction, steering her back to him. She hadn't made this kind of connection with any other male on the planet and even with her lack of experience, something screamed 'uniquely different'.

What will she do when she sees him again? She couldn't let him know how much he affected her. That would be too easy. This time, she'll play hard to get. If he wants her, he'll need to work for it. Could she possibly survive him and his charm? There were other fish in the sea. She just wasn't sure she wanted them. She drifted off to sleep thinking about him and a million possibilities.

Waking up an hour later, she heard the murmurs of her sisters having an intimate discussion in the living room. She poked her head around the door as they stopped talking and stared at her.

"Hey, how was your nap? Are you ready for dinner and dancing?" Raquelle beamed to distract her from their discussion.

"What were you two talking about? It seemed pretty intense." She wanted some answers and wouldn't tolerate being left in the dark again by anyone.

"We're talking about you and Brock. I can't believe what a son of a bitch he was." Leigha didn't swear often.

She sighed as her shoulders sagged under the weight of her past. "Well, can I pick them or what? You know, after I got the wax today, I looked at myself. I don't see what the big deal was. From what I can tell, I look like everyone else between my legs. I realized just how cruel he could be." His needling words stung her.

"He was a douchebag. He probably suffered from small dick syndrome. I can't believe the way he treated you and we didn't know it." Raquelle expressed herself creatively when she was angry, known for her one-liners.

"I guess it would have helped if I had opened my mouth before now. But to tell you the truth, I was scared. I walked on eggshells around him. He got angry over nothing. I was never sure what would set him off. I tried to keep the peace."

A memory roared back to her. His voice rang in her hears. "Mara, are you a moron or what? Why didn't you give me the message that he called? I told you I needed to know right away. Are you trying to ruin my career, 'cause you're doing a great fucking job of it. Get away from me. You make me sick! You spoiled brat!"

He always stormed off, slamming things along the way. In the beginning, she always ended up in the formal living room to cry. She refused to bring that negative energy into her studio. Besides, she hated the formal living room. He insisted picking out the decor with ugly burgundy and purple accents. If she vomited in there, no one would be the wiser.

As time went on, she became used to his rants and they rolled off her back, hardening her self-imposed prison. But then he would amp up the verbal assaults. Examining it closely, she realized he made it a point to hurt her in every way possible.

Leigha knew all the answers to any question you had about yourself, even those you didn't even think to ask. "What he did was so detrimental to you and your relationship with him. Promise that you won't hide from us anymore. As for the sex thing, I think you should book an appointment with a therapist when we get home."

A therapist? Shouldn't she see if it isn't better with someone else first? Besides, did he really have a small dick? Compared to Mac, she was beginning to wonder. The fact that she had no clue spoke volumes about her experience in the sack.

"I think you need to find yourself some booty. We're going all out tonight and find you a man. Maybe we'll run into Mac again. He's hot! As for the two bimbos, forget about them." Raquelle planned out their evening, making it sound so damn easy. Men were effortless for her. But for the rest of womankind, men were like navigating a testosterone-filled labyrinth. You kept guessing where to turn next.

Their heads jerked up at the knock on the door. Raquelle bolted to answer it, coming back with the most beautiful bouquet of flowers Mara had ever seen, a colorful array of dahlias. The card that came with them was addressed to her. Raquelle put the vase down on the glass tabletop and handed her the card. She opened it and softly gasped at the words.

> *Marabella,*
>
> *I will be with you again. This isn't an end but a beginning. I know what you must think happened, but looks can be deceiving. Please, let me explain it to you.*
>
> *Dahlias are the native flower of Mexico. They are everywhere I look, much the way you are everywhere in my head. These flowers remind me of you. The cream-colored flowers with rose-colored tips remind me of the blush on your skin. The blue-purple ones remind me of the color of your eyes the first time I saw you on the plane. You captivate me.*
>
> *I think I need to clear up some things between us.*
>
> *Mac says, see you soon.*
>
> *P.S. I'm holding your red dragon hostage, but he's drying out quickly. Time is running out.*

He left his cell number. She would have the next move. Reading the card a couple of times, she noted the balance of romance, charm, and humor. Damn him anyway. He wasn't going away anytime soon, which gave her mixed feelings of want and revenge.

She showed the card to Leigha and Raquelle, hoping they would guide her. They hummed at the heartfelt words. At the very least, she would text him, thanking him for the flowers and the effort of putting it all together.

She began to text as Raquelle reached over and snatched the phone away from her, sprinting for the bathroom before closing the door behind her. She ran after her, but was too late.

Pounding on the door furiously, she yelled, "What the hell are you doing, Raquelle? Do not send him some perverted text. Do you hear me?"

She turned around as Leigha snapped pictures of the flowers with her Nikon 7100—her casual camera, as she liked to call it. She took every opportunity to take photos everywhere they went, even with her phone. No doubt the scrapbook would be very full after this vacation. Her other obsession was putting together photo albums of all events of their lives. They had volumes of all their big events from the time they were children, thanks to Leigha's avid picture taking.

Raquelle stepped out of the bathroom with a wicked smile on her face that said she had done something left of center.

"I thanked him for the flowers, informing him you'd be out dancing tonight and you would catch up with him sometime tomorrow. You can't let him think he holds all the cards, darling." She tossed her the phone with the smile of a Cheshire cat.

"Fine. But I was going to thank him for the flowers and leave it at that." Her voice held a pissed off tone. She hated when Raquelle took too much control of other people's decisions.

"Don't worry, Mar. You may get yourself some booty yet." Raquelle giggled like a teenager going to the prom.

"Mara, I, for one, don't think you need a booty call. You've got a lot to sift through before you move on. By the way, what's the reference to the red dragon?" Leigha used the voice of reason and curiosity.

"I must have dropped the new muse I was working on in the sand. I guess he picked it up. God, I'm so confused I don't know which way to turn any more. I really like Mac but I can't believe I'm attracted to another player. I know I need to get out there and take a chance, but it needs to be a calculated chance with my eyes wide open this time. I want to feel connected to someone, someone genuine. What Brock did was abusive, but I've got to move forward and try not to move backwards." She choked on the last sentence. Hearing it said out loud confirmed what she already knew—her marriage almost destroyed her.

Confusion set in as another rivet come loose, letting a small ribbon of light into her world. She wanted to bathe in the light. Just talking about her emotions made part of the wall fall away. She needed to let go of her past destruction with Brock. Dead and buried was where she needed to leave him.

"You don't know for sure if he's a player. Keep an open mind until you get to know him better. I have a good vibe about him. I don't know why." Having one of her serious moments, Raquelle's instincts were usually dead on about people, which gave her a bit of hope.

They ordered a light dinner in the suite and

lounged in the hot tub before getting ready to go out. They needed the relaxation and playfulness of just being together. Being in Mexico finally felt like they left The City behind, ready for frolicking and fun. The stress slowly ebbed away from all of their pressured lives back home. But there was a storm brewing that they would all need to brace for, relying on each other like never before.

# CHAPTER 14

*Mac sat back* and took stock of the events of the last couple of days. His phoned binged as he received a text from Mara thanking him for the flowers. His card might have been a little much, but he needed to get across that he hadn't given up on her. He'd never taken this kind of leap before. No turning back. His sailboat sensed the change in the winds, forcing him to alter the sails.

Her text was short, sweet, and to the point. She would see him when she was ready. Really? He twirled the red dragon in his hand while he plotted his next move.

———◆———

*Raquelle picked out* Mara's dress for the evening, what was left of it. Featuring a tightly fitted sleeveless bodice in azure blue, it plunged in the front and back with crisscross silver ties in the V-shaped neckline. The flare at the bottom was more than a couple of inches above the knee. Shorter than she was comfortable with, it was time for her to step out of her comfort zone.

The silver metallic shoes sported four-inch

heels, making her butt look great and her legs look longer. The cups in the dress pushed up her breasts nicely as she braved a G-string. She lacked the courage to go commando. Wearing next to nothing under her dress and minus any hair made her feel naked and nervous.

Breathing deeply, she applied makeup, her coping mechanism in place for the evening. She hardly recognized the person in the mirror from twenty-four hours before. Where had she been for the last five years?

She worried the evening out might be a little too much too soon but her sisters made her feel adventurous. She craved more of the light on the other side of her walled existence. Standing back to look at her mask, she hoped her night out would give the steel rivets the push they needed to find their way loose, letting in all the light.

She came out of the bathroom and stopped to give Leigha the once over. Her red dress had a slit up the thigh as the material draped seductively in the front and back making her look statuesque. Red shoes matched her dress as she stood over six feet, a striking Amazon woman. Of course, her red clutch came equipped with a camera.

Raquelle, on the other hand, dressed to kill. Her silver dress had a scoop neckline that hugged every curve and left nothing to the imagination. She wore it like a second skin. Her shoes, black with crystal accents, made her shimmer from head to toe. Mara hoped Fish Boy knew what he signed up for.

"Well, don't you two look stunning? You're going to turn every head in the club tonight." She wore a huge grin as her nerves played underneath her skin.

"I'm not worried about that tonight. I want to party with my sisters. It feels like a block has been lifted between us. I'm not even sure we knew it was there. As soon as we started talking about that asshole Brock, things changed. I guess in the end, he was good for something." Raquelle's moment of introspection took Leigha and her by surprise.

Leigha voiced her intuition. "You're right. I feel closer to you both. We've never talked about sex before, and I had no idea what was going on with Mara. I just felt something was off."

The more intimate parts of their lives were never talked about. That all changed with her confessions of being an abused wife.

A small tear formed in her heart. "I'm sorry I didn't come to you sooner. I didn't know what to do. I was stuck with nowhere to turn. I thought what I was going through was normal for a married couple. Now that I know differently, it pisses me off. But I also need to move forward with my life and leave him behind, where he belongs."

Leigha and Raquelle came over and gave her a tight Italian hug. She didn't realize uncovering her secret would bring them so much closer.

"Enough of this. Let's go. You two should loosen up tonight and get wild, although I doubt you will." Raquelle twirled around and headed for the door.

Down at the club, the music thumped as bodies kept time out on the sunken dance floor. The lights created a hypnotic atmosphere as Usher sang 'DJ'. Bars flanked either side of the dance floor. Colored light reflected off the brushed nickel swirled bottom as white lights shifted underneath translucent onyx tops. The barstools donned metal saddles that gave you little security if you had one too many drinks. The back of the club opened up to one of the pool areas. Candles floated in the water while white lights twinkled in the trees. There was something for everyone.

Mara started to relax, looking forward to the evening. No pretending allowed. The real her would be out on the dance floor, wanting the steel curtain to fall away and let life happen.

They sidled up to the bar as they ordered their usual drinks: She had a Blue Dragon, Leigha chose a dry martini and Raquelle sipped a raspberry vodka tonic with lime. They say you can tell a lot by what a woman drinks. Their tastes were very distinct, a little sweet with a little bite. It was a good start to what she hoped would be a fun night.

Raquelle yelled over the loud music. "Hey, let's go dance and turn up the heat."

They swiveled their way through a sea of bodies to the center of the dance floor. Their dance moves drew attention from people around them. Raquelle danced front and center. Her silver dress reflected the lights above making her look like a disco ball.

Mara twirled around so her dress flared out slightly at the bottom. The music soaked into her skin, consuming her, as she realized how much she missed dancing. Everything around her seemed to melt away as her body took over. She got lost in the feelings of freedom and happiness.

The heavy erotic bass pumped through her body sparking thoughts of Mac.

One of the onlookers in the outer circle grabbed her and started dancing. She obliged, but kept space between herself and her dance partner. The song ended and her sisters headed off the dance floor. She tried to leave but her companion pulled her back for another dance.

She introduced herself. Her new dance partner was Jack. His dark curly hair and brown eyes made him fairly good looking, but his smile was insincere. Glaring at her up and down, he kept licked his lips as if he saw an ice-cream cone. Whether it out of nerves or because he was a lech, she couldn't be sure. He made her uncomfortable.

"So, where are you from, Mara?" His lips twitched. She wanted to smack the disgusting smirk off his face.

"New York City. My sisters and I are here on vacation. Where are you from? Do I detect a Boston accent?" She needed to keep one step ahead in this exchange.

He moved closer invading her space. "You would be right on the money. Are you having a good time in Cancun, honey?"

"Yeah. I'm having a good time. I love the weather and the people are really friendly." Too friendly from the looks of it.

He moved his hands around her waist, but she managed to spin out of his grasp. Grabbing her by the hand, he twirled her around a couple of times, hooking her into his body. As he turned her around to face him she put her head down, smacking into his chest. Her nerves got the better of her, realizing she wasn't ready for any of this. Her senses were assaulted by the smell of his sweat and cheap cologne. His sweaty hand had found her leg and started moving up the back of her thigh. She tried to push him away.

"Relax, baby. We're just dancing and having a good time, right?" His purr came out like a hairball.

She pushed against him again, but he held her tighter. No one would notice among the distractions of gyrating body parts and wild lights. Her breathing became shallow as her panic began to rise. This was what her body did before the world closed in, making her nauseous. A trickle of sweat ran down the valley of her spine. She was overwhelmed with the urge to run off the dance floor before she went into a full-on anxiety attack.

"It's hot out here. How about we go to the bar to have a drink?" She hoped he would take the hint.

He had an all-knowing smarmy look plastered on his smug face, as if he held some secret. "Sounds good to me, baby. Lead the way."

She closed her eyes briefly relieved that there was space between them. Ordering her second Blue Dragon of the night, she hoped it would take the edge off. He ordered a Crown and Coke.

As the bartender put the drinks on the bar, he turned to her. "Hey, can you help me find my friend in this crowd? He's tall and blond. He's supposed to meet me here, but I haven't seen him."

She turned away to scan the crowd. Her internal compass pointed in the direction across the bar. Gazing over her shoulder, her eyes locked onto

Mac. She took him in from head to toe—black jeans that hugged his ass and thighs, with a white, button-down linen shirt.

———◆———

*Mac walked into* the club and made his way to the bar. His poison of choice was the smooth, fullness of a cool Guinness. He didn't care for the ale warm, like some of his mates. He scanned the crowd curious to find out what interested everyone in the middle of the floor. Moving closer to the banister surrounding the top edge of the dance floor, he peered down to three goddesses dancing, to everyone's delight. They drew a crowd of mostly men, hoping to score. His eyes zeroed in on only one.

She was stunning in her blue dress as it floated around the tops of her legs. Those legs would be the end of him. She looked like a little sex kitten, grinding around, making him hard for her. He was going to need to tame the beast tonight. God, how he wanted her. Combing his fingers through his hair, he blew out a breath.

Each time she raised her arms over her head, the hem hiked up to expose her firm thighs. She was hypnotic. He remained mesmerized by her grace and how well she coordinated her hips and legs. Taking out his phone, he snapped pictures of her. His eyes followed her legs up to a tight bodice that enveloped full breasts as his possessiveness took over. No one would be getting lucky with his lady. She might not know it yet, but she was most definitely his.

A guy from the outer circle grabbed her in for a dance. He stepped back out of sight to observe the scene in front of him. Keeping a protective eye on the situation, he waited for it to play out. He would give her space, but still needed to keep tabs on the situation.

They played a slower, seductive song and Sleaze Boy made his move. It looked like a game of tug of war. Her body language screamed defensive and anxious.

They walked off the dance floor and sat at the bar. He observed, with interest, as his protective side kicked in.

She looked over her shoulder and his eyes locked onto her. He rapidly ate the space between them as he made his way through the crowd, leaving a wake of people behind him.

Lifting her drink to her lips, she only took a small sip before he grabbed out of her hand. "Don't drink that. Your friend here put something in it." He growled as he glared at Sleaze Boy.

"Hey, I don't know who you are, but you need to back the fuck off, pal." Sleaze Boy stood up, but his height brought him eye level with Mac's chest.

"What did you put in her drink? A roofie?" He grabbed him by the shirt as he hung by his sleeves.

"I don't know what the fuck you're talking about. Roofie? Do I look like I need to drug girls to get them to go to bed with me?" He rambled on about his male prowess while being hauled across the bar and out to the pool.

Mac threw him down on the stone deck, raising his fist to punch him across the jaw. "God, don't hit the face. I'll tell you anything you want to know." He covered his face and cowered.

Mac got within inches of his face. "What's your name?"

"Jack." His eyes cinched closed.

"What are you doing putting drugs in her drink?" He managed to say through gritted teeth, his blood was at the boiling point.

Jack opened one eye. He raised his fist again as a threat hoping Jack might wet himself before he was done with him.

"Okay, okay! When I came in the club tonight, some guy approached me. He pointed out Mara and said he would pay me five hundred dollars to put something in her drink. Then he handed me a vial of white powder. After I put it in her drink, I was supposed to lead her out to the pool. I figured the guy was desperate to get laid." He squirmed around on the ground, flinching under a very pissed-off Scotsman.

"What did he look like?" His eyes pinned him down through the interrogation.

"He had dark blond hair, baseball hat, and tinted glasses. The dude was a mess, like he'd been out partying one too many nights. He was shorter than you, but not by much. That's all I know, man." He covered his face with his hands.

Leaning down, he picked Jack up by the shirt. He got in his face, nose to nose, seething. "If I see you anywhere near Mara again, it won't be your face you need to worry about." Pushing him away, Jack took the hint and ran out of the club.

What the friggin' hell was that all about?

# CHAPTER 15

*Mac stood there* with his hands on his hips and head down. Some holiday this turned out to be. He played defender for his Italian goddess but was spinning his wheels with more questions than answers.

"Mac? What's going on?" She stood behind him with fists at her sides as tears glassed her eyes.

He spun around wanting to grab her and hold her in his arms. But he stalled knowing that move might be too much for her. "Mara, are you okay? Did he hurt you?" He tried to keep the anger from his voice.

He was amazed how well he knew this woman in such a short time, working off his gut instinct about her every time.

She ignored his questions, sharing her new epiphany instead. "Do you know that no one outside of my sisters has ever come to my defense? Not even my late husband." Her face contorted with pain. Seeming shocked by her own admission, she collapsed on the lounger behind her as her head hung down.

He straddled the lounger and sat behind her, cradling her with his arms and legs. Stroking her arms up and down, it was a gesture of comfort, nothing more. He needed to be careful and gentle with her so she wouldn't run away again. He spoke in a soft voice as he nuzzled her ear. "I would say you were married to the wrong man. You're a treasure, Marabella, both inside and out. But I need you to be more aware of things around you. That guy tried to slip you a roofie."

"A roofie? What the hell is that?" She turned around, sounding alarmed and irritated at her own naïveté.

"It's also called the date rape drug. It renders you unconscious while your date has his way with you. You don't remember anything. The next day is accompanied by one hell of a hangover. It's nasty stuff." He hoped the explanation put her more on guard around strangers. Revealing that Jack had been paid by some stranger to do the deed wasn't in her best interest. He'd be looking into that later.

Her panic started to fade away. "How would it make me feel if I did ingest some of it?"

"You might feel drowsy or tipsy. I don't think you took in enough to have any effects from it." He saved her from a fate worse than death.

"Mac, you have no idea what you've done for me. I can't imagine how all of that would have ended up. I want to share something with you. Not only was Brock, my late husband, the wrong man for me, but I recently woke up to the fact that he was abusive, as well." She closed her eyes.

He scooted back and turned her all the way

around on the lounger to face him. She folded her legs under her.

"What are you talking about, Marabella?" He didn't lose physical contact her with as he tenderly stroked her forearms with his thumbs.

"What I thought was a normal progression in my marriage turns out to be abuse behind closed doors. He was verbally abusive, as well as other things that I don't want to talk about right now. When Jack held me on the dance floor, not letting go, I started to panic, which is all too familiar for me." Tears trailed down her cheeks.

Brushing his thumb along her jawline, his shock left him mute. He let her information sink in as angry bile rose to the surface. "That explains a lot. I saw you tense as he tugged you closer. I wanted to put him through a wall. But never again, Marabella. No one is ever going to hurt you again, you understand me? I'll make sure of that. When you're ready to talk, I'll be here to listen." He sounded a tad possessive, but hoped it came across as protective in her ears.

She nodded her head with a faint smile.

"I'll walk you back to your room." He assumed it would be the logical conclusion to the evening.

***

*Mara shivered* and goose bumps appeared on her arms. Those eyes were on her again. She looked around but saw no one.

"What's wrong?" He held her upper arms.

"I have this uneasy feeling like someone is

watching me. It gives me the creeps. It's happened a couple of times since I came to Cancun." She surveyed the pool, a little braver with him by her side. Then the feeling left as quickly as it came. She turned back to face him. "And no, I don't want to go back to my room. I came here to dance and have a good time. I'm not letting some asshole keep me from that." She surprised herself with her own fortitude, refusing to let anyone control her emotions.

At first, taken aback by her response, a smile spread across his face. She hoped she had surprised him.

"Hey, watch your mouth, young lady." He teased her.

She earned the right to swear after realizing what could have happened.

Jumping back off the lounger, she offered her hand. "Mara says, let's dance."

She led him back to the club with her head held high. The circus-like atmosphere accosted them. There perched at the bar were Bimbos One and Two. They waved over to Mac.

She snapped her head in his direction. "So, I pegged you correctly. You're a player." She wasn't sure she wanted to hear the answer, but it was an evening full of surprises.

"About that, I think I need to clear something up. I wasn't with those two the other night. Yes, I went to the bar and had a couple of drinks. They happened to be there as well, but I went to my suite alone. I used to be a friends with benefits kind of guy, but then I met this Italian beauty on holiday. She's making me reevaluate things.

You're in my head, Marabella, and I want to get to know you, all of you, good and bad." His statement held commitment. Holding her hands, she felt his determination, no wavering. He firmly pressed his lips to hers.

Her stomach flipped at his words. It sounded like he might be going through some changes of his own. She stood there, as her heart leapt in her throat. Secretly, she was very pleased because that kiss took place right in front of the two bimbos as well as every other woman in the club.

He may be a one-woman man after all.

She didn't want to admit out loud that he was in her head, too. Staring at him, she wanted to know more about her protector's change of heart. More rivets waited to pop out of their secure location. Would the real Mara please step forward? She felt herself come back to life. "Let's go dance and have some fun."

As they made their way to the dance floor, she did a visual check on her sisters. Raquelle cozied up to the man she 'caught' the other day as Leigha entertained one of his friends with a standoffishness that said, "I'm taken". She made eye contact with them as an unspoken vibe let them know she was okay.

Enrique's song "Tonight" started to play. She took the opportunity to turn him on the way he turned her inside out. Starting to move her hips, she swayed back and forth with the heavy bass, hands above her head, never losing eye contact. He matched her grind for grind.

The man had moves. Grabbing her waist, he brought her closer to him as they began to dance.

Together they were simple and effortless, moving in sync with one another. Her hands traveled up to his broad shoulders, wondering what other surprises he had in store for her.

The next song slowed down with a sexy groove as Paula Cole sang "Feelin' Love". He pulled her in even closer. In her heels, her forehead came right to his lips. He brushed them across her forehead before he circled his arms around her waist. She inhaled his masculine scent then closed her eyes, leaning into his shoulder, such a contrast to her encounter with Jack. Her thigh rested between his legs as she felt him rise to the occasion. Smiling to herself, she decided to get a little daring. She rubbed her thigh up and down against his hard cock. Hearing a groan come from him, she giggled in his chest.

She looked up at him using her most innocent voice and batted her eyelashes. "Did you say something?"

"Woman, you know exactly what you're doing. Don't play innocent with me." His eyes were stern but playful.

The butterflies fluttered in her chest as she turned her head into his shoulder again, heady with the idea that just dancing with her turned him on.

His cock strained against the zipper of his jeans, pointing to the exact location it wanted to go. Her giggle made him even harder, as if that was even possible. Lightly caressing her back, he skimmed his hand over her ass. She tensed a bit but then relaxed into his touch, melting into him. He let his hand linger but not for long, just a taste. His lips found her neck as he kissed his way up to her earlobe, giving it a light bite. Her breath hitched at the spark of pain mixed with pleasure.

When the song ended, he led them off the dance floor to get a drink. As she mounted one of the saddle stools, he stood to the side of her in a guarded stance. She ordered another Blue Dragon while he got a Guinness. An overwhelming need came over her to share her abusive past. She wanted to move forward with him. With liquid courage in hand, she would feel the fear and do it anyway.

"Thank you for the flowers and the kind words. It means a lot to me. It's the most beautiful thing anyone has ever sent me. You certainly have a way with words while cutting right to the chase. By the way, Raquelle was the one who sent the text. She's a sneak." She eyed him to gauge his reaction, glancing at his lips. Her eyes flitted between his mouth and eyes.

"You're welcome, and I meant every word of it. You are a classic beauty and need to be spoiled by beautiful things and words." He drew his thumb across her lower lip as he tilted his head in wonder.

The alcohol was going to her head. "I suppose you're just the man to do it." Her gaze kept returning to his lips as she licked his thumb.

"Oh, *leannan*, I'm the only man to do it and if you keep looking at me like that, I can't be responsible for my actions." He leaned in and gently brushed his lips against hers as his tongue grazed her lower one. She let out a small moan.

"Hmm, we'll see about that." Her face warmed

as the alcohol settled in.

She knew if her abuser were still alive, he would have taken advantage of her. Sometimes she used alcohol to numb the pain. Now she needed it to spill her secret.

He nuzzled his mouth near her ear. "Mac says, we call it a night and I'll walk you back to your room."

She glanced at his mouth again, licking her lower lip. He picked her up under her arm leading her to the door.

Moving toward Raquelle and Leigha, she filled them in on the night's events. It was anyone's guess where Raquelle would be sleeping that night, but she knew Leigha would be coming back to the suite later.

He held her hand as he led them out of the club, past Bimbos One and Two, who were trying to gain attention on the dance floor. They looked at her with pure disdain in their eyes. She couldn't help but wave to them as she left with Mac. There was great satisfaction in letting them know just who he had chosen from the group. Take that, bitches.

She wavered. Once she shared her secret, he may decide to leave, despite his committed words. Her journey with him may end before it ever gets started.

# CHAPTER 16

*Mac held her* hand as they rode the elevator to her floor. The sexual tension hung between them like a petit thunderstorm. His body was charged up but he had to tap it down. He may be playing the long game after all.

At her suite door, she turned into him, body-to-body and giggled. She kept up her assault, undoing him brick by brick. If she invited him in, he would decline, claiming he needed to get some sleep. He refused to screw this up by having sex with her when she clearly wasn't ready. He couldn't make it about sex this time. His curiosity ran deep.

"Would you like to come in and get a tour of the suite? The terrace balcony has a priceless view of the ocean. I promise not to bite." She was being cheeky and fun. The alcohol had taken its toll.

Those big, blue eyes made him cave like a house of cards. "Don't make promises you can't keep, but I'll take my chances and come in anyway. I want to be clear. I'm not the kind of guy who takes advantage of a girl who's tipsy. I want you completely sober when we're together so you don't miss a thing." He winked at her as she opened the door. Dropping her stuff on the table, she headed for the second-floor balcony.

Climbing the stairs behind her, he stared at her luscious ass. When he got back to his suite one long, cold shower waited for him, which would do nothing to abate the craving for this woman.

The view from the balcony was priceless. He had the same view from his suite at the other end of the resort. She walked to the edge holding on to the railing and breathing in the crisp beach air. The ocean breeze wisped softly on her skin and rustled her hair. He walked up behind her.

He needed to reel it in and wait it out. There were feelings here that needed his attention more than what his cock needed. Sliding his hands around her waist, she leaned back to put her head on his shoulder. He smelled the honeysuckle in her hair bringing him back to thoughts of home again. This time they were replaced by the thoughts of her with him in Scotland. He rarely brought anyone home and oddly the thought didn't scare him.

"It's beautiful, and the stars are incredible." He just stood there, holding her. Peace came over him. He nuzzled her neck, brushing her hair to the side as she turned in his arms with lusty eyes. He wanted to kiss her, but this time would be different.

They say kissing is one of the most intimate things two people can do. You can tell a lot from a kiss. It just may be the direct line to the heart. Things had changed since he last saw her, not only for him but he sensed there were changes for her, too. While she continually broke through his roadblocks, he'd gotten her to trust him a little bit more. He needed to make this count, making sure she was well aware of how much she affected him.

The breeze gently moved her hair. He took her face in his hands, rubbing her rosy cheeks with his thumbs while his fingers cradled the back of her head. Her eyes never left his, like two beacons searching his thoughts.

His heart winched at the thought of how she would react when she found out his secret. She would figure it out sooner or later. He banked on later, though, after her heart was safely tucked away. That would go both ways. Once she made her way beyond his fortress, there was no turning back. She would capture him mind, body, and soul. He would be all hers, moving heaven and earth to make it work for both of them. She interrupted his train of thought with a question.

"What's a *leannan,* Mr. Creighton?" She said smugly, knowing how she affected him as the evidence poked her in the belly.

He continued to stroke her cheek. "*Leannan* means sweetheart in Gaelic. My grandfather used to call my grandmother that all the time. It came out naturally and seems to fit you." The gentleness in her eyes held him captive.

"I bet that's what you tell all the girls." She stood back, testing him and searching for the truth in his eyes.

He held her waist firmly. "Actually, you're the only one, because of its special meaning for me. My grandparents were married for sixty years before they passed away. They loved one another very much, dying within days of each other. It's like they were made for each other." He held her gaze to make sure she understood his implication. She was significant to him in many ways. He had just thrown it all out there. Nothing ventured, nothing gained.

She sucked in her breath, aware of the shift. "I'm sorry. I didn't know the name meant so much to you. Otherwise, I wouldn't have made light of it. Thank you. I love the way *leannan* sounds when you say it. Now that I know how much it means to you, it makes me feel special." Her eyelashes fluttered down with the apology.

He grabbed her chin to face him. "You are special, Marabella. I don't want you to forget that, ever." He believed it down to his Scot blood. He wanted to erase whatever harmed her at the hands of her dead husband.

"You never call me Mara, always Marabella." Her eyes sparkled.

The back of his fingers ran down her neck. "It's a beautiful name for a beautiful woman." He let out a restrained sigh.

Leaning over, he touched his forehead to hers. "I need to go before things get out of control. I want you too much."

His soul-altering kiss would have to wait. The evening became heavier than he intended. He gave her a chaste kiss on those lips he would be dreaming about later. Passion would have to wait in the wings to make its debut.

# CHAPTER 17

*Emotions rolled through* Mara as she thought about telling Mac everything. As things progressed, all her broken pieces would be revealed. If she got honest with herself then she needed to start by getting honest with him. She had to reveal what haunted her. Standing on the precipice of something bigger, she warred with herself on what to do. The moment had presented itself.

"Wait." She grabbed his arm as he turned from her. "Can we sit down? I need to talk to you." His eyes assess her as silence screams ran in her head. The combination of her liquid courage and his words of endearment made her braver than ever before.

This was the risk she needed to take. She was exhausted from living behind the shield in darkness. She needed to share this with a man she trusted. He expressed his willingness to wait. Sexual tension pulsed in the air between them but he would walk away until she was ready. She looked over that edge again, and this time the jump felt right.

"Marabella? What's wrong?" He frowned as worry covered his face.

She plopped herself down in the nearest lounger while he sat across from her, knees touching.

Gripping her hands tightly together, she began to strip her layers away. "I want more with you. What happened between us in the water was incredible. It felt different than anything I've ever experienced. Not that I have that much experience." She dropped her head to hide her embarrassment. "You're not going to like what I tell you next."

She looked up as she locked her jaw concerned for what he might think of her confession. Afraid that she would appear to be the most naive woman on the planet, her hands began to twist.

He put his hands over hers. "I want you. And yes, damn it, I want more, too. I took your lead and held back. It takes every ounce of self-control I have not to ravage you. You're struggling with many things right now. I don't want to go too fast and ruin everything. I want to know every-thing about you. You aren't like any other woman I've ever met. As you've already guessed, I've had more than a couple of women, but none have got-ten under my skin like you have. Whatever you have to tell me, I can handle it. I'm not going to run, *leannan*." The green in his eyes darkened.

She blinked a couple of times, taken aback by his raw honesty. Her own family didn't read her as well as he did in the short amount of time they had been together. The wheels were set in motion. She couldn't turn back.

Taking her hands out from under his, she gripped them together to the point of pain in her lap. Using them as an anchor, she took a deep breath and looked up at him. If he rejected her after her confession, she wanted to witness it firsthand. "I talked to my sisters about my sex life with Brock. They informed me that I was abused by him." She waited to see his reaction as he cursed under his breath. His features strained trying to understand.

She continued on before she chickened out. "Before my husband, I had only been with one other man, once, and not successfully. During most of our marriage, he more or less forced himself on me. Sex was often painful for me. And..." She hesitated, as her shoulder slouched, debating whether she should paint the whole picture for him. As this layer peeled off, she would shed some of the pain in the process. Taking a deep breath, she continued, "Sometimes, I bled. I don't want to go into all the details, but I thought you should know at least that much. The doctor said there is nothing physically wrong with me. Some women just encounter painful sex. I may be one of them, although I don't know for sure."

Lost and confused by her own conflicting words, she steeled herself to finish what she started. "Raquelle seems to think this was more his fault than mine. Honestly, I have no idea. The last year of our marriage, we didn't have sex. I suspected he was having an affair, which my sisters confirmed for me. I thought that sex, or lack of sex, between us was normal for a couple married five years. To go along with all of that, he always made many nasty and hurtful comments about my lower area, which makes me incredibly self-conscious. There was always something in the back of my mind that said maybe this wasn't normal, but I was too embarrassed to tell anyone the real details of what was going on. Now, after talking to my sisters, I feel stupid and naive."

She debated whether she wanted to confess her true feelings about her dead husband as the tears started to crest at her bottom eyelashes. Her voice cracked at her next truth. "This is going to sound awful but when he died, a huge weight lifted off me. That's when I began to question everything about him and my marriage. It sounds wrong, but it was an awakening for me. The clouds parted so to speak. I wanted to tell you so you can run now and spare yourself from being with a frigid incapable woman."

The tears streamed down her face as a sob broke out. "I'm so broken, Mac. You should get out while you can. But it was important to me that I was honest with you." Her tears made a path down her blushed cheeks, clearing the way for what lay underneath, the real her. Not wanting him to turn away from her, she needed him for so many reasons. She prayed he wouldn't run. This was the real her, a whole picture of the stained glass window and not the shattered pieces of colored glass created by her despicable husband.

He pulled his hands through his hair with a huff and gritted his teeth. His anger spewed forth without control. Standing up from the lounger he began pacing. He seemed bigger to her, puffed up and pissed off, like a raging bull. His eyes tightened. "It explains a lot. That goddamn son of a bitch! It sounds like he enjoyed being cruel. He knew exactly what he was doing. I could show him what cruel is. I can torture a man with the

will of steel till he cries like a baby. Friggin' asshole. My God, if he were alive now, he wouldn't
be for long. I'd pull his cock out through his nose
and make him bleed."

With his hands on his hips, he blew out a long
deep breath to gain some control. Standing there
for a long moment, he stared at her, anger edged
with disbelief. He sat back down on the lounger,
never looking away from her. Her heart pounded
with fear.

He leaned forward, grabbing her hand as he
stroked her fingers. Holding her face tenderly
in his other hand, he caught her tears with his
thumb. "I'm not going anywhere, Marabella.
Your husband was a real bastard. He knew he was
hurting you. The fact that he didn't try to find
out what was going on with you said a lot about
him. I still want us to be together. I want to try
and find out what happens. I don't see a frigid
woman in front of me. I see someone who is inexperienced, scared, and abused. You are a victim of
ignorance. How could you recognize if something
was wrong if you didn't know what was right to
begin with? Yes, your sisters are right, he abused
you. Sex between two people should be trusting,
loving, slow, and with awareness—playful but
not painful. Don't let him break you. Don't let
him stay in your head and rule your body. You're
stronger than him. It's a weak man who preys on
a woman and chips away at her self-confidence."
He took in some of her pain as he choked on his
words.

If there was any man who could help her
through this, it was Mac. He was cut from a dif-

ferent stone. He would stay. She couldn't believe
what she heard. She didn't know many men who
would have stuck around after hearing her story.
His words were like hearing your favorite song
on the radio bringing you back to a serene place.
This incredible man wanted to be with her damaged
and all. He might even be able to help her
put her broken pieces back together.

More of the rivets wiggled in place, ready to
pop out. She was ready to emerge from her self-
made cocoon of steel. The tears making their way
down her cheeks weren't ones of sadness. These
were the tears of relief that he heard her truth and
still wanted her. The heaviness of her past left her
as she revealed her darkest secret to a man willing
to see it through. A huge relief coursed through
her, washing over her body like a clean ocean
wave. One of her prayers had been answered.

Her heart felt lighter yet stronger. The dark
cloud dissipated replaced by a ray of sun. She
viewed him like a savior.

Leaning in closer he said, "Oh, *leannan*. You're
so unique and don't even know it. Don't cry." He
kissed her softly to show her how gentle he could
be with her, continuing to solidify her trust in
what could be between them. He would take her
just the way she was, imperfectly perfect.

———◆———

*Mac had a* new appreciation for his goddess. She
had been through so much. Some of it without
knowing things were drastically wrong. She was a

survivor. He would wait for the lioness that hid in her somewhere. He wanted to be strong enough for both of them but in the end, she would be the stronger one.

Guilt gripped him as he realized what it took for her to tell him her secret. What would she do when she found out his secret? The shit would hit the fan, no doubt.

She kissed and tugged at his lower lip showing him she was up for the challenge. "These are happy tears. The best kind." A new light shined in her eyes as his understanding seemed to eclipse the pain of Brock. "I can't believe you want to be with me."

He continued wiping away her tears with his thumb. He hummed with content.

"What's that hum for?" She caught his thumb with her fingers.

What passed between them had ignited with a new understanding and a profound respect. "I admire you so much. I feel content when I'm with you. You're stronger than you know." He couldn't believe she still wanted to try to be intimate with any man. And she picked him.

The passion between them was palatable. He needed a taste of his *leannan*. The tension threatened to kill them, but first he needed her to be comfortable with him. "Mac says, come lie over here with me." He stood, offering her his hand, leading her to an oversized lounger.

"Funny, I thought it was Mara says." She smiled through her tears.

He liked that she was into the game of 'Mac says'. She used it to her advantage one too many times. After all, the game was 'Mac says' not 'Mara says'.

He lay down directing her to lie between his legs. She lay on her side with her head on his chest. "I can hear your heartbeat," she mumbled.

"Yes. And you send it into a gallop." He kissed the top of her head and reveled in her smell. He stroked her arms and back.

"I can't believe you want to see this through with me. You're a brave one. This could be a real disaster." She looked up at him skeptically. Her eyes scanned his lips.

"You didn't give me a choice. Once I saw those big, blue eyes and those long, strong legs, I was a goner. Eros helped too. Did you know the green dragon is part of the Creighton family crest?" He waited for a beat. "Marabella?"

"Ummm?"

"How did his wings break?" He cringed, suspecting he already knew the answer.

Her fingers curled into his shirt. "I would keep him in a shadow box with some other little creatures. One day, Brock got mad and threw a glass at the shadow box. Everything fell out onto the floor. Some of them couldn't be saved, but I'll always keep Eros no matter what shape he's in." She smiled, realizing the double meaning in her statement.

He pulled her up so she straddled him. She was in the position of control. "So, even when he's an old dragon and has no fire left in him, you'll still keep him?" He wore a sly grin and ran his hands up and down her thighs.

She continued the banter. "Oh, yes, absolutely.

Besides, I can always find a way to keep his fire burning." She smiled and leaned over to kiss him tentatively, teasing her tongue into his mouth, letting him know she would be okay.

Passion made its entrance in a grand way. The spark ignited a flame quicker this time, as his hands traveled up her thighs. His hardness grew underneath her apex. She began to rock back and forth. A low hum came from the back of his throat. As his hands traveled farther up, he stopped, breaking the kiss abruptly. "Marabella Luccenzo, are you wearing any knickers?"

"Yes. It's called a G-string. Raquelle suggested it so I don't show any panty lines. Why? Don't you like it?" She taunted him.

"I like it very much, but let me be clear. When you aren't wearing panties at all, it will only be when you're with me." His eyes locked onto hers, deadly serious with no room for negotiation.

"Understood, Mr. Caveman. I mean, Creighton." She started to laugh.

"Oh, so you have a smart mouth, too, eh?" He laughed with her.

He pulled her down and crushed his mouth to hers, a kiss of possession. Pushing his hips up to meet hers, it elicited a moan from her that made both of them pant. He gripped her firm ass and used it as leverage to move her up and down his cock. He knew he couldn't take it any further. He just wanted her to feel. His kitten had her head thrown back and eyes closed.

"Look at me, *leannan*." He commanded.

Her eyes popped open with her pupils dilated and filled with lust. Her skin flushed. She was the most incredible sight. She made him want to claim her, but he knew what she needed instead.

"How do you feel? Are you wet?" He said through a pant. He wouldn't push things by finding out for himself. She needed to become more aware of her body and what it was doing.

"You're amazing. I should be wearing a sign that says 'slippery when wet'." Her words hung on a raspy voice.

Throwing his head back, he let out a belly laugh as she laughed with him. He stopped moving his hips and stared at her. There was power in how responsive she was to him. "Will you ever stop surprising me?"

"I hope not." She gave him a soft smile that cast a shadow of doubt.

"We need to call it a night. I've got special plans for you. I think we should have dinner tomorrow night, but with a request." He gripped her thighs. "I don't want anything to be between us. When you come tomorrow night, I want to see you and not all the makeup you hide behind. No makeup, Marabella. You hide behind a mask in order to draw attention away from your luscious body, and now I know why. He made you believe you're ugly, but I see everything about you. Under all that is the real you. That's who I want to be with. Can you handle that?" He challenged her.

---

*Mara gasped* and her body tensed, not because of his demand but because he admitted seeing right through her. She wanted to jump in the deep end with him. It was time to sink or swim. Other rivets moved slightly, waiting patiently in their holding places. The light that he shone on her wrapped around her and made her more secure than ever.

"Yes, I'm ready to handle that. I trust you and right now, that's enough." Her words held sincerity still laced with a touch of fear. Lust simmered beneath the surface and was amped up, ready to explode.

"I'm going out fishing for the day. I think it might be a good idea for you to spend some time with your sisters. I'll pick you up at your suite tomorrow evening." His hands continued to stroke her legs.

"Sounds good. I'm looking forward to it." She smiled as she leaned over and gave him a kiss of things to come.

She hopped off his lap and followed him to the door. He could have had his way with her, but he chose not to. His ability not to act on impulse spoke to his character and how he respected her journey. Maybe she *could* trust him with everything. She floated behind him as if carried by a life raft.

Perched up on tiptoe, she gave him a kiss and said good night. After closing the door, she got ready for bed. Her body hummed with excitement and a new energy. She felt revived but the feelings were unfamiliar. As her heart yearned for this uncharted territory, her body winced at the potential outcome of the evening with him. Were the winds of change powerful enough to overcome her past?

# CHAPTER 18

*Mara slept soundly* despite the emotional roller-coaster of the night before. Her mind kept going back to why anyone would want to drug her. She had so many questions, but her focus was on the man who saved her from a potentially hor-rific situation. His actions spoke volumes about his character. He was a perfect combination of passion, playfulness and gentleness.

She still reeled from the idea that he wanted her even after he found out about her secret. She wasn't sure any man would want to be with a woman whose body betrayed her with sexual pain instead of pleasure. She believed her body's reac-tion was her fault.

The thought of telling him about her past with Brock had made her break out in a cold sweat. Since she crossed that abyss, she couldn't be hap-pier. They would be spending time together that night. Looking forward to whatever he had planned for her, she hoped things would just hap-pen between them. The whole evening could end in disaster, but she needed to push forward and take a chance. The doubt about what her body might do still haunted her.

He was her protector on more than one occasion. That strengthened her bond to him. She wouldn't lie to him about anything, facing her demon head-on. If he didn't want her after that, then she was better off without him.

She climbed out of bed, tentatively. As she came out of her room, there sat Queen L drinking her white tea and eating breakfast. "Good morning! How was the rest of your night at the club?" She asked cautiously.

"Well, well, well, and what do we have here, sis? You seem very bright eyed this morning. Did something happen last night that you want to talk about?" Leigha couldn't help but give her a wondering grin.

"Nothing dramatic. Unless you call getting almost drugged, being saved and then having a hot guy's hands all over you your average evening out." Her face warmed everytime she talked about him. These things didn't happen to boring people like her. On TV, sure, but in real life? Never.

"Are you okay? You had me worried but Mac said he got to you before the drug did. He texted us last night to fill us in on more of the details. I have a good feeling about him." Leigha sat back and looked into her teacup. A dark cloud of pain came over Leigha's eyes, like she was remembering something. When she glanced up, the cloud had disappeared.

"He wanted to beat the pulp out of Jack, the drugger. I guess now that I'm single again, I need to be more careful when I go out someplace. I felt those eyes on me again last night at the pool. It creeps me out. I told Mac about it so he could keep an eye out."

As she replayed her story, she began to eat her breakfast in earnest, having built up an appetite. She wanted to push down all her negative thoughts.

"So...tell me about the rest of the evening, Marabella." Leigha, using their motherly tone, left no stone unturned.

She sighed heavily. "What went on between us was better than anything I could have imagined. He's a wonderful man in every way."

"Kinda makes you wonder what else he's good at." Leigha interjected while she absently stared into her cup.

"Okay, *Raquelle*. By the way, where is she? Did she spend the night with Fish Boy?" She frowned. She didn't like Raquelle's taste for men who were strangers.

"She texted to say she would see us sometime today." Leigha shrugged. It was typical Raquelle, but she always let them know where she was staying after a night out.

The door flew open and in strode the one who walked on the wild side. "Hey, how's everyone doing this morning?"

She and Leigha wanted to slap her for being just a little too 'I'm lovin' life'.

Leigha's body stiffened. "I take it you had a wonderful evening of partying and great sex."

"Actually, I had a great night of partying, but the sex? Not so much. He was a little too drunk and not very creative. Good thing this is just a vacay thing." She looked away seeming truly disappointed. "How was your night with Big Mac?

And how big is he?" Raquelle winked at Mara.

"Really, Raquelle? That was bad. It didn't get that far. I'm not some slut. We had a wonderful time and that was it." She cringed when she realized how her slut comment came out, feeling a little indignant in her response to her overly zealous sister.

Raquelle let the comment slide because her sisters didn't know what they were missing when it came to men. "Yeah? So, how was your wonderful time?" Raquelle wanted all the details. She wasn't taking no for an answer.

Mara sat up straight ready to reveal her excitement about Mac. "The evening was one of the most wonderful times I've ever had with a man. He's exceptional, saving me last night from a horrific moment. I guess I need to be more careful." She paused, distracted by her tipped coffee cup and set it down with a clink. "I told him everything last night. I needed to be honest with him. He has a right to know what he's getting into with me." She glimpsed at her sisters who were looking at her with compassion in their eyes. "I told him about Brock and the abuse. He became furious with everything that happened, but he didn't waver in his conviction to me. He wants to continue to be with me and try to make this work for us. He said making love should be playful and fun, not painful. He actually wants to be with me intimately." She let out a sigh. "I'm worried that if I just let things progress, my body will betray me." Her bottom lip started to tremble, the doubts flooding in. She bit down to stop the tears.

"If he's the man I think he is, he will understand and be gentle with you and take his time. You need to be honest with him about how you're feeling in the moment. If he walks away afterwards, it's better to know now instead of later. I don't want you to be hurt again, Mar." Raquelle's hand covered hers.

She needed to keep the lines of communication open with him. It was a strange feeling to be understood and cared for by a man but she desperately wanted to give them a try.

Leigha turned to Raquelle. "Who are you and what have you done with my sister?" Spinning back to Mara, she continued, "For the record, I think Raquelle is right. You need to be honest with him about everything you're feeling—before, during, and after. He obviously cares for you for more than a one-night stand."

She would need to be brave and see this through, but would her body be able to make it to the finish line?

———————

*Mac woke up* the same way he went to bed, thinking about Marabella with a raging hard-on. The cold shower did nothing to abate his craving for her. The memory of her body on his only added to his morning wood and needed to be taken care of right away. He always slept au naturel, so his cock led the way to the bathroom.

He took a good look at the suite he splurged on. High, white ceilings and beige, swirled-marble floors, with furniture in neutral colors spoke to the understated opulence. The accent pieces such as throw pillows and other decor were in turquoise, reflecting the colors of the ocean. The large balcony featured a beautiful blue hot tub with a waterfall feature coming out of a privacy wall. He hoped to entertain on his vacation, but the only woman he wanted to be with was Marabella.

The sound of her name rolled off his tongue. He loved his affectionate Gaelic name for her, *leannan*. When the word just fell out of his mouth it was like a tap on the shoulder from his grandfather. He never used that word of endearment before because it never fit anyone. She was special.

Sensing that she might be overwhelmed with everything that happened, he wanted to prove to her what making love could be, not the horror show of her dead husband's abuse. The connection between them was too strong not to fight for. Fighting was born in his blood and now, so was she.

He made his way to the bathroom big enough for a party of ten. The floor was covered in flat river rocks and the walls were cream travertine. The shower stall was over-the-top with glinting glass tiles in shades of bronze with LED lights that colored the ceiling. He planned to take advantage of the rain shower, six jets, bench and satellite radio.

Turning on all the water features and the radio, he relished the jets as they pummeled his body, hitting all his tight muscles. After a thorough massage, he turned off the jets and let the rain shower cascade down his body.

The music blared with Robin Thicke singing

about blurred lines and wanting a good girl to go bad. He knew that girl. Lathering up with a spicy, woodsy bath gel, he started to think of everything he wanted to do to her body. Even though his libido wanted her, no holds bar, his head told him to be cautious and gentle. His claiming of her would take time.

The head on his shoulders played cock blocker as his body screamed for release. Based on her reaction in the water and in light of the new information, he knew he needed to move carefully not to scare her off. He finally knew what held her back and scared her, her fuck-nut of a husband.

How would kitten feel under him? Would she purr with delight when she came?

His thoughts led to how he would please her as he began to stroke himself. He wanted this pleasure to last, remembering how her breasts filled his hands as he rolled her nipples between his fingers in the warm ocean water. His lips would replace his fingers, sucking gently on her hardened nubs, listening to her moan with satisfaction. Cupping that gorgeous ass of hers, his fingers would find heaven between her legs. She would be wet and ready for him, but he would take his time. God, at this rate, he wouldn't last long.

He tightly stroked himself up and down at just the right pace. As if he could grab her, his fingers curled on the hard tile above his head. The thought of her beautiful body and the way she smelled tipped him over the edge. He wanted to know what his cock would feel like inside her, rocking her slowly, watching her face as she had the first of many orgasms he would give her. She would arch her back and cry out his name. That visual shot him off like a rocket, saying her name over and over again, wishing like hell she were there with him.

Panting like he had just finished a marathon, his cum slid down the shower wall as he braced himself with both hands. He needed to pull his shit together. Relaxing on holiday always made him horny. Normally that would be a good thing, but he needed to find a balance if he didn't want to blow it.

Sex was usually done out of necessity, not because he was involved emotionally. It had been a long time since he felt anything at all for anyone outside of his family. Longer than he cared to admit. Fear clawed at his chest when he thought he almost lost her at sea. She felt good and whatever this was between them felt right. Yeah, he leapt into the deep end, treading water in a sea of emotions. He would slay his demons to be with her. She would be worth the wait.

He finished his shower and got dressed. The red dragon glared at him from the nightstand. It had dried out looking pissed off and evil. The face was contorted and the ends of the wings and tail were sharp. He didn't think it was what she had in mind when she made the creature.

A chill hit him, giving him goose bumps on his arm. Something nagged at him, a gut feeling that wouldn't let go. What was the drugging really all about? He needed another set of eyes. There was only one person he trusted for this situation.

He decided to reach out to his CIA contact and old partner, Sydney. As a highly trained agent and computer hacker, she would have some insight into the night's encounter with Jack. He needed her expertise and recon. Confident that no matter what happened, she would always have his back. They saved each other's arses on more than one occasion. Having worked together for so long, they had memorized each other's moves, in and out of the shadows.

During the phone call he found out that she was on her way to Mexico for holiday. He filled her in on all the details and requested she bring plenty of ammo for any situation. She would be on the next flight out, catching a ride on a company jet with a layover in Cancun. Security wouldn't be a problem for her clearance level. Sometimes, fate *did* work in his favor.

After making some arrangements, his only focus was a day of fishing, wind surfing, and relaxation. The evening with his goddess could end many different ways. He needed to be prepared for anything.

# CHAPTER 19

*Mac came back* to his suite after a day of ocean fishing and wind surfing. He needed to relax and unplug from the world while getting in a workout.

Sitting on the table was the dossier he had been avoiding. His boss, Neil McFadden, had passed it to him on his way out on holiday. McFadden mentioned that he wanted him to just keep an eye on things for the time being. He wasn't sure he wanted to know what those things were.

He sat back on the couch and closed his eyes. Moments later the phone rang snapping him out of his deep sleep. Astonished that two hours had gone by, he picked up the phone and confirmed the location and meal with the caterers for dinner.

Everything had to be perfect for Marabella, from the atmosphere to the food. He wanted to make sure the evening was casual to set her at ease. What he didn't tell her was what he had in mind for a little romance. Having about an hour before he needed to get her, his heart pulsed in his throat.

MI6 with nerves? He could fend off a shark, but got nervous having dinner with a woman? Okay, not just any woman, *the* woman. Bloody hell. Where did that come from? He needed to keep cool.

He managed to pull himself together and he made his way to her suite. He took a deep breath before knocking on the door. She yelled, "Come in" as he turned the doorknob.

He stood in the doorway as she sauntered around the corner and stole his breath away. Her hair was up in a loose bun. A few strands curled freely around her face. She wore a simple blue and white floral sundress that hugged her curves and fell to mid-thigh. A pair of blue wedge flip-flops accentuated her legs. The red welt left by the shark was barely visible. Seeing her in person was so much better than anything he could possibly imagine.

He leaned forward and gave her a kiss on the cheek, lingering near her ear. It would take all his control not to take her before dinner. "How are you feeling today? You don't have any after effects of the drug, do you?" He looked at her intently.

"I'm actually fine. I don't think I took in enough to have any aftereffects. Come on in." She moved aside to let him through. As he brushed past her, sensuality poured off her in waves, crashing over him. He wanted to lose himself in her undertow but needed to calm down.

"You're naturally beautiful without any makeup. The red mark is barely visible." He drew his thumb softly across her cheek, not wanting to stop touching her. "I really like you this way. I might start to worry that someone is going to steal you away from me." His mind latched onto the word *mine*.

He didn't miss her checking him out from head to toe with mischief in her eye. His hair was tousled with sun-kissed highlights. His pale Scottish skin tanned from being out on the boat all day.

She smirked. "I iced my face more today. It looks like you got some sun." She walked over to the table and handed him a bottle of red wine. "I figured we're having Italian since I won at 'Mara says'." She bit her lower lip while trying to hold back a smile. Oh, this woman would bring him to his knees.

He took the bottle from her while securing his arm around her waist. He whispered. "First of all, the game is 'Mac says'. Second, you can win anytime you want to, but wait and see what happens when I win." He peppered kisses across her jaw and down her neck. Her body shivered at what the night would bring. Relaxing, she melted into his embrace.

"I don't know about you but I'm starving." He winked at her, knowing she got the double meaning from their encounter at the pool.

"I know, with all that saving damsels in distress." She giggled as her hand covered her mouth.

They turned as Leigha and Raquelle came into the living room.

"Raquelle and I just want to thank you for what you did last night. I'm not sure what we would have done without you. That date rape drug can be pretty powerful." Leigha's hands were clasped tightly in front of her and spoke as if she was familiar with the effects of the drug. He hoped he was wrong.

"It's not a problem. But let me ask you both

something. Have you felt like someone has been watching you?" He needed to gather more information on this whole situation and test his instincts. He might leave his job but his job never leaves him.

Raquelle spoke after glancing at Leigha. "We haven't felt that way at all. What do you think is going on?" She frowned curious about his spin on the situation.

"I don't know, but I need you all to be extra careful until I can figure this out. Just be aware of your surroundings." His focus was aimed at Raquelle, knowing she might not take the situation seriously.

"Thanks, Mac. We will. We promise. Don't we, Raquelle?" Leigha wanted to make sure Raquelle got the message.

"I get it, I get it. Let's face it. Brock's death is still suspicious and until we get the DNA results back, we need to be careful. Who knows what that sack of shit was up to?" Raquelle spat venom when it came to anything related to Brock.

Okay, so he didn't need to worry about her. If someone ever took her, they would give her back on feistiness alone. He would question Marabella about the DNA testing later. He turned to her. "Shall we?"

They turned to leave as she mouthed over her shoulder. "Don't wait up!" Then gave her sisters a wink. "So, where are we going?" She leaned into his shoulder as their fingers intertwined.

"It's top secret. You'll have to wait." He kissed the top of her head. The smell of her relaxed him.

They walked along the beach as they came

upon a small tent in the distance with a warm glow. Dusk on this side of Mexico painted the sky various shades of blue across the horizon, making a beautiful contrast to the amber tent. Small, white-capped ocean waves lapped onto the beach as the cool sand wisped over the tops of their feet, leaving a light dust. The sound of the ocean completed the mood.

He led them toward the tent as she suddenly realized where they were having dinner. "This is what you planned for dinner? I think you went overboard, Captain." She beamed at the idea of dinner on the beach.

"Nothing's never overboard when it comes to you. I wanted to do something special for you because you're turning into someone special to me." He put his hand behind her head and kissed her deeply. "Leave your shoes and step inside."

———◆———

*Mara loved the* feel of soft sand between her toes. She glanced down and noticed his feet. There was nothing sexier than a man with tan bare feet.

They stepped inside to find a chef at a grill with a server. Hurricane lamps sat in the sand casting a glow of warmth. They surrounded a table and loveseat filled with overstuffed green-and-blue patterned pillows. Large coral-colored conch shells were scattered in the sand. An iron chandelier hung above the table filled with short red candles. The top of the tent was vented sending curls of smoke into the air.

She became speechless with awe. He came up from behind, wrapping his arms around her waist. He leaned down. "I never want you to forget this night with me."

"How could I? You've thought of everything. The whole thing is simply beautiful." She turned in his arms looking into the eyes of a very happy man. "Thank you." She pressed a kiss to his lips, smoothing her fingers down his freshly shaven cheeks.

"How about we start off with a glass of wine? I'm not much of a wine drinker, but I'll give it a go. We'll have scotch after dinner back at my suite." He held an air of confidence as he took control.

The thought of going back to his suite had her in knots. She was nervous, scared and excited all at the same time, not knowing if she would ever be ready for this. But the time was right and so was the man.

He read the uncertainty in her eyes. He took her hand rubbing his thumb over her fingers and led her to the table. The wine might calm her nerves.

She gave the toast. "To a handsome, honest man who doesn't run away from any of my challenges."

He held his glass up to hers. "To a brave woman, willing to face her challenges, and who will conquer them." He looked into his wine before drinking as if it held a secret.

The red wine ribboned its way through her body, warming her to the core. Dusk settled in as shadows came over the tent, adding to the ambiance making it warm and cozy. One thought did flash through her mind—for someone in security, he seemed to have a lot of money. She knew putting this together wasn't cheap. She tucked that thought away in the back of her mind, not wanting to spoil the evening with twenty questions.

The table was set for a romantic dinner for two. Candles of various sizes, shapes and colors were placed everywhere. Their flames danced as the gentle breeze came off the ocean, making the sides of the tent billow. The delicate white china and multi-faceted crystal caught the light leaving sparkles on a blue tablecloth. There was a colorful arrangement of varying shades of red dahlias interspersed with delicate baby's breath. Her artistic eyes roamed to take everything in.

"Mac, everything is so beautiful. You put so much thought into tonight. I can't believe you did all of this for me." She paused and twisted her hands together. He glanced her hands and waited for her to tell him more. "I don't remember the last time any man did something like this for me." She talked into her lap.

"You seem to appreciate the beauty in simple things. You deserve to have someone spoil you rotten and I want it to be me. Honestly, I've never done anything like this for a woman. Kendall would always say the way to a woman's heart is through romance. I guess I heard her whispering to me tonight." He swallowed the lump in his throat. Every time they shared a moment like this, he sank a little deeper into her soul. Reaching out his hand to her he opened his palm.

She took his hand, loving the way they melded together. Her heart sped up as she looked into those eyes that saw straight to her soul. She stretched up on tiptoe to give him a kiss that she hoped conveyed her readiness for the evening ahead.

Catching a glimpse of something on the table, she leaned back and started laughing. "What's on the plate?" She started to move toward the object.

"Your evil red dragon. It doesn't look happy." He stood next to her, peering down at her malformed creation.

"It does look kind of pissed-off, doesn't it? I don't want to look at that during dinner, so let's put him somewhere else." She picked up the offensive object and walked toward the opening of the tent. Cranking her arm back, she chucked the evil looking creature out. They watched as it sailed through the air before landing on the beach with a soft thud.

"Well, that's one way to get rid of it. Let's eat. I almost lost my appetite looking at that thing." A kid's smile spread across his face as a curl fell on his forehead.

He informed the chef they were ready to begin. Soon, more servers appeared to make sure they had the leisure of eating without worrying about anything else.

They sat down on the loveseat with knees touching. His body stiffened. She was sure the skin-on-skin contact sent electricity through his system. The tingle was certainly making its way into her body.

She cleared her throat and asked, "So, where did you learn how to dance like that?"

He tried to ignore the energy that danced between them by plying himself with more wine.

"Kendall said if I was ever going to be any good with the ladies, I needed to learn how to dance. We would practice in the barn before school dances. Well, I should say she did most of the dancing and I did more watching. By the time we got to the dance, I already had a few in me so I could cut loose." He stared down into his wine glass. "I haven't thought of her dancing in years. It's a fond memory. She was a good dancer. Her laughter could fill a room." His smile reached his eyes at the warm but distant memory. "I always seem to remember the good times with Kendall when you're around." He pressed his lips to her forehead with a secret thank-you. "Kendall would have loved you. You're so easy to talk to when it comes to remembering her."

A server interrupted the moment to bring them an appetizer of oysters.

She couldn't help but make a comment. "I don't think you need to put any lead in your pencil." She slipped an oyster between her lips.

His oyster almost shot out of his mouth as he clamped his hand over his lips. "Did you just refer to my cock as a pencil? I assure you, it's no pencil. Maybe you need a reminder."

Her cheeks warmed. Having him say the word cock made warmth pool low in her belly. "It's just a saying. And yes, I know for a fact you're not a pencil. I think I might need a reminder later, though." She looked at him through daring eyes. Tilting her head to the side as she slipped another oyster through her lips.

He leaned over to her ear with a gravelly voice and said, "After tonight, your body will know without a doubt how generous I can be."

Her nerves played havoc with her as excitement took over about seeing him in all his glory. She wanted to experience every inch of this man, but her body might not want him.

The next course offered salad and the main course was a fresh pasta primavera, perfect for a warm evening. It was almost as good as Mama's fresh pasta, but not quite.

"Tell me more about your brothers. What are they like?" She was curious about the other people who helped shape his life.

"Declan is the oldest. The name Declan means warrior and that he is. He's very stoic and serious. We always made fun of him growing up since he didn't smile much. He and I look a lot alike but are polar opposites in personality. He's very driven and making his way up the ladder pretty quickly in military intelligence. A lot of his missions are top secret." He had a hard edge in his eyes she couldn't figure out.

"That must be scary for your family, not knowing where he is or what he's doing. Do you worry about him?" She looked at him wide-eyed and curious.

"No, I don't worry about him because he's very well trained. I tend not to worry about things I have no control over. I worry more about him mentally than anything else. The job's demanding and it takes a lot of psychological stamina. It can be hard on you." The faraway look in his eyes did little to hide the true worry he had for his brother. He snapped out of it to talk about Campbell.

"Now, Campbell is another story altogether.

He's the jokester of the family. He loves to laugh and play pranks on people, sometimes to the irritation of the person on the receiving end. He could have been Kendall's twin leprechaun brother with auburn curly hair, green eyes, and freckles. He grew into all of that and definitely has a way with the women." He looked at her with expectant eyes.

"I see that runs in the family, too." She laughed as he laughed along with her.

"I see Raquelle has a way with the men. Maybe some of that runs in your family."

"Well, that's one way of putting it. I wish my late husband had less of a way with women." Her eyes cut down to where her fingers curled around the stem of the crystal goblet filled with blood-red wine.

"Speaking of your late husband, what's all of this about DNA testing? I assume they suspect foul play. Does it have to do with the business he was in? I hope that's not going to come back to you." She knew he wanted to know what kind of man she dealt with all these years. Was he dirty or clean?

"To be perfectly honest, I didn't know anything about his business dealings. I know he worked for an investment firm, but that's about it. We're waiting for the DNA tests to find out if that was really him in the car that burned up. But enough about him." His body relaxed. He had a wicked gleam in his eye and she caught on. "What is running through that mind of yours now?" She was curious to see what game he would come up with this time.

"Did you say running? Now would be a good time because when I get a hold of you, you're mine." She knew this game and was ready for him.

They shoved back from the loveseat at the same time and she turned around to run out of the tent, toes gripping into the cool sand. He captured her from behind, caging her in his arms, and twirled her around. She shrieked like a little girl and turned around to face him when he put her down.

"That's not fair! I needed a head start. You're faster than me." Her body and soul felt light and airy. She loved his games.

He leaned down with his nose in her locks. "I know, but now that I've caught you, you're all mine for tonight." Those words made her quiver and flush with warmth. "Let's go back to my suite. I want you all to myself without any prying eyes."

They walked arm in arm back to his suite in comfortable silence. The warm ocean breeze was cool against her heated body, which only added to her anticipation.

# CHAPTER 20

*Mara noticed his* suite was about the same size as hers. The space opened up full of earth tones and splashes of ocean colors. A hot tub for six was centered on the huge balcony, a perfect setting for a bachelor on vacation. She wondered if he had anyone else up there, but she pushed that thought away. The night was about the two of them. Her psyche didn't need to bring any unwanted third parties to the evening.

He came up behind her, wrapping his strong arms around her waist as she leaned into him. Her mind flashed back to the pool as she inhaled, taking in his masculine scent. "Go make yourself comfortable on a lounger on the balcony and I'll get us a scotch. It's my favorite after-dinner drink. Although, after tonight, it may be my second favorite." He gave her a light kiss on the cheek and turned away, building anticipation with every touch and kiss.

As the warmth of his body left her, she wanted to grab him back. There was no doubt in her mind about him. If she had her choice, she would wrap herself in him for a very long time. But she kept vacillating between willing her body to cooperate and fearing this evening could end badly.

She stepped onto the balcony to find the same warm ambience as in the tent. There were candles everywhere with dancing flames that created shadows on the ochre-colored walls. A two-person lounger was tucked away on the far side in a little nook where the lights weren't so bright. The night cast its curtain on this side of the world and the stars winked in the sky. She lay down and viewed the flickering lights in the sky while the ocean breeze kissed her skin. A shiver went down her spine, knowing where her next caresses would be coming from.

The sound of the waves calmed her into her comfort zone. She remembered going to the shore for vacation when she was younger. The three of them would curl up in beach towels on lounge chairs. They searched for falling stars while listening to the waves that lulled them to sleep. Mama would always have to wake them up and herd them inside for the night.

He came around the corner with a glass of scotch in hand. Her head came up as he walked toward her. The power in his stride and sheer dominance made her ache for him. The wine had worked its magic by settling her nerves and relaxing her body.

Stopping mid stride, he stared at her. "I see someone's looking very relaxed. We're going to put that to good use." He winked at her.

"I see you stay true to your promise of scotch after dinner. Is that your preferred dessert?" The wine and the ambiance made her sassy side come out.

"Well, let's get a couple of things straight, me lady. First, this isn't just any scotch. It's Talisker single malt made on the Isle of Skye in Scotland, my personal favorite. Second, I have many preferred desserts." He grinned as he tilted the amber liquid to his lips. "Do you want a taste?" Daring her to come and play with him, again.

She grew braver by the minute. "I would love a taste. But I'm afraid I might really like it and want more." She would show him a little of her seductive side that said 'take that, Highlander'. She loved his playful side but needed to keep it interesting and challenging.

He slid in beside her on the lounger and held the glass to her mouth, watching as her lips sealed the edge of the glass, the scotch slipping past them. Her eyes never left his face, landing on the scar above his right eye. She ran her finger over it.

"I consider it my lucky scar. The bullet grazed me and missed entering my head. Otherwise, I wouldn't be here with you. You are a gracious gift." Said with such conviction and intensity, he took her breath away. He was hardwired to her soul with a direct line to her heart.

The scotch went down smoothly with a hint of a smoky taste followed by an after-bite, reminiscent of her Scotsman. It warmed her all over. They never broke eye contact as he put the glass down on the table on the other side of her. He leaned over and kissed her passionately. Suddenly she became aware of how big he was as he loomed over her. She didn't feel fear but protection. Grabbing on to his hair, she tugged it, making him moan. She affected him in ways she never imagined, just running on instinct.

His kiss was hungry, as if he had gone without for a very long time. This wasn't any woman he wanted. He wanted only her. She was his dessert. This night would hold the answers to so many questions. Slipping his fingers into her hair, he unclipped it. He expertly ran his fingers through her waves, making her aware of how many times he might have done this with other women. But she didn't care because he was there with only her. Soft brown tresses cascaded around her shoulders and face.

"I like your hair down. It accents your face and you look carefree." He played with the end of a wandering piece, wrapping it around his finger, tugging and letting it go.

"I'll make sure to wear my hair down more often." She had a sudden urge to please him. This felt natural and normal, to want to please some-one, not to shun them.

More rivets found their way out to let the light filter in. Hammer in hand, he could break through. Could she afford to totally trust him? He had proven himself trustworthy so far. She would have to take the leap. Her body responded to him in ways she never expected or had ever experi-enced.

He kissed her jaw and made his way down her neck and shoulder. He propped himself up on his forearm as his other hand slid over her breast, across her belly and down her thigh to her knee. That handsome hand she fantasized about slowly made its way up the outside of her thigh and cupped her ass.

He bent his head down. His hot breath whispered on her neck. "God, Marabella, you're trying to kill me. No knickers?" He stopped moving, wearing the smile of a hungry wolf.

"G-string. Compliments of Raquelle again." Her naughty finally came out.

He slid the hem of her dress up. She lifted her hips and trembled at the thought of him seeing her. Bathed in the soft glow of the candlelight, she was used to being cloaked in darkness. The darkness protected her, but he lifted her veil of protection. He wanted *all* of her in the light.

"You're a friggin' beauty, Marabella. I want to take in every bit of you. Let's get this dress off." His impatience started to show. She needed him to slow down, but like a dam that sprung its first leak, it wouldn't be long until it burst.

She sat up, her heart racing as he helped her up to stand in front of him. He turned her around and unzipped her dress. She watched as it floated to the floor. Pivoting around, she stood before him, adorned in a blush-pink lace bra and matching G-string. His eyes raked in every inch of her, from her round breasts to a flat stomach and firm thighs. His hands shook as he grabbed her thighs.

His intense stare made her wet and excited. She could see how much she affected him by the bulge in his pants. Her nerves were taken over by excitement. The dance had begun and she would dance until her legs gave out, which could be very soon. She would go to the end, no matter what.

He moved his hands up to her waist and pulled her toward him as he nuzzled her belly. She cradled his head in her hands, running her fingers through his thick, soft hair. Feathery kisses trailed down her belly to her lace-covered mound. His warm breath was on her sex as his hands held her to him. Her knees almost buckled. He inhaled her scent through the lace and pulled back to look up at her. She started getting nervous again, but she bit her lower lip to stop herself from questioning anything in this moment. He reached up to rub her nipples through her lace bra. They pebbled under his touch becoming more sensitive.

"Take off your bra, *leannan*, and relax. You don't even know how gorgeous you are. Turn the old recording off inside your head and listen to my voice." She loved when he called her *leannan* because of it's meaning to him. His voice was deep and hypnotic. His accent complemented his gravelly voice.

Unhooking her bra, she let it fall to the ground. Her arms automatically came up to cover herself but his eyes told her no. She slowly rested her hands on his broad shoulders.

"You're perfect." He said on a whisper. Her nerves calm down a little.

He hooked his thumbs in the little elastic at her hips and pulled it down her legs. She stepped out of the small scrap of fabric, standing naked before him, exposing it all.

Goosebumps covered her arms as the breeze caressed her skin, making her aware that she stood outside, bared to the world. He would finally see the offensive area. She began to tremble, worried what he would think. This was her moment of truth. She didn't want him to turn away.

His eyes followed the curves of her body, from

her breasts all the way down. He groaned out loud like a man holding on by a thread. She looked down as his large cock hardened and strained against his pants and smiled. It gave her more courage.

"You are so beautiful bare. How can anyone look this good naked?" He lovingly stared at the area between her legs.

"I just did this. I wanted to see it for myself." She spoke softly and sucked in a breath, waiting for his reaction.

"You are so brave. You surprise me all the time, Marabella." He said her name as if he owned it all along. He stood, taking her hand, and kissed her open palm. "Come with me." He gave command, not a question. She followed him, tethered to his hand. Having him fully clothed and her completely naked intoxicated her. He had complete control and she willingly gave herself to him. She needed courage to give him her fear.

He led them to the master suite bathed in candlelight as the scent of sandalwood hung in the air. The candlelight cast shadows behind the pieces of grey driftwood art placed on the dark, sand-colored walls. Their true beauty masked by the dark outlines on the wall. Like the pieces of driftwood there on display, she was uneasy about how she would measure up in the light. She wanted to hide in the shadows, her place of comfort.

The pitch-black of the bedroom always helped hide her shame. Darkness detached her from the numbness and pain. She would be totally exposed, both physically and emotionally. Ready or not, she was about to jump in with both feet. She took in a deep breath to try and steady her nerves vibrating beneath her skin.

Laid out before them was a fluffy, cream-colored down comforter accented by a dark teak bed frame, a stark contrast to the rest of the room. Her calm crumbled and her nerves got the better of her. She stopped short and jerked her hand out of his.

"Can we put out some of the candles? And the bedding is light colored. What if I..." Her bubble burst as panic set in. Taking her trembling arm, she moved it to cover her breasts. She took her other hand and covered her bare sex, hiding her overexposure.

He turned to stand in front of her, blocking her view of the room. He moved her arms down to her sides, piercing her with his eyes. "I want to see all of you. Every reaction to everything we do tonight. Nothing gets hidden for either of us. All I want you to do is feel. Let me take care of the rest. I won't hurt you, I promise. This is about you and me together, erasing the past. I'm not worried about the bedding."

He said it with all the confidence of a man who had been with his lion's share of women. His eyes never left hers as he spoke, making the moment about the two of them, not just her. He wanted her to know that he was in this with her, that they were a team. The events of the last couple of days proved that. When the night came to a close, they would be more than teammates or a holiday fling. They would be lovers who would know each other inside and out. He would know her most intimate secret and she needed to trust him with it.

He stepped back from her. "I want you to take my clothes off."

Her body froze in place. He pulled her hands up to his chest placing his hands over hers.

He kissed her. "You and me, baby."

She pulled his shirt over his head, exposing the firm pecs and well-defined abs that drove her crazy. Her breath hitched as her hands ran down his chest, exploring the ridges under her fingertips. Next, she unbuttoned his shorts and pulled down the zipper, reaching for his hardness, sliding it along her palm. Her eyes were transfixed to the places where her hands explored him. He took rapid, shallow breathes, trying hard to keep control. She ran her hands down into the back of his briefs, gripping his firm ass. They fell to the floor along with his shorts, freeing his cock, which pointed in her direction. It was definitely bigger than Brock's, by a lot. She gasped and took a step back.

He chuckled as he saw her reaction. "I have to say I've never had a woman step back from it. That's a new one." She looked up at him and giggled nervously. "I'm still chasing you, *leannan*. When are you going to come to me?" She took the hint and took a small step toward him.

They stood in front of each other with nothing between them, just like she had wished for. Closing her eyes, she took in the heat that radiated off him. Breathing deeply, she wanted nothing more than to touch him, but she needed to be patient.

———◆———

*Mac gave her* time to take it all in. Truth be told, his nerves were getting the better of him, which was a new and uneasy feeling for him in this particular moment. There was the added pressure of wanting this to be perfect for her. He wouldn't hurt her in any way, stopping long before that happened, but she needed to open up and not shut down.

He prayed his gut was right, that she was normal but abused. Her body reacted so beautifully before. He needed to get her there again. He sucked in a breath as he watched her hand slowly made its way toward his needy cock.

She reached out to wrap her strong but slender fingers around his impressive length, hard as granite, yet smooth as silk. She stroked him lightly up and down, weighing the heaviness of his balls in her other hand. He tried to suppress a moan in the back of his throat, but it came out like a grunt. She looked up into his hooded eyes and seemed tentative, aware that his control could snap at any minute.

"I don't think it's going to fit." She lowered her eyes to the oversized part of him that was rock solid in her hand.

He wanted to laugh at her comment but thought better of it. "Why don't you leave that to me? I promised not to hurt you, Marabella. You can tell me to stop at any time and I will, immediately." He placed his hands over hers as the two of them stroked him. He kept his eyes on the place where her hands gave him so much pleasure. "We need to stop before I lose it completely. God, I love your hands on me. You're stronger than you know." He wanted her to understand that he saw her strengths not her weaknesses. There was no doubt about it. This woman was made for him inside and out.

Leading her to the bed, he whipped back the comforter to expose more light-colored linens. He laid her down on her back, climbing on top without putting his full weight on her. His eyes seared into her. He wanted to make sure it was what she wanted since they were to this point. "Are you sure you want to do this? I can wait for you to be ready." His rubber band was near the snapping point.

"God, yes. I've come this far, but I need you to do this with me." Her words caught in her throat as her body tensed. He picked up on her signals.

"Then let go, *leannan*. This is more than physical for both of us." He tried to comfort her with a smile. "Mac says, trust me. I promise not to hurt you." He used the playfulness of the game to calm her down.

He licked her bottom lip, teasing her to come play with him. She responded by sucking on his in return. They locked into a passionate kiss that made all kinds of promises. His warm, tender hands caressed her breasts, rubbing them and lightly pinching her nipples. It was the perfect amount of pressure that he hoped went right to her sex, making her even wetter.

She closed her eyes and whispered his name as he latched on to her nipple with his mouth. He circled the harden nub with his tongue suckled and released it. He did this several times before he moved to the other one. With each moan that came from somewhere deep within her, warm pool of wetness slid between her legs. He wanted each touch to heightened her awareness of her body and sooth her nerves. There, laid out before him, was the woman of his dreams. Her body relaxed and a smile graced her lips.

Her moans drove him higher and higher, fueling the fire between them. He needed to taste her and make sure she was ready before he took her. He moved down her stomach, feathering kisses across her hipbones. Lost in this new, comfortable world she sat straight up. "You don't have to do that. I don't think it would be a good idea." Panic rose in her voice. He suspected she heard Brock's caustic voice play in her head.

"Who am I?"

"Mac." She refocused on him.

"I'm not him, Marabella. I want you, all of you. I want to know you intimately in every way. I want you to know that I will love every part of your body. Tonight, I'll make love to your body and soul. You should only ever be made love to."

She nodded as the tension started to leave her body. Breathing in and out, she anchored herself to those big, green, compassionate eyes. He got on all fours, meeting her face to face. It gave her the space she needed but with the understanding he was in still control. His words were enough to calm her down so she could take the leap. He kissed her while pushing her on her back again. She sat up on her elbows, giving her a false sense of control over the situation. He stroked her thighs, trying to calm her down and relax her closed legs.

"Spread yourself for me, *leannan*. Nothing between us." He pushed her knees apart. She glistened between folds of rose-colored flesh. Kissing the inside of her thighs, he made his way up to what would be heaven. Leaning in, he licked her tiny, hooded nub. She arched her back, moaning as she reacted by gripping his hair with one hand. He couldn't believe her sensitivity and responsiveness considering her history.

For all the women he had been with over the years, no one reacted to him like this. He would've had to put more work into it. He was high from the power he had over her, realizing she had the same power of him.

"Um, Marabella, are you sure your husband wasn't gay, because you are divine. I happen to love the way you look."

She smiled. "Thank you. I needed to hear that. And no, he wasn't gay, just incredibly cruel." A flash of pain came across her face. He suspected she remembered the hateful things Brock said that had chipped away at her.

"I want you to lie back and feel you and me. Let go of the past. Will you try?" She needed to let go of those memories so they could move forward.

"Yes." As she lay down on the soft sheets, she put her hands on his head. He loved the way her fingers played in his hair, with enough tug to keep him harder than he had ever been.

He returned to that place that could give her so much pleasure. Licking up and down her folds then circling around her nub. He listened for her reaction. As she relaxed, she tugged harder on his hair, arching her back and moaning loudly. This was how he wanted her—unleashed, lost in the sensations running through her body. He continued as he pressed one finger into her. Tight didn't even begin to describe her. As she tensed slightly, he stopped.

"You okay? Relax for me." He didn't want to go any further until she let him know she was okay. She relaxed again as he stroked her with his tongue. She needed the reassurance that he was listening to her body and would stop when necessary.

"Yes... More... Please." Her voice staggered with a husky urgent edge.

He started to move his finger slowly in and out, adding another to stretch and push her. She was so snug he could only imagine what it would be like to be wrapped in her. He might lose it right then without ever being inside her.

She started to flex her hips upward to match his rhythm. "Oh, God, Mac, please!" She begged for release. He moved his fingers in and out of her more rapidly and sucked on her clit until she tightened around his fingers.

Her ragged breath matched his. His fingers were a tight fit inside her as she bore down. He was seeing her in the light with no shadows, nowhere for her to hide. She had let go. Letting go of his hair, she gripped the sheets.

Closing her eyes, she screamed his name as her climax claimed her. She trembled and shook as he slowed down and finally stopped as she came back down to Earth.

"That was incredible, *leannan*. You are incredible." He climbed up her body and kissed her lips, as she tasted herself on him, his new favorite flavor. It might even beat the Talisker. At first, she moved away, but then it aroused her. "You taste good, don't you?" She licked and kissed his lips.

"Yeah, you have very talented tongue and fingers. I've never experienced anything like that. The strongest orgasm I've ever had, given to me by the strongest man I've ever known." She touched his face. Hers was still flush with desire. Her eyes were wild with passion.

He leaned over and opened the nightstand drawer to pull out a condom. In one fluid, expert move, he ripped it open and rolled it on. Panic crept into her eyes.

"Relax, Marabella. Listen to your body. It will tell you what to do. Look at what your body just did. You let go. I can tell your body was made for sex. You're ready." He sounded so sure of himself, yet he trembled on the inside. Wanting in her so badly, he was afraid he would hurt her, but she was ready for him, all of him. He made sure of that.

He eased the head in and out slowly. Then a little bit deeper, watching her eyes for any indication of discomfort. Her eyes closed as she instinctively wrapped her legs around his waist. Moving until he was buried in her, he stopped to feel her encase him. This required the most control he ever had with a woman. She fit him like a glove. Even after her climax, she was still tight. This was where he belonged.

"Eyes on me." Her eyes fluttered open, full of

hazy lust. As she smiled there were tears in her eyes. He started to back away. She gripped his ass with both hands, holding him to her. "Talk to me. Tell me what's going on."

"These are happy tears. You feel incredible. I never thought it could be like this. It doesn't hurt. I'm so full with you." His cord of control snapped as he started to move inside her. He cupped her ass angling it so he was buried balls-deep in her. In this position he would hit her sweet spot. She started to match him thrust for thrust. He wasn't going to last long. Two more and he would be done.

A powerful orgasm ripped through him, leaving him with stars behind his eyes. This woman made him come completely undone, losing the control he valued so much. His body shuddered several times as he came down, collapsing on top of her. Her nails stroked up and down his back to his delight. He never wanted anyone as much as he wanted her. She felt perfect to him. He lay there for a while to catch his breath. She amazed him. Worried he was too heavy for her, he rolled off as he slipped out of her.

She gasped. "Did I...?" She began to move and examine the bedding underneath her.

"Are you okay?" He slid down her body to examine her. "No blood."

She laughed from sheer exhilaration of the experience and the thought that she may be normal after all. That laugh speared him differently this time and made him smile with her.

"That was the most delicious dessert ever, Mr. Creighton." Her face was rosy, hair mussed, lips red and plump. Little beads of sweat covered her body. She wore the look of a ravaged woman, every man's wet dream. But she was his and *only* his, even if she didn't know it yet. This was no holiday fling.

———•———

*Something deepened between* them. Mara was closer to him than with anyone in her life, having fully opened herself up to him. The bond sealed them. For the first time in her life, she trusted a man with her heart, soul, and body. She was ecstatic that her body accepted him and enjoyed sex. Her body had tried to tell her something about Brock years before. She just didn't listen. She didn't know enough to listen, but she would be paying attention from now on.

When Mac returned from the bathroom, she had started to fade. He blew out all the candles, casting them in total darkness, but even in the dark she could feel exactly where he was. She was attuned to his essence. Just on the edge of sleep, his arms wrap around her from behind, "Sweet dreams, *leannan*." He was her dream, but could he keep the nightmare that awaited her at bay?

# CHAPTER 21

*A fresh breeze* billowed the curtains signaling another morning in paradise. Mara couldn't imagine paradise existed before Mac. The generous man next to her snored, his face peaceful and serene. She ran her fingers down his morning stubble as he rolled onto his back still sound asleep. She hoped she gave him as much pleasure as he had given her. Feeling impulsive, she wanted to wake him up in her own special way. The song "Sex for Breakfast" by Christina Aguilera floated through her head.

Peeling back the sheets, she uncovered his well-endowed lower half. His body called to her. She would never tire of wanting him now that he opened the gates. Her eyes followed the hairline beneath his belly button, leading to the hard shaft that had given her so much pleasure the night before. After their first encounter, her appetite for sex had amped up to ten.

She kissed the head of his cock and licked down to the base of the shaft. Gripping him at the base, she moved her hand up and down as he disappeared in her mouth. She ran her nails under his balls as he let out a moan and started to move his hips up and down. She could feel herself getting wet from his moans.

His eyes shot open. Casting his eyes down, his cock was buried in her mouth as she drove him wild by gripping his balls from underneath. He surrendered to the moment. She had pulled out yet another surprise.

"Oh, God, Marabella. You know how to wake up a man." He pulled her up by her arms as she laughed. "Are you sore this morning? Straddle me." His voice strained as he ran his thumbs up and down the indents of her stomach.

"No. I'm good, thanks to you." She gave him the satisfied smile of a kitten.

"Are you on any birth control?" His fingers gripped into her sides. There was wildness in his eyes.

"Yes." She said softly not understanding where he was going with his questions.

"Are you clean?" His eyes locked onto hers.

Her words stammered out with confusion and curiosity. "I...took a shower last night before I came here."

He chuckled at her naïveté. "No, have you been tested for any venereal diseases?"

"Oh, I feel like such an idiot again." She covered her mouth as she laughed at her own obvious inexperience. "Yes, I got tested a couple of months ago. I wanted to make sure he hadn't given me anything."

"Good girl, because I want you with nothing between us. I've only been with one woman without a condom, a long time ago. I get tested regularly. I'm clean."

There was a heat in his eyes she had never seen before, a need to feel her around him. His thumb moved over her needy clit and began circling. She started to move her hips into his thumb. His other hand played with her breast, rolling and pinching her nipple. In a short period of time, this man had memorized all her buttons, pushing them at just the right time.

"Lean forward." The move tilted her hips back perfectly, placing a nipple in his mouth as he brushed her hair over her shoulders. He sucked and nipped at each one, driving her desire higher, creating an ache between her legs. The head of his cock teased her entrance as he thrust up slightly.

"Take me. The way you want to, at your pace." With that, she pushed her hips back so the head of his cock slid inside her. She closed her eyes, praying she could do this. The morning light completely exposed her and yet she was comfortable with him. He would see her in all her wild abandonment.

"You're going to have to help me. I've never done it this way." She closed her eyes to cover the doubt and embarrassment that settled in wiping away her self-confidence.

"Open your eyes. I want to see you. You're so beautiful. Pretend you're riding a horse and roll your hips," He said with husky rawness in his voice. Their eyes locked. They were ensconced in each other.

Opening her eyes, his gorgeous green ones stared back at her with wonderment. With each rock of her hips, she took him a little deeper. She stopped to take in what it was like to be filled with him. They understood that this moment reached well beyond a one-night affair. She saw herself by his side for a long time but questioned what he wanted for them. It made her wild to think about. This intimacy was deeper than she had ever experienced.

A piece of her soul was safely tucked away in his heart and she willingly gave it to him. She wouldn't leave without taking a little piece of his as well. Not wanting to hold back anymore, she totally let go, giving him everything inside and out. The last rivet popped free from the steel barricade, bathing her in the light of this man, the man who set her free. He accepted her, all of her, down to her true self. She started to rock back and forth while his fingers dug into her hips, helping her set the rhythm.

She was content and free in her abandoned form like something had dropped away. Taking his cues from her, he moved his hips upward. Her clit rubbed against his pelvic bone. Breathing turned into pants as sweat beaded across her chest.

A spark started at the point of contact, building like a wildfire, spreading through her body. She wanted him there with her as she finally let go.

"Mac, I'm going to come. Please." She desperately held on, digging her nails into his chest. She begged fueling his fire.

"Hold on, baby." He pumped up into her as she threw her head back in total release, crying out his name. His orgasm rocketed through him as he came with her, inside her, and marked her as his.

An all-consuming orgasm shook her body to its core, coursing through her veins like a drug.

Craving more, this man had fast become an addiction for her. She realized she never had an orgasm during intercourse as she slumped on top of him trying to catch her breath.

Covered in sweat and breathing hard, her emotions collided. Hitting her all at once, she started to sob, overwhelmed by the warring emotions of ecstasy and profound sadness.

"Marabella, what's wrong?" His voice was panicked. Groping around her, he tried to get her to move.

Sobs racked her body. She had never heard these cries of pain come from her before. It scared her.

"*Leannan*, look at me. What's going on? Talk to me." He was frantic trying to figure out what went wrong. He slipped out of her, trying to move her off him, but she lay there like dead weight.

Behind a waterfall of tears, she lifted her head and peered down at him. Her body twisted with emotional pain as her mind tried to absorb it. Her bubble of denial finally burst. She whispered. "He meant to hurt me. He abused me and he did it on purpose. Why did he want to hurt me so much? I'm not sure I ever really trusted him. It never felt like this, this intimate. It hurts so much now that I know what it can be. I wasted so much time with him." Anger set in as she gritted her teeth together. "I was so stupid. I let him do it over and over again."

The pain of being tortured came out in a flood. The realization hit her that her husband was a mean abusive man. She could barely speak, her voice weak and body limp. She had never been so emotionally raw, torn between the freedom of being with Mac and the intentional abuse of her late husband.

He moved her to the side, wiping away her tears. "Shhh, you're not stupid. You never knew what making love could be. And yes, he was abusive and hurt you, but you're strong enough to heal. This is the first step. Let go of him and the past, Marabella. Let go of all of it. Focus on us and how far you've come in such a short period of time." He got out of bed to get a washcloth. She reached out and clutched his arm.

"Please, don't go. Hold me. Please." She wanted comfort from a man she'd bared her soul to. She wasn't ready for the loss of him, feeling strangely empty without him, wanting to keep him inside her forever.

He didn't hesitate as he crawled back into the bed. Holding her tightly, he curled himself around her body in a statement of total protection. He was her new wall with windows. Rocking her back and forth, he gently stroked her hair.

"Always. I have you now, *leannan*. You're safe with me." He whispered into her hair as he continued to stroke her body.

Those were the only words that consoled her. She needed to feel safe more than anything else. Her mind went numb. It had all tumbled out in one moment. She might be in love with a man for the first time and only after a couple of days of knowing him. Maybe she was confusing love with lust and great sex.

———◆———

*Mac's heart broke* for this woman, his woman. Her words tore at him like something sharp raking across his skin.

Too bad Brock was already dead, he would have relished killing him. She shined spectacularly moments before, free and rising out of the ashes of her recent hell.

He felt something for this goddess. Love? He didn't know. She completely stripped him. He had lost all control. His self-imposed fortress of loneliness crumbled. This woman made him connect again. If she could do it, given everything she had endured, then so could he. She proved to be stronger than she knew and inspirational. She was one of the strongest women he knew, next to his sister. Facing all of her demons head-on and coming out on top. Watching her transform and build her self-confidence made her even more attractive. He seemed insatiable when it came to her.

She needed to know he would always be there for her, no matter what. While her protective wall came down, he still held on to a thin veil he thought could shield his heart from her. But that veil slipped away as she spoke to something so primal in him he couldn't put into words. Clearly, she trusted him enough to be vulnerable with him. He saw it in her eyes and sensed it in her body. He came undone and fell under her spell. He would never get tired of hearing her say his name.

Her body went lax as she fell asleep in his arms. He couldn't sleep with this much on his mind. Getting up so he didn't wake her, he decided it would be a good time to distract himself with the case McFadden wanted him to review on his holiday. Sydney should be arriving soon. Funny how she planned a trip to Mexico the same time he did.

———————◆———————

*Alone in bed*, Mara tried to gain her bearings. Oh, yeah, she'd had an inner core meltdown about her life with her abusive late husband. She felt drained, naive and stupid. But no more. A sense of relief washed over her as she realized she let it all go. He was there to catch her fall from grace. An awakening shifted in her making her grow up a lot in a short period of time.

Her marriage to Brock would be the last time a man would ever take advantage of her or hurt her. She didn't need to worry about that with Mac. He might not have said the words, but his love for her came through his body and the way he held her the night before with those expressive eyes. He stayed attuned to everything that happened with her. She smiled when she thought about the moment she had normal sex with no pain. She had an orgasm with him inside her. It didn't get more intimate than that or more spectacular. Lost in thought, she didn't see him come in the room.

"What are you grinning at? You're positively glowing. I like that look on you." He stood over her with his hands on his hips, shirtless with a pair of low-slung shorts. The V of his abs pointed down to his pleasure point. "I guess you've moved on from earlier this morning." Concern crossed his face.

"I need to leave Brock behind and everything that's happened with him. If I could, I would tell him off, but he's not here. Thank God. I was thinking about you and how you make me feel treasured. I want to scream out loud that I'm normal. I never thought being normal could feel like this. I never knew any different." She stood up on the bed, stark naked, with a double fist-pump in the air, shouting, "Yes!"

He laughed out loud at her childlike playfulness. Grabbing her hips, he lifted her off the bed. "Just so we're clear, if your husband were alive, he wouldn't be for long." His face grew dark. Letting the moment go, he switched gears. "You did enough screaming last night but I happen to like listening to it, especially when you scream my name." He growled and playfully bit her neck.

She held on to him and wrapped her legs around his waist as he carried her to the dining area. "Well, I'm glad you don't have a big ego or anything. By the way, I enjoy screaming your name. You're talented in many ways." Lightly biting his lower lip, she leaned back to watch the gleam in his eyes. He held her in place on his hips and gave her a chaste kiss but she sensed a strange detachment from him. His eyes lost their merriment.

He let her slide down as her bare feet touched the cool floor.

"I think I need to get some clothes." She started to cover herself with her arms and put her head down.

"Oh, no, you don't." He spoke firmly like he would with a child. Her head snapped up. "You've got nothing to be embarrassed about. I've never seen a woman more exquisite in my life. It makes me want you more. If I had my way, you'd walk around in my suite naked all day long."

Honesty and gentleness shone in those big, green eyes, but she also detected a sadness that hadn't been there the night before. It made her wonder if he regretted being with her.

"We need to talk about earlier this morning. How are you really doing with it all?" He cupped her cheek tenderly like a porcelain doll.

"I'm okay. I didn't realize I had all that stored away. It was a relief to let go of all my anger and sadness. I needed to get rid of it. I'm coming out the other side. I know I have some work to do. But I won't let anyone take advantage of me again." She looked hard into his eyes confirming her determination. She had a newfound confidence and strength.

"How about some breakfast, my little warrior princess?" He said without being condescending.

Eggs, pancakes, waffles, fruit, and biscuits were ordered to replace the burned calories of the evening's events.

She grabbed a t-shirt he'd flung over the back of the couch and put it on. The oversized shirt hung on her like a rag resting at mid-thigh.

He gave her a sly smile. "You look sexy as hell in my shirt." He never had an unkind word for her.

A little sore from the morning's activities, she sat down carefully, but her appetite raged. She took one of everything and filled her plate. Her appetite was back in full color.

He started to laugh out loud. "So, now I know

how I can get you to eat more food, burn calories with great sex. Are you going to eat your weight in food? I guess I'll take this as a good sign."

His mood shifted abruptly as his brows hung halfway over his eyes. "So, I was hoping we could get together later. I have some work I need to catch up on today," he said cryptically.

She saw hesitation in his darkened eyes as he cast them down away from her. She didn't want to push him. Let him come to her.

"No problem. I need to catch up with Leigha and Raquelle anyway. Give me a call when you're done." She was weary and concerned their night of bliss was over. The cord between them tightened, wrapped in uncertainty, leaving her unsettled. The other shoe was about to drop. She could sense that he was hiding something from her. Her instincts about him took another hit.

She finished breakfast quickly and got dressed. Before she left, she gave him a deep, lingering kiss making it understood that she would be there for him no matter what.

He hid some demons of his own. Not knowing what they were, she prayed it wouldn't ruin everything they shared together. As she left, the darkness continued to consume his eyes. She hoped he could work it out, for both their sakes.

# CHAPTER 22

*Mac tried desperately* to hide his emotions from Marabella over breakfast. Leaving Sleeping Beauty in bed, he caught up on the case the boys back home wanted him to keep an eye on. In his wildest dreams, he never expected what waited for him in that folder. He hoped this case would be his last one because he wanted to move onto the next chapter in his life.

Tired of running, he needed to put some roots down. He couldn't think of a better place than New York City. The global security firm of McKenzie, Bryan, and Knight, or MBK Global Security, handled security all over the world and was expanding their international division. They were head hunting for another team member with international experience. He had gotten a reference from an old friend working for the CIA out of the New York office. His current job gave him exposure to international as well as domestic arenas. He seemed like the perfect fit, hoping to hear from them by the time his holiday came to an end. He worried how Marabella would fit into his puzzle as he made an ironic discovery that rocked his world.

He opened the thick dossier with the case McFadden had given him before he left. It gave a run down on the long-time surveillance of a man named John Walker Junior. John worked at the investment firm of Chaplin, Zaret & Roman, or CZR Investments, located in New York City. Both the CIA and British Intelligence were watching this firm very carefully because of indications of suspicious trading in the U.S. and the UK. The implications included ties to prominent families of the Russian mob. The agencies called them 'czar' investments for a reason. The Russian mob had expanded globally in recent years getting their hands in hi-tech espionage, along with the old ways of doing business—drugs, money laundering and racketeering.

John came on as a rookie about nine years back and headed up the ladder pretty quickly. He made a lot of money very fast in some shady investments. Using some loopholes in a financial system that relied more and more on digital frameworks, he made offshore accounts seem invisible.

A string of shell companies seemed to be linked to the Russian mob and indirectly connected back to CZR Investments. However, the agencies were having trouble connecting the dots. Some of the shell companies had holdings in some of the most powerful banks in Britain, Japan, Dubai, San Francisco, New York City, Zurich and the Cayman Islands. They had covered their tracks very well. It was clear they had one badass tech guy. Top-notch hackers got hired all the time, just not always by the good guys.

The timing of John's death was very convenient

given the fact he just made some bad investments and lost a significant amount of money for many clients. Some of those clients might have been in the mob. His fatal car accident in Brighton Beach was questionable, considering the lack of head or hands, making identification almost impossible.

The hair on Mac's neck stood on end. He continued to read the profile, as his gut gnawed at him. Up until that point, John seemed to be living well, with a home in Greenwich, Connecticut and an apartment in New York City, a far cry from the poverty-stricken community where he grew up in upstate New York. However, John studied hard in high school, earning himself a scholarship to NYU. He graduated with a degree in finance and economics summa cum laude, which made him very attractive to CZR Investments.

The agencies were currently waiting on DNA evidence to confirm it was John's body in the car. His hunch, probably not. There was also the matter of a five-million-dollar insurance policy taken out with his wife as the beneficiary. Only, she seemed surprised it existed. Being quite wealthy, she didn't need the money. According to the value of her accounts, five million would be a drop in the bucket.

Right around the time John started to work for CZR Investments, he got married to... *Oh, fuck no!* Marabella Luccenzo. His head screamed as he clutched his chest to try and stop his heart from dropping into his gut. Fate always had a cruel twist to it. As a postscript, the profile mentioned his family knew John as Brock. He never used his legal first name.

The dossier included pictures of Marabella and Brock. In every shot, they were dressed to the nines, not a hair out of place. Tall with short blond hair and blue eyes, he was very good-looking by anyone's standard. Custom tailored suits fit him well. He used it to his advantage. Surveillance photos showed that he'd tasted fifty-one flavors when it came to women.

His rage boiled to the surface, but he kept it in check for her sake. She deserved so much better than that piece of shit. He tried hard not to show her what he found out at breakfast, but a pit sat in his stomach. In a blink, things turned a hundred and eighty degrees. He felt more protective than ever and hated keeping secrets from her, especially after she bared her soul to him.

During his abrupt change in topic that morning, he had the impression she sensed something was up. Based on the start to his day, the rest of it was going to suck donkey balls.

He needed to contact headquarters and bring them up to speed on the situation. It seemed his job at MI6 wasn't done with him yet. He would protect her with his life if Brock were still among the living. Calling in reinforcements, his brothers would be his back up. He would keep tabs on her for the rest of this trip. Whether she liked it or not, he had just become her guardian angel—or stalker. Since she was involved, there was no rest for the weary.

Contacting his boss, he let him in on the current situation in Mexico. "So, mate, a holiday in Cancun, eh? You didn't suggest it for a reason, did you?" He didn't let Neil off the hook. They worked together for many years. He could take a little ribbing.

"Why, what do you mean, Mac? You don't love the sun, surf, and bikinis?" Neil chuckled.

"By the way, I don't know if you also control fate, but I've met the potential asset in this case. I assume she's the one you wanted me to keep an eye on. Met her on the plane ride down here, before I knew who she was to the deceased. We're staying at the same resort. Coincidence? I don't think so. I doubt she will be of any use to us. She's only now discovering things about her husband she wished she didn't know. Where are we with the DNA?"

He didn't give him the whole story about his relationship with the asset. The less he knew, the better. He wanted McFadden off her scent, not only to protect her but because he truly believed she didn't have a clue about Brock's other life. She vaguely seemed to know what he even did for a living.

"The DNA isn't back yet, but I suspect Walker may be very much alive and kicking. If he *is* alive, the question is, what's his next move? Will his wife be in danger, or is she in on it? Stay close to her and see if you can't get more information from her about her husband. That won't be a problem, will it?" Neil baited him to see if he already slept with her. He knew Mac's appetite for beautiful women.

"Won't be a problem, boss. She's here with her sisters and staying occupied. Will she get notified about the results of the DNA?" He wanted to know where he should stand when the shit hit the fan.

"I don't know. That will be up to the discretion of the CIA and NYPD. I'll talk to you soon." Neil clicked off, leaving him with an empty plan.

Of all the women he could have been attracted to, she caught and held him captive. This might make him a believer in fate after all. If Brock were still alive, he might come after her. He wasn't sure what made him think that, but once again, he was running on instinct.

He caught up with his brothers, Declan and Campbell. Both worked for the RAF and had leave coming to them, so they could come to Mexico if necessary. He felt like he might need some serious back up for this, depending on which way the wind blew. He would feel more in control after he touched base with Sydney. His secret was about to be revealed.

# CHAPTER 23

*Mara returned to* her suite as her sisters waited for her. They wanted to appear casual. Raquelle shattered that illusion the minute she opened her mouth.

She had a battery of questions to unearth what she didn't want to talk about. "Hey, so how did things go last night with Big Mac? I can see by your rosy cheeks all went well." She was an easy read for Raquelle. "So, did he give you the big O? If so, I would say that man has talent and heart, a rare combination. How did it feel to be with someone who actually cares about your needs for a change?" Raquelle's voice dropped off, wavering, which made her curious. But since the door opened, she might as well step through.

She beamed. "Yes. Everything went very well. My body had no pain and no bleeding. I guess I'm normal after all. I can honestly say it was because of my partner that things went well. Having sex with him was beyond incredible. I never experienced anything like that. He's an amazing man and very talented." She wiggled her brows. "But it's more than that. We made a connection that I've never had with anyone. He knows me so well. He's so tuned in."

"Way to go, Mar. Are you having dinner with your demi-god tonight?" Raquelle ran over and gave her a high five. She was the poster child for the word fresh.

"Yes, I'm seeing him later. He's really special and definitely pushes all the right buttons." Her light came from the inside, relieved to be talking about the enjoyable part of the evening. It felt comforting to speak openly with her sisters about intimate things, giving her a sense of belonging and closeness. "I dread once this vacation is over, it's all going to seem like a dream. He and I are just getting started, but where can it go?" The joy faded as reality set in. "I wish I understood him better." Her voice drifted off and she turned her head away.

When she glanced up at her sisters, she noticed sadness in their eyes. Hidden somewhere in their subconscious, that statement took on a much deeper meaning for all of them. It was a silent communication about their distant father.

Leigha piped up first. "What's going on, Mara?"

"I'm not sure. I got the sense he's struggling with something, but he's not sharing it with me. It has me on edge. He acted odd this morning. I could tell something was off." She felt like he was about to drop his own bomb.

Raquelle was a dictionary when it came to men. "I'm sure it's nothing. This might be all new for him as well. Men can be hard to read sometimes. They don't always know how to handle their emotions." She knew more about men than the two of them put together.

Mara's feelings ran deep enough to fight for him. "Well, I guess I'll find out eventually. I'll give him some space, but things can't continue like this. I won't let it, not when being with him feels this fantastic. I'm willing to fight for this." A fierce determination came through in her voice that hadn't been there before. She wouldn't give up on him because he might be running scared.

"I'm going to take a shower and freshen up a bit before lunch." Some alone time was necessary to think things over and regroup. She needed energy to figure out what was bothering him.

*Mac's frustration level* peaked after doing some asking around about the guy in the baseball hat. He needed to contact Sydney and ask her to do more recon on the mystery man who was behind drugging Marabella. His phone binged indicating he had a text message. It said she had arrived and to give her a call.

"Hey, I'm down at the pool. What's up?" Sydney knew who it was without looking at the phone. They had a good rapport and a sixth sense for each other. It had developed over many years of working together.

Although she found him to be a nice-looking guy, men didn't appeal to her. She was attracted to beautiful women and had her lioness' share. The one thing she and him had in common, an appetite for women.

"Can you meet me in my suite? I want to go

over a couple of things with you and read you in on what's been going on." He called the shots in his work zone.

She acknowledged his all-business tone. "Sure. No problem. I'll be there in ten." He knew she'd want all the intel she could get before moving forward.

When she arrived at the suite, he sat slumped over the edge of the couch feeling worn out.

"I thought you were suppose to be a vacation? You look exhausted."

He saw the worry in her eyes and addressed it. "So, this hasn't been the most relaxing holiday I've ever had, but I'll fill you in." He needed an extra set of eyes because with the distraction of Marabella, he probably missed something. This was the reason why he didn't become emotionally involved with women other than a quickie. They were too damn distracting, but she was the total package he didn't even know he was looking for.

Sydney sat at the aqua glass dining table, one arm flung over the back of the rattan chair, looking causal but listening intently.

She had long, black hair that framed her bright blue eyes and creamy fair skin. Her body was that of an athlete, lithe and sleek, due to all her training as an agent. She had been gifted with the best of both sets of genes from a Ukrainian father and a German mother, a match made in hell. Their very volatile love-hate relationship ended in a fatal car crash when she was ten years old. At that point, her Ukrainian uncle took her into his home and she became one of them.

He explained everything to her about the case,

from Brock's death to the drugging incident. "Jack, the motherfucker who tried to drug her said some guy with long dirty-blond hair in a baseball cap paid him to put the drugs in her drink. Said the guy would take it from there. I think he's also the one watching her, but I haven't told her about any of it. She didn't say anything about any enemies or admirers as of late." He puzzled over the situation as he tried to piece it together.

"Other than you, of course." She could see right through him. He kept rubbing the scar above his eye, a dead giveaway to his nerves. "Your eyes light up from the inside when you talk about her. The mark of true happiness, for a change."

His body tightened. "That obvious, eh?" He sighed heavily. "She's a very special woman. You know better than anyone I don't usually hang around, but this one's got me and I hope to hell I have her." He flinched at his own proclamation. Stating his emotions out loud to someone who knew him so well made it that much more real. He loved everything about her.

Whoa, mate, love? Was he sure about that? Yeah, he was sure. Kitten had so much more to show him. She was just getting started and doesn't even know it. He wanted to take the next steps not knowing if he was ready for them and not sure what they were. He'd take his cues from her.

"Oh, you always were a charmer. I'm sure you've got her hook, line, and sinker." Sydney smiled, but it didn't reach her eyes. Her smile fell as sadness tugged at her face. He knew the last couple of relationships for her were epic failures with some beautiful yet seriously fucked-up women.

"There's a chance her late husband is alive. But God, I hope not. I've got a bad feeling about all of this. I'm waiting for the DNA test results to confirm it was his body. If he's still alive, that could mean trouble for her. We would need to find him before the Russians do or he'll be dead before we get the information we need. From what I can gather, she knows little to nothing about his goings-on or what he did for a living." As he finished he let out the breath he'd been holding in all day.

"I'm going to start doing some recon and try to find your guy in the baseball hat. That will be about half the guys here. I'll throw on a bikini and do a little sightseeing. I think I'll start at the pool with some drinks." Wiggling her eyebrows, she had become a master at how to play the game to extract information from people. "I need some downtime. It's been awhile. I don't need to tell you how it goes."

A silent understanding traveled between them. They were caught in the agencies' spider's web always at their mercy. Traveling from one assignment to the next left little time to think about what the job really entailed or what else life had to offer.

"I can't tell you how much I appreciate you being here. I know you'll have my back if I need it. We'll touch base tomorrow to see if you came up with anything. I hope to hear from McFadden by then." He felt relieved as he handed her the dossier hoping all his focus could be on Marabella.

She let herself out as he lay back on the couch and shut his eyes. After all the events of the day, he was totally spent. He had to tell Marabella about his assignment. She had a right to know everything about him. There would be no more hiding behind his wall. He fell asleep thinking about the different scenarios to tell her. None of them seemed right. He woke up an hour later with a start. The time had come to reveal his secret.

He walked through a thick haze making his way to her suite. He cursed under his breath as his heart sank in molasses. His nerves were back again, only this time for a much different reason. He dreaded how she would take the news that he worked for an Intelligence Agency. Life always had the last laugh.

# CHAPTER 24

*M*ac stood at the door of her suite as courage leaked from him, trying to pull himself
together. He relented knowing he would never be
ready, so why put off the inevitable.

Leigha answered his soft knock. "Hi, Mac,
come on in." She sensed his somber mood as her
body straightened. "Mara, Mac's here to see you."
Her eyes never left his face as she stepped aside to
let him enter.

Marabella bounced into the living room, smiling, glad to see him, but then came to an abrupt
halt. The claws of dread gripped him.

"What's wrong?" The bad news written on his
face struck her head-on. She started twisting her
hands together.

He gave a heavy sigh. "Where's Raquelle? You
might as well all be here for this." She and Leigha
looked at each other, more perplexed than ever.

"I'll get her. She's sunning on the deck." Leigha
left them alone as tension strung tight between
them.

She watched Leigha leave as a heavy silence
invaded the space between them. Turning back
to him she said, "What's going on, Mac? Why do

my sisters need to be here? Whatever you have to tell me, I won't fall apart. I'm a big girl. I can take being dumped." She crossed her arms over herself. The tears welled up.

He watched as fear and hurt wove their way into her heart. God, does she think he would dump her after last night? The whole night was beyond his expectations. She still doesn't get that he wanted her, no matter what. He took a step toward her. "I'm not dumping you, Marabella. How could you think that after last night? It was incredible. You're perfect for me. I think I'm falling—"

Leigha and Raquelle rushed into the room, with worried faces. He was so totally focused on her he didn't even register Raquelle's micro bikini, barely covering her gorgeous curves.

"I need you all to sit down. I have something to tell all of you, not just Marabella." The sisters slowly sat down on the couch, not sure what to make of the situation, eyeing each other cautiously. He stood in front of them with his hands on his hips. "First of all, I'm not in security, per se. I work for British Intelligence, which I shouldn't be telling you but there's no way around it at this point." He let that sink in before he dropped the second bomb.

She sat there stone-faced, no emotion whatsoever. Her sisters each wore a frown. He didn't take her reaction to his first piece of news as a good sign.

He continued, not sure where to go. "Second, I was given this assignment to look into Brock's death because of his possible connection to the Russian mob. And here's the kicker." He laughed nervously hoping to lighten the mood, scratching his scarred eyebrow with his thumb. His eyes pinned her as he gave the next piece of information. "My boss suggested a holiday in Mexico with the idea I would make a connection with you. You're a potential asset in piecing this case together for us." The minute the words left his mouth he waited for her reaction.

She continued to wear a blank stare for a couple of seconds, while his new information sunk in. All eyes turned to her as she stood up with her fists at her sides. "You fucking son of a bitch! You were on assignment this whole time and never told me. British Intelligence? You played me so you could get information about your case? You're a lying fucking asshole! I knew it. I knew there was something you weren't telling me. And to tell the truth, I really don't give a fuck. I want nothing to do with you from this point on. Tell your boss you just lost the 'asset'." She sneered using finger quotes.

Her arm swung back ready to slap him. His automatic defensive mechanisms kicked in to catch her arm, but he thought better of it. Her hand connected with his face, slapping him hard. She jerked back and covered her mouth, shocked at her physical assault on him. The pendulum of passion seemed to swing in both directions. Tears formed in her eyes. "I've never slapped anyone before." Her voice trembled.

His cheek warmed from her slap but he didn't flinch. He wanted her to feel in control. That slap was meant for Brock. The mention of his name brought back the feelings of betrayal and lit the wick. He received the brunt of it. He made her want to do things she'd never done before, feel like she never had before, find the real her but he turned out to be a fraud.

He remained frighteningly calm. "I was in holiday mode and met you before I saw what the assignment entailed. I swear that's the truth. I read it this morning." His level and calm voice made him appear to be under control, but his accent always grew thicker as he became emotional. He pleaded with her to believe him.

"So, now I'm an assignment? I shared my soul with you and opened myself up to you. All you saw was a pathetic woman you could take advantage of. Well, you know what, Mac? Mara says, fuck you!" She trembled from head to toe as tear flowed down her cheeks. There was nothing for the tears to reveal. She was fully exposed.

Leigha and Raquelle looked like spectators at a tennis match, watching the words fly between he and Marabella.

She held her head in her hands and whispered. "Will I always be stupid and inept when it comes to men? I need a break from everything and everyone."

He wanted to get down on his knees, begging her to understand the severity of the situation. "*Leannan*, listen to me. You weren't an assignment. What's between us is real. Unfortunately, there's more. Remember Jack, the guy at the bar who put the drug in your drink? Well, he was paid by someone to drug you. He described the guy in a baseball hat with long dirty-blond hair and sunglasses. Does that sound familiar to you at all?

Part of my job is to protect you, but I would have done that anyway." He needed to get through to her how dangerous this had all become.

She glared at him with coldness in her eyes that shot straight through him. "Do you always fuck the women you're protecting? Wait. Don't answer that, because I already know the answer. And no, your description doesn't sound familiar at all. By the way, don't. call. me. leannan." She yelled but her voice cracked as tears continued to fall from her cheeks. Unable to hold in her emotions in any longer, something snapped in her. After showing him her deepest scars, he possessed the one that cut the deepest. "I need to get away from you right now." Her voice was a decibel above a whisper as she snatched up her cell phone, stuffing it in the hidden zipper pocket in her skirt.

He caught her by her upper arm and spun her around to face him. "Please, be careful. Whoever this guy is, I'm convinced he's out there and may want to hurt you. He might be the one spying on you."

She didn't pull out of his clutches right away. He knew she felt the jolt of electricity going through her. Even angry she recognized the truth through his touch. Sucking in her breath, confusion crossed her face. Wanting to believe him, she needed time to process. Tears cascaded down her face, accentuating her pain. She looked him straight in the eye. "How could he possibly hurt me any more than you just did?" He flinched as her words slapped him. He released his grip on her. She turned and stormed out, slamming the door behind her.

He whipped his head back to her sisters, who were still as statues. "I have completely fucked this up. I may lose her, but she better be ready for the fight of her life because I won't give up." He grabbed his hair until it hurt and folded himself into an oversized chair.

"I can honestly say I have never seen Mara quite that explosive or passionate. She must have very strong feelings for you." Leigha spoke from a position of shock. She glanced at Raquelle, who had the same look of surprise on her face. They had never seen her so emotional over anything, not even Brock's death.

"I agree with Leigha. She never swears. She went straight to DEFCON 5. You need to leave her be for a while. She obviously needs to cool off. I can't predict where this leaves you." Raquelle dropped the smart-mouth routine to deal with all the new revelations of their so-called vacation. The hurricane lurking offshore hit them all full-force. They wondered if they would survive its intensity.

"You both need to know I'm telling the truth." He rested his eyes in the palm of his hands and gathered his thoughts. "I met Marabella on the plane down here. She scared the shit out of me. We had an instant connection I've never experienced with anyone else. I know it sounds crazy after such a short period of time, but I'm in love with her. I don't want to live the rest of my life without her. I won't go away without a fight. I hope you'll help me." The words spilled out of his mouth before he could retract them. There was no turning back. He loved her and wouldn't let go, having lost too much in his life, too much time and too many people. He desperately sought their support. They were her back up, but he had the feeling he might need them more.

"I can tell you love her. Your actions were obvious before today. I understand your need to keep this all to yourself until now. I'm not sure she will be as understanding. Let's not forget her husband betrayed her on so many levels. Given that, I'm not sure any of us knew the real him." Leigha, the voice of reason, calmed his nerves to some degree, but the engine in his chest still ran on high octane. He needed her to see that what was between them was different. He had changed his ways.

"In the meantime, I need you two to be on your toes and watch out. Awareness and safety are key here until we can figure out this guy's angle. I assume he's going after her, but he could just as easily go after one of you." He went right into MI6 mode. He needed to take the reins and fast. Otherwise, this would spiral out of control quickly.

"Contact me the minute you hear from her and try to think why someone would want to get to her. There may be something you remember. Even if you think the information is insignificant, let me know. I don't need to be here when she gets back. We both need a little space and I need to keep eyes on this." He left the suite like a man on a mission.

# CHAPTER 25

*Mara hurried out* the door, down the elevator and through the grand lobby to the pool. She felt those eyes zero in on her again. She spun around to see who it might be. Examining everyone thoroughly, no one stood out and no one looked like the guy Mac described. She headed to the beach to get away from all of it, seeking much needed space and quiet.

The sun started to settle in the sky casting a cool light on the sand and a soft breeze whispered off the water. She didn't notice any of the surroundings as she focused on deceitful Mac's words. Walking along the shore, she took her shoes off so she could feel the warm sand between her toes. The sensations brought her thoughts back to the evening with him in the tent. The memory twisted in her chest. On one end was love, on the other, betrayal. Love and betrayal seemed to be the continuing themes in her life.

Her mind and emotions ran through Mac's maze. Confused about where to go next, she tried to avoid her own roadblocks. She had been a fool, again. A big, betrayed fool. He took what they shared and made it about an assignment. He played her but good.

She guessed when you work for British Intelligence you have to sleep with the mark sometimes. Well, she hoped his little romp was well worth it. Scumbag. She fell for his lines, head over heels. The pain of betrayal threatened to crush her. He had said and done all the right things to make her feel special, being led blindly to believe what he wanted her to believe. She had to admitted it. She'd fallen in love with him. Deep down she wished he meant the things he said over the last couple of days.

Her phone chimed, indicating she had a text from her sisters. Without reading it, she turned the phone to vibrate. With her mind and emotions so jumbled, she didn't want to talk to anyone. She certainly didn't want to deal with his shit. This was going to be another battle for her to take up. But she already felt defeated.

As she made her way further down the beach, the number of people began to dwindle. Absorbed in her muddled thoughts about the events of the day, she wasn't paying attention to anything around her.

A change in atmosphere crept across her skin as a warning. The hair on the back of her neck began to tingle as goose bumps formed on her arms. Before she had a chance to turn around, someone grabbed her from behind and clamped something over her mouth. She struggled as best she could but her attacker was bigger than her, holding the cloth tightly in place. She clawed at the hand in panic for several minutes before the blackness took over.

———➤———

*Mac paced in* his suite with no word from Marabella. He'd been going out of his mind for hours, unable to stop thinking about how he could have done things differently. His timing had been off when exposing his real job. She hadn't been ready.

He had betrayed her, but not the way Brock betrayed her. His rationale sounded like he was splitting hairs but his betrayal wasn't at her expense. He hoped she would see it that way. The hope that he could defuse the situation before letting her know who he worked for vanished when his heart got in the way. He broke a lot of rules when it came to her, but he couldn't have ever stayed away. The pull to her was too strong. Stopping to look out over the balcony, dusk bore down as his panic set in.

His phone rang to his relief. "Hi, Mac. It's Leigha. Mara never stays away this long, even when pissed off at the world. We haven't heard from her and she's not answering our texts. We're trying not to panic, but—"

"Fuck! I'm on my way to you. I'm bringing my partner Syd. See you in a few." He hung up.

Thank God Sydney came for back up because this shit was about to get real on a whole other level. He didn't think Marabella would be ready for what lied ahead.

Less than ten minutes later he was at their door. He strode in with Sydney close behind. Leigha and Raquelle stood as their jaws dropped staring at the gorgeous Sydney. The day had become a merry-go-round of surprises. They crossed their arms in front of them wearing scowls.

Judging by the looks on their faces, he needed to clear the air before he got wrapped up in a game of twenty questions. "Before you think or say anything, this is Sydney. She was my partner for many years and has only ever been my partner."

"Besides, Mac's not my type. I'm not into penises, if you get my drift." Sydney emphasized her proclamation with a cocky grin. She locked eyes with the tall, gorgeous blonde spotlighted in the middle of the room.

"I'm Leigha, and this is my sister, Raquelle. It's nice to meet you." Leigha extended her hand, receiving a firm, warm grip from Sydney. She couldn't keep her eyes off Sydney. Based on physical appearance, they completely contradicted one another.

"The male population is pissed they're missing out on you." Raquelle couldn't help herself. Sydney and Leigha sized each other up with curiosity. Raquelle smiled with glee.

He didn't have time for this bullshit. He was already in agent mode. "Sydney is a highly respected hacker and agent. We're going to need her skills. We'll start with where you two think Marabella may have gone. We need to spread out and search those areas. Getting out there before dark is our best shot at finding her." His intuition glared like a neon sign, his gut was rarely wrong. He needed to keep his head on straight if they were going to find her in one piece.

The plan was to split up. He took the pool, Sydney the hotel grounds and the sisters would search the beach.

———————◆———————

*Leigha and Raquelle* separated from Mac and Sydney as they began to process everything.

"Who do we know that would want to hurt Mara? Does she have a stalker we don't even know about?" Raquelle tried to make the pieces fit together but came up empty.

"I think it's possible, but I can't put my finger on why. Do you think this has anything to do with what Brock was mixed up in? Mac said something about the Russian mob. So much for knowing your brother-in-law." Leigha put on her CSI hat again, examining all the angles.

"I don't know. Some vacation this turned out to be. How the hell did anyone even know we were here?" Raquelle wasn't as dumb as she led on sometimes. Lately, she felt the need to step out of the sandbox and play with the big kids for a change.

They continued to talk as they walked farther down the beach questioning whether Mara would even go that far. Scanning the area a couple her feet ahead of her, Raquelle saw a couple of objects in the sand sitting at an odd angle.

"Leigha, what's that up ahead?" Raquelle started running toward the objects. They both stood stock-still over them, recognizing them immediately. Her shoes were haphazardly thrown in the sand rather than carefully placed like someone going to take a swim.

"She didn't walk into the ocean and kill herself, so don't go there." Raquelle knew how Leigha's mind worked sometimes when she was in over-drive. She turned three-sixty to scan the area to see if she could spot her. It wouldn't be hard since very few people ventured that far down the beach at sunset. "I don't see her. Look, footprints. Oh, my God, do you think she was taken?"

They followed the footprints to the road, but that's where they ended. Mac was a phone call away as needed to get to him fast. They jogged back to the hotel, all the while trying to call but having every one of them drop out. The clock was ticking. Leigha carried her sister's shoes, hoping that whoever took her needed her alive and not dead.

# CHAPTER 26

"*Wakey, wakey, Princess.*"
Mara woke to someone slapping her in the face. Her head felt foggy as a sweet aftertaste filled her mouth. Her eyes cracked open to a place she didn't recognize. Her breath hitched. She couldn't move her body. Blood rush in her ears as her heartbeat picked up. The fuzziness in her head started to dissipate and panic set in. The voice was familiar but she couldn't make sense of it.

"Wake the *fuck* up, Mara. The sooner we get this over with, the better." Brock's rough, threatening and irritable voice seeped into her skin like permanent tattoo.

Wait... Brock's voice? How can it be? Oh, God! No! Her nightmare continued. Fear ran through her veins as she finally raised her head to see him standing in front of her. Secured to a chair, her wrists were zip-tied to the arms and her ankles to the legs. Her fingers curled over the ends.

She scanned her holding cell. It appeared to be an abandoned building in the midst of completion. Bare walls surrounded her as the smell of concrete filled her nose. The floor was covered in a grey dust. In the middle of the room hung a naked light bulb. She spotted a bare, dirty mattress wedged in the corner. This was a new kind of hell. The darkness outside came on quickly, which meant she had been unconscious for a while.

The sparseness of the room wasn't what bothered her but the sight of her dead—make that undead—husband. He stood in front of her in a pair of dirty jeans and a t-shirt with long greasy hair beneath a ratty baseball hat. His weary blue eyes stood out from the dark circles around them.

Shocked by his appearance, she wondered what happened to the clean-cut man she was married to for five years. The Brock she lived with wouldn't have been caught dead looking like this. A combination of anger and fear rolled through her. She would fight him this time, on her terms. But first, she wanted some answers. She deserved them.

"Ah, I see her majesty has awakened. Thank you for joining me, your highness." His exceedingly sarcastic tone made her skin crawl.

"Well, look who's back from the dead. I guess I don't need the DNA results to see you faked your death. What's that god-awful taste in my mouth?" She squared her shoulders determined not to show weakness.

"Yes, well, I never really left. Obviously, I faked my death to escape some unpleasantness. The aftertaste in your mouth is from the chloroform. I could have predicted you wouldn't come with me willingly, so I went with Plan B." Stepping forward, he positioned himself directly in front of her so she had to crane her neck back to look at his face.

"You're right. I wouldn't have come with you. What do you want from me? Haven't you taken enough already?" She stared him dead in the eyes, not backing down. She wouldn't be intimidated. He had been the coward, feeding on an ignorant woman, but not anymore. The game changed. She was different.

He moved around behind her and ran a finger through a stray wave in her hair, making her shiver. There was no way to keep him from touching her. Her anxiety kicked up a notch, but she fought to breathe through it. He leaned in close as his breath whispered across her ear, a silent threat that he could do what he wanted with her.

"Well, did someone find her big-girl voice? For the record, I never took anything that wasn't mine." He snarled, "Right now, you have five million of my money that I need ASAP. I tried to get to you several times, but your new boyfriend kept getting in my way. Tell me, does he know how fucking frigid you are? You know what that means, Mara—a dead fuck." He laughed in an evil, maniacal way that made her blood run cold.

Who was this man? Something's snapped in him. He was cruel but not nuts.

"I'm guessing the answer is yes. Poor guy. He probably ran for the hills. I guess you're destined to be an old maid." He chuckled.

She knew the less she said, the better. This man differed greatly from the one she had married. He appeared to be a new demented version. He was always the epitome of cruel, but this version of him seemed a lot more twisted.

She wanted answers, not a fight. His desperation

became evident, as he kidnapped her in broad daylight. She would need to protect Mac and his job. This called for a change of tactics to get him talking and answer her questions.

"Why?" Her whispered voice caught him off guard.

His laughter broke, puzzled by the question. "Why what, Mara?"

"Why do you hate me so much? What did I ever do to you? I know you cheated on me, but it didn't explain your cruelty." She choked slightly on her words, fighting to keep her tears at bay. Her head fought to prevail over her emotions.

He sighed like it was all so trivial and threw his hands up. "You were a means to an end, Mara. That's it. I needed someone of social status to get me where I needed to go. You were a sweet, innocent young woman who grew up in a sheltered lifestyle. You moved in all the right circles and looked beautiful doing it. I needed someone who had the ability to say all the right things and introduce me to all the right people. You were my 'in' to that world, especially after I got hired at CZR Investments." His eyes darkened as he tilted his head down. The air became still. "But I resented you. You are so fucking clueless to the world around you, living in your precious glass case. You take for granted the way you grew up and the money given to you. You don't need to work for the rest of your life. But what really got me was when your sculpting took off. It's as if you were born with a lucky horseshoe up your ass."

His old recording played in her head. "Jesus, get serious. Grow the fuck up! Those creatures are childish. You need to make some real art. How are you ever going to make a name for yourself? I guess your father's right. You're not an artist and never will be."

His fingers bit into his waist. Staring at her intently, she waited to see if he would reveal his secrets. He shook his head as if trying to rid himself of thoughts. "Do you really want to understand how I grew up? Well, let me paint a pretty little picture for you. Yes, I told you I grew up poor, but what you didn't know is I grew up dirt poor. My mother left my brothers and me when we were young and we had to fend for ourselves. She was beautiful, with long, dark hair and big, blue, loving eyes. There was a hole in our hearts where she once lived." Turbulence crossed his face. "Oh, and my father? He was a drunk, spending time at the bar between jobs. His drinking got worse after she left. He'd come home ranting, blaming us for her leaving and we got beatings on a regular basis. I took the brunt of it to spare my brothers. We scraped by for food and clothing. I'm the oldest, so it fell on me to take care of my younger brothers since my father wasn't available. Can you even comprehend what it's like to go hungry?"

Squatting down, he sat back on his heels with his forearms on his knees, glaring at her with dark hate in his soul. "No, I bet you don't. I don't think you can imagine going dumpster-diving, eating other people's leftovers, or have hunger eat at your stomach as it turns in on itself so bad you can't sleep at night. How about when you grow out of your pants and they're too short, exposing your dirty socks? The only saving grace was we weren't the only ones like that at our school."

He gripped the arms of the chair, caging her in, a captive audience. Looking down, he paused to regroup before continuing his story. He shoved her chair back making it tilt before it hit the floor again. She let out a scream, trembling. The gentle fawn to his wild boar.

"When I got my scholarship to NYU, I got out of town as fast as I could and went straight to New York City. I left all of it behind and never looked back. By then, my brothers were old enough to fend for themselves. For me, there was no time for partying. My sights were set on making money and plenty of it. I was willing to do anything to get there. I didn't want to be like my father. Even though I was named after him, I never used his name. He disgusted me." Looking for sympathy in her eyes, he wouldn't find any. There was a wisp of regret that crossed his face, but it quickly faded. He turned his head away. When he looked back at her the blackness in his eyes was shrouded by intense sadness.

She never met his family. He used his estrangement from them as an explanation for his lack of contact with them. "I didn't know. But then again, you never told me. You never really let me in. Sounds like you're still holding onto a lot of anger and sadness." She said it so quietly she didn't think he even heard her.

The stark contrast between him and Mac made her realize how genuine her feelings were for Mac. He let her in behind his shield where some of his secrets lived. Secrets of loss and life that made him the man he turned out to be. She saw it in his eyes and felt it in her heart. Even as awful as she had been to him, she hoped he was searching for her. He kept his secret to protect her, not to betray her. Brock kept things hidden to further his greedy agenda. Her lower lip began to tremble at the reality of her situation. Her head snapped up at his next words.

"Why, thank you, Dr. Freud! I hated my mom for leaving us. But in the end, the anger fueled my motivation to become something more. Besides, do you think if I told you the truth about me, you would have stayed with me? It's only when I became successful that your father even considered me worthy of you. He would've always viewed me like the dirt I used to be." The pain etched on his face made him look like he had lived a thousand lives. He let out a deep sigh while staring at his fingers. Tapping the tips together was a nervous habit.

She was stunned to discover so much in his face that he never revealed before. She visualized a small boy with the anguish of his childhood that led to the bad choices as an adult. It wasn't lost on her that no matter how hard she tried he shut her out and abused her without remorse. In a way, he punished her the way he wanted to punish his mother for leaving them.

Raising her voice, she wanted closure to all of the drama that enveloped her life with him. "First of all, you never even gave me a chance, never let me in. You punished me and abused me over and over again. There are a lot of people out there with crappy childhoods, but they don't all grow up to abuse their wives. You were supposed to love and protect me. But instead, you took advantage of the fact that I was naïve and inexperienced to move yourself forward."

"Well then, I guess the saying is true, you become your role model. Why do you think my mother left us? My guess is she hated all men at that point. My father was cruel to her and she couldn't take it anymore. My mother was so gorgeous she could have had anyone. Why she married him, I'll never understand. Maybe he was kind to her in the beginning, but poverty has a way of destroying everything in its path." He wore the face of his child, scared, alone, and hungry. He watched her intently. "What to you want Mara? An apology?" He threw his head back and laughed. "You're not getting one. I didn't become a better man. I became the bitter man. The hatred I have for my mother for leaving us runs through my veins. But I don't need to get dragged back down by my past. I needed to focus on the future."

She got pissed with all his reasons as to why he abused her. She didn't hate him anymore. Worse, she just didn't care and wanted to be away from him as soon as possible. "What do you want from me?"

"Well, princess, you inherited the insurance money that belongs to me. I was going to move it from your account to mine, only you fucking changed the usernames and passwords with high security encryption. It makes it impossible for me to gain access. So, you and I are going to go to the nearest free Wi-Fi place in the morning. You're going to tell me the passwords so I can make the transfer." He ran a finger down her jawline. She recoiled at his touch, her body remembering her tortured past with him.

"I don't know the passwords by heart. They're stored in my laptop back at the hotel." She threw a pebble in the lake. The ripple instantly destroyed his streamlined plan.

"Fuuuuuuuck! You never were the sharpest knife in the drawer. Shit!" He whipped off his hat and started running his trembling hands through his greasy hair over and over again, pacing back and forth in front of her.

Her anxiety spiked, as he became unpredictable again. She had never seen him this on edge, making it hard for her to read him.

"Okay, so we're going to have to go back to the hotel tomorrow. Thank God my IQ is near genius, it makes up for your fucking stupidity. You must know your arrogant sisters well enough to guess when they'll be out of the room." He focused on her as if she held the answers to the rest of his plan.

"They're probably looking for me, so I don't know where they are or what they're doing." She didn't want to give too much away about their situation.

As angry as she was at Mac for lying to her, this situation was ten times worse. Brock's anxiety was amped up. While she sat there, her phone had been vibrating in the pocket behind her waist. She tried to reach it, but couldn't get her wrists free.

"I need some water. Can you untie my hands, please?" She thought appeasing him would be better than flaring his anger.

He stared at her for a long moment as he wiped

the sweat from his upper lip. Clamping his hands on her forearms, he brought his face inches from hers. "If you try anything, Mara, I will hurt you in ways you have never experienced. Am I making myself clear?" His eyes were wild and intense. He was a man on a mission. She was nothing more than a means to end, again.

"Yes," was all she was capable of saying. She couldn't stop from trembling as fear ran across her skin. He gave new meaning to words cold and calculating. The great manipulator fed off her fear. She needed to break that pattern, but she didn't know this version of him and didn't have time to figure it out. She kept reminding herself, the less said, the better.

He cut the zip ties holding her wrists together and handed her a bottle of water from a bag on the floor. "You need to eat something. I wouldn't want you to pass out on me or anything." He smirked. "Then we'll tackle this clusterfuck tomorrow. I need time to think things through. You'll be my little pet for the evening."

The water cooled her throat as she scanned her new imprisonment. The windows appeared to be covered with holey black curtains, but she realized it was the night sky in window frames absent of glass. The only light came from the dim bulb hanging from the ceiling. The harshness reflected the severity of her situation.

He went back into his bag and pulled out some sandwiches and snacks, shoving one at her. She reached out to grab it, accidently brushing his fingers. A sensation of cold steel coiling up her arm speared her heart. She flinched from the absence of warmth that she lived with for so long. Like an out of body experience, her former self examined her new self. She couldn't understand how she lived with him for so long and not see who he really was.

As things continued to change, she questioned if she ever loved him. Time after time, she cowered, living in the shadow of his brutality. Her naïveté kept her from knowing the difference between healthy and dysfunctional. Growing up in a family with an absent father and a protected lifestyle had its downside, but Mac helped her become a changed woman. The old fear left, replaced by hope.

No wonder Mac seemed like that ray of sunshine. He showed her what made up a real man. She felt worshipped by him. He attended to everything about her, every nuance of her body. She hoped he was helping her sisters find her despite what happened between them.

She heard Brock's voice but was deep in thought, ignoring his words.

# CHAPTER 27

"*Hey, princess*, where did you go there? Thinking about how your boyfriend is going to save you? I doubt he'll get very far. I've covered my tracks very well. God knows I spent a lifetime doing that." He casually bit into his sandwich and stared at it as if his past life was half a thought.

Mara ate her sandwich in silence, but things still nagged at her. She knew enough not to ask about the connection to the Russian mob. Holding her cards close would be the wiser move. No sense in making a bad situation worse. But she wanted answers to some lingering questions. She would take the opportunity to find out how wrong her choice had been when it came to him. She shouldn't care, but she did. Her ego reared its head and wanted some attention.

"I get that I was a means to an end, but were you ever attracted to me? Did I repulse you that much? You always made it a point to tell me how ugly I was. What was the purpose of all that?" The crack in her voice gave away her vulnerability.

"No, Mara. You're one of the most beautiful and innocent women I've ever met, but anger took over. I wanted to hurt you like I hurt. You had everything growing up and I had nothing. You weren't even aware of poor people. You just lived your overpriced life in ignorance. I wanted what you had and more. I said you were ugly to keep you from leaving me. It was a brainwashing of sorts. If you believed you were beautiful and desirable, you would have left before my plans were complete. If you really knew me, you wouldn't love me. I kept you where you needed to be. You served a purpose. Besides, I enjoyed seeing you weak." The ice in his voice and the reality of his words cut like shards of glass.

She had no defense for this news. It seemed incomprehensible that someone like him existed on the planet. The rivets had already popped out of place. Her steel wall had already come down. She wouldn't rebuild it.

Her dam of emotions broke. She couldn't believe what she heard. The final nail hammered in the coffin for the old Mara. He was about to meet the new Mara, or was this the woman who hid in fear for so many years? She couldn't believe there was anyone capable of such deceit and cruelty to satisfy their own delusions. Something clicked over inside her. She was about to unload with nothing to lose.

"You are so fucking twisted. You make Ted Bundy look like a dream. At least he had the decency to *kill* his victims. You just torture them for years on end. You know what, asshole? I grew up a lot in the last three months. You weren't worthy of me then and you sure as *hell* aren't worthy of me now. Your shitty childhood is not an excuse for what you've done. You can have your fucking money and stay the hell away from me and my family."

She wasn't surprised by her words. They seemed to flow of their own volition. While she spoke, his face contorted into the ugly mask of a demon. It reminded her of her angry red dragon she had flung out of the tent at the beach.

He slowly stood and stalked toward his prey. A lump formed in her throat. She might have poked this red dragon a little too hard. Before she could see it coming, he backhanded her hard across the face. It stung worse than the shark's tail due to its point of origin. She refused to cry. Refusing to let him feed off her weakness.

"Oh, so now you're all grown up? Don't forget who's in charge, Mara. I had every right to do what I did, you rich, uptight bitch. I deserve it all. I deserve to be happy and wealthy. Besides, you have no idea how much it's cost me. Ted Bundy, eh? What makes you think I won't put you out of your fucking misery once I get the passwords?" He reached in his pocket and threw her red dragon in her lap. "Here's one of your childish trinkets to keep you company tonight."

Stunned, she picked it up, remembering what Mac said about red dragons. They represented anger, danger, aggression and a warning. Her subconscious sounded an alarm, because this red dragon was very much alive and standing in front of her.

He laughed while he bent down to cut the ties on her feet. Grabbing her by the arm, he threw her across the room to the naked soiled mattress that lay on the floor.

"Where did you get this?" She was bewildered at seeing her ugly creation again.

"I watched your every move, princess. I was so close to grabbing you but the doors of the elevator closed. You got lucky then. As I was walking on the beach, you threw it out of the tent. Did you and lover boy have a good time? You should cherish that moment, because I can't wait to see the look on your face when I put a bullet in his head." He started laughing again. She turned in his direction as horror gripped her.

"Leave him out of this. He has *nothing* to do with this!" She screeched in panic.

"What's he going to do when he finds out he's been fucking a married woman? Eh, Mara? You *did* fuck him, didn't you? Or were you worried it would hurt too much." He chided her with a pouty face. When she didn't answer, he went on. "Poor Mara. It doesn't matter. That's probably all the dead fuck he could handle for a lifetime." His face, hardened like stone, lacking all emotion. She remembered a time when his eyes seemed softer, but that softness faded shortly after the ceremony.

She followed his eyes as they moved to a place on the floor. A chain attached to a bare pipe went from floor to ceiling. He dug his fingers into her wrist, and handcuffed her to the pipe. Fear swept across as her face flushed. This was it. He's going to rape her one last time. One final round. Something to remember him by, as if she could ever forget his torture.

He watched her, deciphering her facial expressions. He used it to manipulate her with the greatest of ease. Bending down, he grabbed the back of her hair and hissed. "Don't worry, princess, I have no desire to fuck you. I'm just not that desperate for a stale fuck. Besides, I don't do leftovers." The hatred in his voice rivaled the devil himself.

She curled up on the mattress, remembering her phone in the zipper pocket of her waist. Even if she could text someone, she couldn't tell them where to find her. The mattress dipped as he moved behind her. He didn't touch her, but she wanted to run away from his burning breath on her neck.

"Go to sleep and don't worry. No one is coming for you. I'm sure you've scared off lover boy." She felt him smile behind her as if he held all the cards. But she had a couple of trump cards of her own.

Her mind drifted back to Mac and what he told her before she left. As an agent he had resources to find her. She prayed she hadn't burned that bridge. This world was unfamiliar to her and became scarier by the minute.

She was out of her element with this Brock, like she hadn't known him at all. All these years, he hid this evil, dark side of himself behind designer clothes and money. In his desperate need just to survive, his true colors were finally on display. They frightened her, feeding her fear.

The facts remained that he killed someone, used the body to fake his death, and had connections to the Russian mob. He certainly didn't care for her one iota, nor did he ever. She would have to watch what she did and said, not wanting to set him off. As her mind ran a mile a minute, it brought her back to Mac.

Tears built up threatening to spill over. Closing her eyes, her thoughts wandered back to her night with Mac, a man so incredible, gentle and knowledgeable, the exact opposite of Brock. She wondered if love could happen that quickly, feeling more for Mac in the last couple of days than she had ever felt for the man laying behind her. Mac got her. When she gazed in his eyes, there was an invisible silk thread of an unspoken connection. They knew each other, recognizing each other's missing pieces. They didn't work at being comfortable and relaxed with one another. He listened when she talked and enjoyed her playful side.

What gutted her more than anything was the thought she might not make it out of this alive. She might never see Mac again. If she did live to tell about it, she would go all-in. She wanted to show him how he affected and changed her life, even if it was for what would be left of her vacation.

As she escaped in thoughts of Mac, her phone vibrated again in her hidden pocket. She froze praying he didn't hear it.

"What the fuck was that, Mara?" He lunged at the back of her, grabbing at her waistband. He rolled her over on her front as they both struggled with the zipper. He grabbed her free wrist, yanking it above her head.

"Keep your hands off it!" Unzipping the pocket, he found the phone as she rolled onto her back. He glared at her with such disgust she thought he might kill her right then and there.

He hurled the phone across the room. Hitting the concrete wall, it shattered into a million pieces, echoing in the barren room. He searched the debris on the ground to make sure the SIM card had been dislodged and crushed it beneath his heel.

He turned to her as she huddled in the corner trembling and moved within an inch of her face. His face was red with fury as he spoke through gritted teeth. "I guess your lifeline is gone. It's just you and me out here in the middle of a deserted Mexico. Don't try anything else or I *will* kill you. I can't afford to get caught for a lot of reasons, none of which I'm willing to share with you."

With that, she rolled over and gave him her back. She couldn't stand the sight of him. This was the situation she wanted to avoid, but life had a way of throwing you curve balls.

He unlocked her wrist from the handcuff and hauled her up to her feet. "We need to move now. I'm not taking any chances that someone tracked that phone. You're a goddamn pain in my ass, as always. But I've always been good on the fly." If he could have spewed venom on her, she would have been covered in it.

Moving out the door and downstairs, they walked into the dark, steamy night.

# CHAPTER 28

*Evening approached as* Mac's ringing cell jarred him out of his thoughts. "Do we have any information on the DNA results of the dead guy?" His words came out quickly as he got impatient for answers.

"Bad news, mate. The DNA came back and the dead body in the car does *not* match Walker's DNA. It's conclusive. There's no doubt that Walker, according to the evidence, is still alive." McFadden sounded relieved.

He felt like a heavyweight boxer that just got knocked out. "I had a hunch. I think he may be here in Mexico. There's a man who sort of fits his description who tried to drug Marabella at the club the other night. My old partner, Sydney, is down here trying to find him. I read her in on the case today. She's doing some recon work for me." His whole body went rigid as the thought of Marabella in danger. He needed to keep it in check. As a trained operative, there was no room for emotions, but he had never fallen in love with the asset before.

"Don't forget there's another player in this game. If we know he's alive the Russians aren't far behind. If he's in Mexico, you need to find him as soon as possible and bring him in. We need him alive, Creighton, to give us information on the Russians." Neil wanted to make sure he understood the full scope of the situation as it escalated on an international scale.

"I had to tell Marabella about my assignment. Needless to say, it didn't go well. She left their suite hours ago and hasn't returned." He mumbled to himself. "I dread telling her sisters about the resurrection of her dead husband." His voice gave him away.

"You've got it bad, don't you, Creighton?" Neil stumbled on his words. "I think they need to know despite what the CIA or NYPD decides to do. Good luck. It sounds like you're going to need to dig deep on this one. Keep your wits about you. I'm not talking about Walker, either. You can handle him." With that, Neil hung up, leaving him to deal with the impending shit storm. Round two was going to be worst than round one. His first contact needed to be Syd, giving her the latest information. Then he would deal with the dynamic duo.

When he called Syd, she sounded a little giddy. A voice in the background indicated he was definitely interrupted something. He guessed she'd had picked up someone at the pool. She got rid of her guest so she could talk to him privately. "So, what's going on?" She recovered quickly, always ready for the next phase of an assignment.

"John Walker, a.k.a. Brock, is alive and possibly down here in Mexico. Did you find out anything about the guy in the baseball hat?" He needed intel and fast to stay ahead of whatever he might have planned for Marabella.

"I got nothing. There are a lot of guys with baseball hats and blond hair at this resort." She was always very thorough with her investigations, talking to everyone necessary. "It may be that he isn't even staying at the resort."

"Keep on top of this and start asking questions off the property and see what comes up. My gut tells me he must be getting desperate at this point. If he has her, I haven't figured out what he wants with her. Let me know what you find out." He only had his gut instinct to go on. There was no proof that he was even in Mexico. His mission was to find this asshole before he got to Marabella.

Now came the hard part. He would have to go to Leigha and Raquelle and tell them everything, giving them an introduction to his world that they could do without.

He got a text from them explain what they had found on the beach. Responding right away, he said he and Sydney were on their way back to their suite. "Tell me exactly what happened and don't leave anything out." His accent was heavier than usual as his words ran together.

Leigha responded first after deciphering what he'd said. "We were walking down the beach when we spotted Mara's shoes, but her cell phone wasn't there. She must still have it on her. We picked the shoes up and started to follow a set of large footprints, probably a man's. The footprints led to a road, but that's where they ended." Leigha wasn't the crier in the group. She continued to stay her stoic and in-control self with her hands twisted in front of her.

Raquelle interjected, "We think Mara was taken." Her voice shook, showing her raw emotions.

"You both need to sit down for a minute. I have some news that I need to share with you." He gave himself a moment to collect his thoughts, head down and breathing slowly.

Leigha and Raquelle each sat down in the nearest available seat.

He eyed them wearily, rubbing the scar above his eyebrow. "I got confirmation from my boss. The DNA results are back. They don't match Brock's. That means there's a very good possibility he's here in Mexico. He might have taken Marabella but the question is why? He's taken quite a bit of money from his clients. I don't think she was in on this with him. She didn't seem to quite know what he did for a living."

Raquelle stood up like a Jack-in-the-Box. "First of all, there is no way in hell Mara is in on anything with that douchebag. Second, if he took her, he just gave me a reason to kill him once we find him."

"Raquelle, take a deep breath. I need you, and she needs you. So before you go killing anyone, can you and Leigha take me back to the beach where you found the shoes?" He gripped her by her shoulders to keep her focused on him. To some extent, it helped keep him grounded as well.

Leigha stepped in. "Yes, we can take you back to the exact spot on the beach. Do you think he has her?" She locked onto his eyes not wanting to miss his reaction. She wanted to gauge his gut instinct when it came to this new situation.

"Yes. It's a strong possibility at this point. Sydney, can you stay here and start putting together your computers for a triangulation of the cell phone? Also, I need you to contact the resort security and get the footage of the last twenty-four hours." He felt in control giving orders. His head was in work mode, but his heart was a mess, a tug-of-war between the job and his emotions. If Brock had her and he was fighting to survive then all bets were off on how this all might go down.

Leigha managed to keep herself together to concentrate on the search. "I think I should stay here and help Sydney set up. I might be more useful here. I have some tech savvy." She looked at Sydney through interested eyes and a slight smile.

"Okay then. Raquelle and I are going back to the beach before we lose light while you two set up shop." With that, he and Raquelle left the suite to search for any traces of evidence that might lead them to Marabella before it was too late.

When they reached the beach, Raquelle showed him where they found the shoes and the footprints. They followed the footprints to where they stopped further down the road toward the resort. He began to search for tire marks of any kind.

"Here. It looks like a car was parked for a while in the muddy sand. If we follow the tracks, the car moved forward and turned around. I don't see the same tracks on the other side of the road. They must have moved down the beach."

He scrutinized the tire tracks, stopping to take pictures of them. After being on the job for so long, he could feel the rhythm of the case, hoping it would lead them in the right direction. Although sometimes, you get sideswiped, needing to change course.

He rubbed the back of his neck remembering her pull on his hair. He needed her back with him where she belonged. There was unfinished business with her, like a lifelong contract that needed to be fulfilled.

He and Raquelle walked back at the suite. Leigha helped Sydney setup the computers while she listened to her explain how triangulation worked.

"Hey, what did you find? Anything we can use?" Sydney worried they hit a dead end.

His face fell, the heaviness settling in his chest that she might be gone for good. Mexico tended to be a place where people disappeared without a trace. "No, just the tire tracks. A car traveled down the beach from that area. I took some pictures to see if we can match the tires."

Raquelle spoke up. "Speaking of pictures, Leigha takes pictures of everything. If we go through her camera, we might find Brock's face in the crowd. Then we'd know for sure he has her. It's worth a try." She would do whatever it took to bring her sister back. "Besides, I'm portrait artist of the family. I know faces from every angle."

"Why don't you and Leigha look at the pictures? Sydney, where are we with security footage from the area?" He pushed his heart behind the walled fortress. If he got caught up in his fear, he would be of no use. Every second counted in a kidnapping. The first forty-eight hours were always the most crucial.

"We need to go to them and review their feeds. They have cameras everywhere, thankfully, but viewing them could take a while. Why don't we meet back here in an hour and see if we can find out who has her." Sydney expertly delegated the jobs and would piece things together afterwards.

"That sounds like as good a plan as any right now." His heavy sigh indicated his growing weariness.

———————◆———————

*For the next* hour, Raquelle and Leigha searched through all of her pictures for anything that resembled Brock.

Raquelle noticed the looks Leigha gave Sydney. She didn't think it was because Sydney was gorgeous. "So, what do you think of Sydney? She's really quite nice to look at, isn't she?" She said with a tone of casualness, without making eye contact.

Frowning, Leigha turned to look at her. "She may be beautiful, but she's also quite intelligent. There's a calmness about her I can appreciate." Her lack of emotion gave her away. She knew her sister too well. She would get to the bottom of what was going on eventually.

"Hmm," She gave a noncommittal response. She didn't want to push her too much, but she got the feeling something had been eating at Leigha the entire trip.

"Wait. Look! Is that a side profile of him?" She turned her head back to the LCD screen of the camera. Her skills as a gifted portrait artist had paid off. "Can you enlarge that one?" She hoped the picture was of him. They could at least identify who they were dealing with. One more piece of the puzzle was in place.

Leigha pushed a few buttons on her camera to enlarge the picture. They stopped on a picture of a disheveled Brock wearing a baseball hat with greasy, dirty-blond hair standing in the background focused on something. They stared at the picture without saying a word. It wasn't the fact that they weren't used to seeing him like that, but the realization that hit them full-force.

Raquelle finally broke the silence in a voice barely above a whisper. "He's got her."

As she got ready to call Mac, he and Sydney came through the door. They looked rather somber. The sisters stood up, making it like a Mexican standoff on who was going to tell the other team the bad news.

Leigha spoke up. "We know he has her. We found a picture showing a profile of him on my camera. That son of a bitch is very much alive. But we're going to do everything we can to get her back and make him pay, right?" She had found her strength again. Knowing who had Mara made it easier somehow. What they didn't know was that the Brock they once knew didn't exist anymore. He replaced that persona with the real him.

—◆—

*Mac didn't acknowledge* the emotion in her voice.

"The question is what does he want with her? He embezzled millions of dollars from CZR Investments that he could access. The money was untraceable and literally seemed to evaporate into digital space." He tried to put all the pieces together. "Let's go back to the insurance policy. It was for five million, but that seems like chump change for the millions he took."

Sydney picked up where he left off. "Maybe he wants the five million as seed money to start up somewhere else. If he accesses the other money, it will trigger a red flag and the agencies will be all over him. The Russians will be alerted as well. That's the last thing he wants." She looked at things through the eyes of a criminal, making her a valuable operative.

He was missing something crucial to the investigation, something they needed to get their hands on right away. "Let's assume he wants the five million in insurance money. If he easily accessed her email accounts to find out she was coming here, why not do the same with her other accounts and transfer the money?" The puzzle pieces weren't fitting together.

Raquelle and Leigha stared at each other as if a light bulb had gone off in their heads. Leigha piped up. "He can't access them anymore. Our lawyers had her change her usernames and passwords to all her accounts. They also added an extra layer of security and encryption features so no one can hack into her accounts. I think she has them stored on her laptop." Her eyes had hope in them. He didn't want to dash them but it wasn't that easy.

Sydney continued his thought. "Well, that explains a lot. More than likely, he accessed all of her accounts before and now needs her to get into them so he can transfer the money. I don't think he counted on that. It's making him scramble to come up with a new plan. I don't mean to scare all of you, but the question is will he need her after he's transferred the money?"

The statement was meant to put everyone on high alert. It was in everyone's best interest to put it out there and deal with the reality of the situation. Otherwise, there wouldn't be a favorable outcome.

He let all the information sink in as he slowly sat down on the couch while everyone stared at him, waiting for his next move. He wouldn't be the one with all the answers. They needed to work together as a team. His mind whirled while his heart beat rapidly. He couldn't think of what would prevent Brock from killing her after he got what he wanted. He would leave her for dead in the middle of Mexico somewhere, and no one would find her.

His worry escalated at the thought of him torturing her or, worse yet, raping her. His hands balled into fists at the thought of any man touching what was his, let alone that motherfucker. He would spend the rest of his life hunting him and then torturing him beyond what he could imagine with no regrets. God, he needed to pull himself together if he had a prayer of making it out of this with her intact. "We need to find her as soon as possible. He's unpredictable, at best, which means he's dangerous. Sydney, where are we on locating the cell phone?" If he kept himself moving forward in this case, he could keep his mind off the dangers of this situation.

"If he lays a hand on my sister, I will hunt him down and kill him with my bare hands." Everyone looked over to see Raquelle vibrating with rage, fists at her sides, teeth gritted, as tears streamed down her face. No one doubted her for a minute. Out of the sisters, she had enough anger and determination to follow through with her threat.

Leigha reached out to grab her hand. "Calm down, Raquelle. We're going to work together to find her," she said it with stoic confidence, folding Raquelle into her arms.

"Let's send her one more text, and maybe she'll respond." Leigha tried to calm herself hoping Mara would respond.

Sydney studied the computers for anything to pop up on the triangulation for Mara's cell phone. "This isn't going to be easy with the spotty reception, but I'll see what I can do," she reported.

"Good. Look for something south, down the beach. We saw tire tracks leading in that direction. She may still have her phone and just didn't respond to the texts. We can only hope." He sounded sure of himself for the sake of her sisters. On the inside he was losing his sister all over again.

He read the profile on Brock. The man presented as desperate, unpredictable, and smart as hell, a deadly combination. He'd dealt with enough criminal profiles to know he would probably be diagnosed as a psychopath. In other words, he was a loose cannon. There was no way of knowing what he would do under extreme stress. They couldn't afford to waste any time to find out.

The night cast an inky blanket on this side of the world, making the air heavy with uncertainty. Raquelle and Leigha decided to order room service for dinner. They needed to distract themselves from thinking about the all dangers their sister faced.

The computer tried to put together the pings off the towers in the area. Technology wasn't always quick. He settled in front of it as his eyes never left the computer screen.

"Mac, staring at the screen isn't going to make it happen any sooner." Sydney mumbled quietly, trying to relieve some of the tension that built up in a room full of nerves.

"I know. I can't stop thinking about her. I shouldn't have let her leave today. She'd still be here with us. Instead, she's out with that maniac. He might hurt her. I don't know." He rested his head in his palms, covering his eyes. "I've never had a case like this before. This is so personal. My head and heart are at war with who should be in the lead. I can't seem to separate them." He would leave Sydney to make the tough decisions to pull them through.

"I don't think I've ever seen you like this. I've got your back, partner. Don't ever doubt that for a minute. We've been in some tough spots before. We'll push through this and have her back here in no time." Sydney's voice wavered. They were all too familiar with what really happens as time slips away.

"God, I hope so. I'm usually not a praying man,

but I'm calling in all my prayers tonight. I don't just want her back, I need her, Syd." His voice broke with a hint of desperation, covering up his sheer determination.

Just then, the computer pinged on two of the three towers they needed to locate her. Raquelle and Leigha joined them as they watched the computer screen. The third ping came up but left the screen along with the other two.

"Shit! There's no signal from her phone." Sydney tapped madly on the keyboard to locate the pings again. "We've lost it."

"We need to move now. We have an idea of where the phone was based on the last ping. Let's go. Leigha and Raquelle, you two are going to stay here and wait for us. Do not answer the door. We'll be in touch."

"Let me go to the restroom before we go. I'll catch up with you at the car." Sydney seemed unusually quiet, but he let it go. His only focus was to get to Marabella.

# CHAPTER 29

*Gripping Mara's upper* arm, he squeezed it tightly. He propelled her down the unfinished concrete stairs. Her bare feet skidded into the dirt streets of the forgotten Mexican resort.

"Ow! You're hurting me! Let go!" Making a scene in the middle of the street, she hoped someone would hear her. She came to a stop. Dark abandoned buildings surrounded her.

He whipped her around so fast she slammed into him. He bent down, nose to nose with her. "Shut. The. Fuck. Up. I would punch you unconscious if I could, but I need you to move with me. I don't need to carry any dead weight. You're going to be quiet and cooperate, or I'm going to cut up that pretty little face of yours. Do you understand?" His teeth clenched so tightly his jaw pop. Spit started to form on the corners of his mouth.

Evil emanated from him as it slithered coldly through the steamy tropical air. Goose bumps traveled all over her body, and her hair stood on end. Her head bobbed up and down in agreement.

"Thank God I had the foresight to scout the area in case there was a problem. I should have known there would be problems with you. Stupidity and naïveté always ran your world. I don't know why you decided to up your IQ points now." His sarcasm always became nastiest under duress. This was the most stressed out she'd ever seen him.

He continued to pull her down the street to another abandoned building very similar to the one they had just come from. They made it up three flights of stairs to the top floor. As they moved down the dark hallway, she stepped on something sharp. She jumped back and stopped dead in her tracks. The blood seeped from the bottom of her foot.

"I cut my foot." Using it to try and slow him down before they reached the room at the end of the hall. She would have done anything not to be stuck in a room with him again.

"I don't give a fuck. Keep moving. We're almost there." He dragged her to the end of the hall to the only room with a door.

As soon as they entered the room, he threw her forward as she slammed onto the concrete floor scraping her shoulder. Her body automatically curled into the fetal position. This room was sparser than the other one with no mattress on the floor. A lantern stood in the corner of the room next to a huge duffle bag.

"You need to stay down on the floor and don't say a word." He went to the duffle bag, grabbed a flashlight and lit the lantern with a match.

She backed herself into the opposite corner. He slid down the wall and propped his elbows on his knees with his head in his hands.

He talked to the floor, never looking up at her. "Fuck all, how did I get here? This was supposed to be so easy, but things are never easy when you're involved. No matter what, by tomorrow, it's done. I can't let anyone know what I've done."

She became unraveled, crying in the corner. His head came up as he viewed her through empty eyes. Her soft whimper didn't tug at his heartstrings. He had become immune to it. He tilted his head as if he were realizing something. "Stop crying. For the love of God, stop crying. You don't get to cry." She sniffled. "What? Not comfortable with the dirt of slum living? Too bad. My mother used to cry after my father beat her. He was always worried that she was cheating on him. Look at it this way. At least I never beat you."

"No you scarred me where no one could see. There's no difference." Her tears stopped as she faced her demon head on.

His face was the coldest she had ever seen it. He rubbed his finger along his chin. "I won't be foolish enough to leave any evidence." He crawled toward her and stopped halfway across the room. "Do you think you deserve a life so much better than mine? Was it just a roll of the dice? Well, princess I'm about to change the odds in this game of craps. I'm going to start a new life with that five million dollar life insurance policy. Why do you think I took it out in your name? It'll get me the lifestyle I want and deserve."

He blew out the lantern. Sucking the light out of the room, they were encased it in darkness. The only light came from the gibbous moon. "Nighty night, princess. You're going to need your strength for tomorrow." His voice scraped like needles across her skin, pain but no puncture. "Here's a towel for your foot." He threw a towel across the room, landing within reaching distance.

She put her hand to the bottom of her foot. The bleeding had slowed down. She wrapped it in the towel and closed her eyes, hoping for a reprieve from her living hell. Finding no escape from the devil himself, she would need to use her head this time. She didn't lack intellectually. Emotionally, she needed to play catch-up. She found out things about him she had never known before, like the motivation for his cruelty.

If she focused on Mac to escape this horror in her mind and get some sleep. She imagined herself wrapped in her protector's arms. If she ever saw him again, *when* she saw him again, she would make it up to him. She would use the darkness as a protective cloak as she dreamt about him. The next day might bring a new opening to an otherwise bleak situation.

———◆———

*Mac and Sydney* drove south down the beach, passing clusters of undeveloped buildings. They didn't pass many cars. It looked like a resort in the middle of construction that had come to a halt. Some buildings were more complete than others. All of them no more than three stories high, showed signs of decay with crumbling concrete and cracked steel.

They parked the car out of sight. His instinct told him if there were a place for Brock to hide, this would be it.

"Here, wear this so we can communicate while we're out here. We need to be on point for this." He handed Sydney a two-way, military-grade communications earpiece.

"Boy, you came prepared. I always liked that about you." She winked at him, hoping to relieve some of the tension before all hell broke loose.

They split up and moved quietly through the streets, guns pulled, searching for any signs of life. The unpredictability of the situation put them on high alert. They searched the outside of several buildings.

"Anything?" He used a quiet voice. The com was sensitive enough to pick up breathing.

"Negative."

"Nothing here either."

"I say we call it a night and come back tomorrow for an internal search." Sydney's voice showed signs of a long day.

He stopped to listen to the voice inside his heart. "I can feel her. She's here, somewhere." His desperation came through.

On the way to meeting up at the car, Sydney stumbled over some debris. A quiet search quickly turned into the crunching sound of gravel under his feet as she hit the ground, revealing their location.

———◆———

*Mara heard the* noise outside and hobbled to the window opening. As soon as she got there to see who or what was in the street, Brock came up behind her and put his arm across her shoulder like a vice. She gasped as he yanked her head back against him.

In the street below were two figures, one leaning over the other. She couldn't make out what they said. But when one of them stood up, it was Mac's silhouette. He had come for her. She sucked in a breath, trying not to give them away. Frantic on the inside, she wanted to go to him. She struggled against the locked arm, but he only held her tighter to him.

He spoke close to the side of her face. "Who's that, Mara? Lover boy? How interesting. Is there something you aren't sharing with me? Hmm? How would he know to come all the way out here? Is he a cop, princess?" He hissed, moving his arm around her neck like a noose. The heat of his breath flamed her ear. "If you so much as breathe the wrong way to give up our location, I will kill him right now in front of you." He took the gun out from behind his waistband and showed her the barrel.

She violently shook her head back and forth to indicate she wouldn't say a word. Mac needed to stay alive. They watched as the two figures walked in the opposite direction and disappeared out of sight.

He spun her around and threw her on the floor. She slammed onto her back. Before she could turn away, he moved on top of her, breathing in her face. Explosive anger radiated off him like a ticking time bomb. She needed to find a way to diffuse the bomb before it went off.

He yelled in her face, clearly at the end of his

rope. "You better fucking tell me everything about lover boy now." As she tried to turn her head, he grabbed her by the throat. "Start talking, you stupid bitch, before I choke the life out of you." His adrenaline spiked causing his breathing to become rapid and shallow.

Gasping for air, she used both hands to grab his wrist. He slowly released enough pressure to let her speak. Since he thought she was stupid anyway, she decided to play dumb. "I don't know much about him. We only met a couple of days ago. He simply said he was on vacation. I have no idea what he does for a living." Thankful for the darkness of the room, it made it almost impossible for him to see her eyes, a dead giveaway.

His words came through pants of desperation. "That's fucking classic. Spread your legs for a man you know nothing about because you are so goddamn desperate to be loved. Who was with him?" He released her throat putting his hands on either side of her head, emphasizing the fact that she existed at his will.

"I don't know. It was only ever just he and I." She hoped her lies would pay off, throwing Mac off his radar.

He used his knees to push her legs apart. She whimpered the word, "no" as her body broke out in a cold sweat. "I think I should claim what's mine again. You might have forgotten what it's like to be with a real man." He lowered his hips to rest on top of hers.

She turned her head, squeezing her eyes shut, readying herself for his assault. The memory she thought she buried as her body realized what was coming. Her old instinct would have her body tense up but she started to shake as fear took over. He may get her body but her heart belonged to Mac.

She could feel his hot wet breath on her neck. "If you lied to me, there will be hell to pay. I will make sure that my torture is slow and painful before you die out in the hot desert of Mexico. So if there is anything you remember in that sieve you have for a brain, you better tell me." She stayed stick still. The back of his hand caresses her cheek. "I used to relish the fear that poured off of you, like I did every time I fucked you. But it doesn't give me the thrill of power like it used to. Hell, I can't even get hard. You would be wise to obey my every command." He softly kissed her ear and whispered, "princess."

As soon as he moved off her, she rolled away into the corner. She held herself with her knees drawn up to try and stop the uncontrollable shaking. He had her right where he wanted her and wouldn't stop until he got what he wanted. She feared him like she feared no one else, especially this unrecognizable version of him. The only relief came when she realized she succeeded in not betraying Mac. She needed to find a way to save herself.

A butterfly only makes its wings stronger when it beats against its cage. Mac pulled back the divider to show her what the other side looked like, fighting her way out of the darkness. She wouldn't be going back. She wasn't the woman Brock brutalized for years. He wouldn't be taking anything else from her.

As the shaking eased, she lay down on the hard floor with her hands tucked under her cheek, finding the calmness within. Her life could end at the hands of a man whose heart was as black and dark as the cage she created to keep him out. Who knew what tomorrow would bring. Hopefully she would find the hole in his plan. She wouldn't allow Brock to hurt Mac or anyone in her family.

———◆———

*Shrouded in darkness*, Mac and Sydney moved between the shadows back to the car. She limped after hitting her knee pretty hard, but during her time as an agent, there had been much worse injuries than a scraped knee. He held her elbow as he helped her along.

"If I were a betting man, I would say Brock's holed up in one of these buildings. Hopefully, we didn't give ourselves away. You're right. We'll do better in the light of day. Let's hope she's with him." Hope lingered on his words.

They arrived back at the resort where Leigha and Raquelle anxiously waiting for them. The disappointment on their faces spoke to how much they wanted to see their sister walk through the door with them. It speared him. They imagined how easy it would be for them to bring their sister back. Civilians always believed the movie version of every outcome.

"We're going to call it a night. Everyone needs to sleep and rest up for tomorrow. It's going to be another long day." Weariness had worn him down. His heart felt like an hourglass, with each minute more grains of sand had her slipping away from him.

After he took a shower, he laid back on his bed. The same bed he made love to her in only twenty-four hours before. Her honeysuckle scent lingered on his pillow. Her spirit was with him. He could feel her strength. His soul seemed to chant the same mantra over and over again. Cherish what you have in the moment because you never know when it will be gone.

He knew he needed some sleep, but his thoughts and aching heart couldn't let go of her. Life could be cruel enough as to take not one loving woman from his life but a second one.

They say when you find the one you're meant to be with, you can see your unborn children in her eyes. He had not only seen them but felt them, running after his little girl with big, green eyes and curly, chestnut brown hair. He closed his eyes as his mind flooded with thoughts of her. A calm came over him that knew she was still alive. He held on to it like a favorite childhood blanket to get him through the night.

# CHAPTER 30

*Mara ached from* head to toe. Her foot throbbed where dried blood covered the cut, a grim reminder of the night before. A chill came over her thinking about the mask that lifted off of Brock's face, revealing more of the real him. He was ugly, sad, and in ruin.

The warm light of the morning sun streamed in, highlighting the middle of the grey concrete floor. Flecks of dust glinting and floating in the air reflected her scattered and insignificant life. She realized that she married him with eyes wide shut. She didn't want to accept what was there all along. It was easier to believe he was the man of her dreams. Her heart recognized the monster behind that mask, but her mind talked her out of acknowledging him. She wanted her 'happily ever after', everything in a nice, neat package. Life had a way of presenting lessons so you had no choice but learn them or relive them.

Her eyes followed the stream of light coming from the window she looked out of the night before, watching Mac down below. Her heart ached with emptiness as hope faded away. By sheer willpower, she stood and slowly shuffled to the open window frame. Her body screamed its disapproval right before his eyes burn into her back. She turned around, peering down into the shadows where the sunlight didn't quite reach him.

"Sweet dreams, princess? Don't worry. Prince Charming won't be saving you. This isn't some fucking Disney flick." As he moved forward into the light, he was smirking, but his eyes gave him away. A flicker of fear passed over them.

She flinched at his words, slapped by the reality of her situation. If he noticed her discomfort, he didn't let on or care. Her sensitivity to him and all his nuances increased dramatically during their time together. As much as she loathed him, she stayed attune to his every move in hopes of finding the crack she could slip through.

He continued to discuss the plan for the day. One that would hand him what he wanted, but the price might be her life, or someone else's. He made that clear throughout his diatribe. She listened with half an ear while her brain tried to find a hole in his plan where she could escape unharmed. Watching him intently, she looked for any signs of a slip-up in his self-proclaimed foolproof plan. She laughed inwardly at that notion. Her life had been the epitome of a foolproof plan.

"Mara. Mara!" In two strides, he shortened the space between them, holding her chin in a vice grip as he glared at her with knowing eyes.

"Don't. Don't try to find a way to escape. Someone is watching your sisters and lover boy as we speak. One wrong move and they die. You forget how well I read you. I have studied you over the years to always be one step ahead. Life is always about being one step ahead, princess." He held her attention to make sure she understood she wasn't the queen in this chess game. He pinched her chin before shoving it away.

There was something there that she didn't miss, his uncertainty. She wondered if he was bluffing. He wanted her to think he was working with someone else. He didn't anticipate her study of him over the years as a way to survive the abuse. She spent time reading him to anticipate when the tide would turn and how she could react accordingly. Call it woman's intuition, but it never failed her. The pain in her heart never lied. Right then, her intuition tapped her on the shoulder, begging her to listen. Something wasn't quite right.

———◆———

*Mac looked in* the mirror at the dark circles under his eyes, giving away his sheer emotional exhaustion. He had a fitful night of sleep, thinking of all the ways he could kill Brock once he got his hands on him. He opened and closed his hands. He wasn't unsure if he was trying to hold himself together or hold down his anger.

By midmorning everyone reconvened in the suite, which had been turned into a command central. They all looked as though they had been shot out of a cannon sideways.

He took control. "Here's the plan for today. Leigha and Raquelle, I want you to canvass the resort. Take the pictures of Marabella and Brock with you. Ask everyone if they have seen either one of them in the last two days." Blowing out a breath, he wasn't operating on all cylinders.

Sydney frowned at him and stepped up. "How about I sit with security and monitor the cameras? There's a chance that Brock will bring Mara back to the resort for the laptop. I'll let you know if I pick up on anything unusual." She needed to make it a productive day.

"I've already contacted local law enforcement, for what it's worth. I'll bring them up to speed. I spoke to McFadden to let him in on what's happening. He gave us carte blanche to do what we need to do to bring Brock in and bring her back. He wants Brock alive. He has crucial information about the Russians that might help them tie this case together internationally." His second wind kicked in. Far from giving up, he would push himself to the brink to bring her back. If they could get one break, he would make the most of the opportunity to bring Brock down.

His vessel was empty without her. His heart wanted her and wouldn't be denied. But that cord between them was stretched to its limit. All he wanted to do was hold her for the rest of his life. A thought he had without reservation. A place he never thought he would be. He couldn't let her go. She was the energy that coursed through his veins. He hoped Sydney would be the one to bring in Brock alive, because he wasn't sure he wouldn't kill him dead in his tracks.

A quiet fell over the group filled with all the things that weren't being said. Would they find them? Would Brock kill Mara when he was done with her? How would they all survive without her?

Suddenly, the heaviness of the situation sat on his chest. He pushed it away because he couldn't go there, not when they may be this close. He needed to keep his head in the game and his heart out of it for the time being.

Raquelle's sniffle broke the silence and Leigha put her arm around her.

"We are going to find her. She's smart and she'll find a way out." Leigha sounded confident but weary. She was always the rock, but the rock was starting to crumble.

For as tough as Raquelle seemed, her heart poured out at the thought of losing her big sister. "I guess I'm dealing with the reality of it all, the possibility that we may never be with her again. I want more time with her. I want to know more about her. We just turned a corner. Now we may be facing a life without her."

He reached over and grabbed Raquelle's hand, getting her undivided attention. He locked on to her eyes with a fierceness that demanded her focus. "On the upside, we're pretty sure she's still alive. Brock needs her. We have to cover all our bases and find a hole in his plan. We need to out-smart him. I never thought I would hear myself say this, but we need to have faith to get us and her through it all." His body vibrated with uncertainty, but couldn't cover the sheer determination and passion in his heart. He was definitely not giving up. Raquelle wiped her tears away and stood up straighter. She nodded in agreement as if he transfused some of his determination into her body.

They decided to order brunch. Each of them ate enough to get them through the day but mostly pushed the food around on their plates in silence. Their minds seemed in different places, going over all the scenarios and possible dreadful endings.

After brunch, they split up to their various assignments and began the search. They found a new reserve of courage and hope through their silent imaginations. They had more fight left in them, fueling them to the end.

# CHAPTER 31

*Five miles away*, in a dilapidated concrete cell, Mara sat awaiting Brock's plan. He pulled a blonde wig out of the duffle bag and threw it at her. Handing her a makeup case full of pale colors, it was a palette for a blonde, from the foundation to the lipstick.

"In case I had to drag you out anywhere. The make up was easy enough to find. They like to cater to the blonde and blue-eyed tourists down here." His smug smile matched his ego. He had covered all his bases. All his backup plans made it seem as if he knew what he was doing on every level. "I know how good you are with makeup, so do a professional job because I will know the difference. I watched you put this crap on your face every day for five years, that mask you wear to let everyone see how perfect you are inside and out." Poison slithered across his tongue.

His words struck like a pit viper. For once, she didn't want to put any makeup on, but this wasn't a choice. Biting her lip, the pain kept her from crying at the irony of her life. She spent so many years creating the illusion of the perfect wife with the perfect house to cover up the not-so-perfect husband. She had finally let the mask go, but she had to put it on one more time. If she made it out of this alive, she might never wear makeup again.

Her hands shook. Applying make up required a steady hand. Stopping for a moment, she clasped them together and breathed through her fear. She hoped to save her life creating a mask of survival. She applied the foundation, eye shadow, liner, blush and the final touch of brown mascara instead of her classic black. By the time she was finished, her own mother wouldn't have recognized her.

She sucked in a breath at the thought of never seeing her parents again. Her nails dug into her palm to keep her from trembling. By killing her, he would create the domino effect and hurt everyone in her family. Lost in her thoughts about her family she didn't notice him standing there.

He couldn't resist making a cutting comment. "Why, princess, you've done a remarkable job. I almost don't recognize you. You might really fool everyone this time around." He had an over confident look on his face that read, 'I'm going to get away with this'.

He held her by her upper arm as they made their way to the car, making sure there wasn't a repeat performance from the night before. She walked next to him with her head down. As they got closer to the car, she peeked up to see a beat-up red rental car with garbage all over the floor and seats. He must have lived out of it for the past week as he watched her twenty-four seven.

She got the creeps thinking about him stalking her. In those moments, she had felt him without ever seeing him. Why did it take her a fake death and five years of hell to figure him out? Her mind didn't want to see what true evil really looked like.

Stopping at a small café on the way to the resort, he commented about not wanting her to faint due to low blood sugar. Given the truth about his past, she recognized the pattern of his concern for always having food. Some things from childhood never went away.

She ate what she could of the stale sandwich and drank some of the sour orange juice, a far cry from the gourmet five-star resort food. As she ate in silence, her thoughts went back to the night she spent with Mac. She realized no one was that good at faking their feelings. She was so much more than an assignment to him. *Was?* If she got out of this alive, she wanted to change that to *is*. She would have some apologizing to do for not believing him, but right then, he was her only lifeline.

Her life was surreal. These kinds of events didn't happen to a girl from Greenwich. They happened to other people in the news, movies or books. She disconnected from herself, needing to play the role of her life. She prayed she'd inherited some of her mother's acting skills. Staring blankly at her food, she sighed deeply, hoping for a window of opportunity in the next couple of hours. If she didn't find it, she would be just another statistic of a vacationer gone missing in Mexico. She'd survived him that long and wouldn't go down without a fight.

He never witnessed the fighter in her as she tried to keep the peace, but she was about to surprise him. More than ever, she wanted, no, *needed* to be with Mac. He demanded she take off her mask then reached into her soul, never shying away from her, even after he learned the truth about her abused life. That amazing man made her stronger, not weaker. She was alive with him. The darkness wasn't there to eat away at her.

"Why so quiet, princess? Worried your fairy tale life is about to come to an end? God knows I like to keep you guessing." He threw his head back, laughing like he owned the world.

She must have let something pass in her eyes he couldn't identify because he faltered. The faint smile on her lips unnerved him as he sat staring at her. His brows furrowed as he swallowed hard. Her smile came from the hint of her newfound self-confidence. The last three months wore him down and challenged his choices. She might find that window of opportunity after all, paying close attention. The ownership of the chess pieces became blurred between the pawn and the queen.

On the way to the resort, he handed her a burner phone. Her eyes shone with hope that this might be her way out.

He laughed at her as she smoothed her thumb over the keys. "Oh, princess, do you think that's your lifeline? How sad. That phone in your hand is linked to only one number—mine. You should never underestimate me." The hard edge in his voice emphasized his warning. Looking away, she didn't want to give attention to the deceit in his eyes with his overbearing self-confidence.

His stiff smile was a reminder that he held the control. She longingly looked at the phone. A man she loathed was cutting her thread of hope, but she wouldn't give up. Mac would be searching for her, but he'd have to out maneuver Brock to get to her.

They drove into the resort and parked behind the main building. He turned to her. "The two o'clock maid shift has just come on. It's the perfect time to get in the mix. The lunch crowd is gone for the day and the buildings are empty except for staff and guests passing through." He handed her a master key to the resort. "Go in the maids' laundry room and put on the first uniform you find. I'll be waiting outside with my computer. I can remotely operate all the security cameras on the inside. Wait for my call at the top of the stairs, enter the suite, grab the laptop and meet me in the parking lot at the car."

He firmly grabbed her face and held her inches from his own. "And don't think about contacting anyone. You picked an upscale resort, as always. There are security cameras everywhere. I will see every move you make. One hint of contact and my inside guy will have his pick on who he gets to kill first. Oh, did I mention he enjoys killing? Despite getting paid, it's a hobby of his. I'll pick Raquelle first. She always was a smart-mouthed bitch," he hissed as he roughly pushed her face away from his in disgust. "Now, go get that laptop so I don't have to look at you ever again."

She gingerly stepped out of the car on her sore foot. Taking a deep breath, she stood upright. He might have won this battle, but he hasn't won the war. She prayed to God that she would find an opening.

He told her how to locate the laundry room and sneak in there without being seen. She got inside using the master key card he gave her to gain access. A rotating rack held a collection of uniforms from maids to gardeners. He had prepared for plans B through Z.

She put on the first uniform she found with a nametag that read Maria. Her sweaty hands shook as she tried to ignore the nausea rolling in her stomach. She had to do this if her sisters and Mac were going to stay alive.

According to his instructions, she needed to make her way to the suite via a back staircase she didn't even know existed in the building. She dragged herself upstairs, hoping her sisters had left for the day. She waited for his call.

<hr />

*Mac met with* local authorities in the lobby, filling them in on the latest in the investigation. They seemed disinterested at best. Their attention veered away every time they heard the calling card of stilettos on the marble floor. They claimed to have hundreds of missing persons reports a year. A lover's quarrel often ended in a missing person's report. They usually dismissed the whole situation, reassuring the person making the report that the missing person would eventually return to the resort. What happened after that didn't concern them.

He tried to impress upon them that Marabella had been kidnapped by her deceased husband.

Even as he said the words, he realized how crazy the whole thing must sound to them. This wasn't the most far-fetched case he had ever been on. He just had the most to lose. As his phone rang, he excused himself to take the call.

"I think I found something on the security feed." Sydney's keen eyes picked up on something unusual.

"What's going on?" It could be the break he was waiting for. He needed Brock to slip up.

"I saw a blip on the security feed, which may mean someone is tampering with the digital connection. Where are you right now?" Her voice had an edge.

"I'm in the lobby with the local officials. Why?" He looked up and around for the cameras.

"That's interesting because I can't locate you on any of the cameras. It means someone is remotely operating the camera feed. My guess is Brock and Mara are on site. How quickly can you get to the suite?"

"I'm on my way." He didn't bother telling the group of locals. If she was at the resort, he needed to find her before Brock took her off the property again.

---

*Mara stood a* couple of feet from the door to the hallway when the burner phone rang and vibrated, making her jump. She never would have made it as a spy. Her nerves were frayed and on edge. Breathing deeply, she needed to pull it together as she answered the phone.

"Hello?" Her voice cracked.

"The hallway's clear. Knock on the suite door and in your best Spanish accent, say it's house-keeping. Swipe your card to open the door and grab the damn laptop. I'm giving you fifteen minutes tops to meet me in the parking lot. Got it?"

"Yes." Her mouth went dry as her composure splintered.

"And Mara, be a good girl and bring the phone back to me. Don't leave any breadcrumbs. I will put you in more pain than you ever thought possible if you do something cleverly stupid." He hung up, leaving her shaking and terrified.

She swallowed her fear digging deep to find her courage. She dropped into the role she would play to save the lives of her loved ones, even if she couldn't save herself.

Knocking on the door, she got no response. She slipped into the suite undetected as the door snicked closed behind her. The living room was filled with computers and technical equipment. Scanning the area, she registered scattered shoes lying on the floor that belonged to her sisters. She squelched her gasp by covering her mouth. The reminder was too much. Gulping air into her lungs, she needed to push past this to get to the laptop. Her estimated time was less than thirteen minutes.

Making her way to her bedroom, it looked exactly the way she left it. It felt like years had passed since she had been there, but it had only been twenty-four hours. She swiveled around, looking for cameras, but didn't see any. This could be her break. She headed for the table in search of pen and paper. Tripping on her favorite pair of Louboutin heels, she landed awkwardly on her injured foot. When no pens or paper could be found, she became frantic. Time ticked away from her. It hit her. She would leave a trail of breadcrumbs. At least they would know she had been there.

She scraped at the dried wound on the bottom of her foot until it opened up and bled. It should have hurt, but the adrenaline coursing through her body overrode the pain. Wiping her foot across the floor several times, she smeared the blood, managing to draw a heart with the letter u. If death was her destiny, she wanted her sisters to know how much she loved them. She choked down a sob but continued to move ahead, aware of the falling grains of sand in the hourglass of death. Grabbing some tissues, she tucked them under her foot, and stuffed her foot back into her shoe.

Looking towards the bed, the next breadcrumb came into view. The bed was neatly made. She ripped the sheets off and threw pillows everywhere. If anything, they would see the mess, hopefully bringing their attention to the words on the floor. Love didn't even begin to describe what filled her heart, knowing this might be the last time she would be this close to them. Her heart squeezed to the point of bursting, making it difficult to breathe.

She grabbed the laptop from the table and with a swipe of her arm, hurled everything else to the floor. By the grace of God, they would put two and two together and notice the missing laptop.

Tick-tock, time wasn't on her side.

She made a mad dash for the door, closing it quietly behind her. Heading for the stairwell door, she heard their voices behind her. She closed her eyes letting her ears absorb their voices one last time as a sword slashed through her heart.

"No one has seen either one of them. I'm running out of hope, Leigha." Raquelle's voice cracked, signaling more tears.

"Well, we know Mac and Sydney are doing everything they can and I have complete faith in them. They're trained for this; we aren't. We have to take their lead and be patient." Leigha sounded confident but she knew those words covered her fear.

Leigha spent a lifetime pretending to be the strong one when all she wanted to do was cry along with Raquelle. Everyone had their defenses in one form or another and all for different reasons. Her facade was in place to keep Raquelle from falling apart.

Who the hell was Sydney? Why was Sydney with Mac? Was Sydney with British Intelligence?

Held by a strong cord of survival for her sisters, she tapped down the urge to turn around to tell them she loved them one more time. She stayed rooted in place. He would stay true to his word and kill them, taking out Raquelle first. His hate for her ran deep, mostly because she saw right through him.

Pushing the door open, she ran down the stairwell and out of the building with tears streaming down her face. Her emotions spiraled out of control with no hope of reeling them in. The pain in her chest was like shrapnel, making her breathing labored. She opened the car door and threw the laptop and phone at him.

"Hey, what the fuck?!" He caught the laptop just before it hit him in the chest. The phone bounced off his leg and landed on the floor. She caught him off-guard, doing something he would never expect.

"Here's your fucking laptop, asshole. Don't you dare touch my sisters or anyone else in my family!" Her scream filled the small space of the car. She had enough. The fear slipped away at last. Weakness left her, replaced by strength she didn't know she possessed. She completed the job she needed to do to save her sisters, knowing she was still at his mercy.

He looked stunned before his mask slid in place. She glared at him dead in the eyes to let him know she could take whatever he threw her way. This was her breaking point, the final freedom she had earned. She wouldn't die as the woman she once was. She would take death as a strong, confident woman.

"I'm shocked you didn't run back to your sisters. Yes, I saw everything in the hallway. Quite honestly, I didn't think you had it in you, princess. Are you finally angry and fighting? I don't think I've ever seen you pissed off before. Congratulations, it's about time. But time is exactly what you are out of," he snarled.

With that, he peeled out of the parking lot and headed back to the concrete cell. He had a death grip on the steering wheel. Glancing at her several times, he looked bewildered.

With her arms crossed over her chest, she kept her eyes straight ahead. Catching his reaction in her peripheral vision, she wasn't the same woman he had left behind. Breaking her was his goal, but she proved to be stronger than he gave her credit for. That thought had him on edge.

# CHAPTER 32

*Mac raced to* the suite with Sydney on his heels. They flew through the door startling Leigha and Raquelle who had plopped themselves down on the couch. Exhausted from a day that garnered no results, their faces indicated they were starting to lose hope.

"Was she here? Did you see her?" His eyes wildly scanned the room.

They jumped off the couch like it was on fire. "What?" Their voices were in unison.

"Look over every inch of this suite. Sydney, take a look at those computers and see if you can get a read on anything unusual." He barked out orders as if his life depended on it. They split up to search the suite.

"Oh, my God!" Raquelle screamed from the bedroom.

They raced in, stopping short at the sight before them. The room looked as though a tornado had raced through it.

"She was here. Look at the floor," Raquelle managed to utter as her shaking hands covered her mouth.

Leigha looked at the floor where Mara's message

glared up at her. She clasped her hands together in front of her. Her eyes gave her away. She broke apart on the inside like fractured rays of light. On the outside, she appeared in control. Turning to Raquelle, she held her tight, letting her sob into her shoulder. Marabella had been there, so close to them, leaving a piece of her behind as a clue.

"The laptop's missing," Sydney said, running to the command center set up in the living room. "Lei, didn't you tell me that laptop is equipped with a GPS?" Sydney typed furiously, concentrating on the screen.

"Yea, it does. I think the GPS works whether the laptop is on or off." Leigha frowned. Silence and tension began to build between them as a glimmer of hope floated in the air.

"Let's see if we can get a ping on that. I bet he's going back to the same place we were last night." Mac's eyes were glued to the computer screen. Time might still be on their side. But once Brock got those passwords, he had no use for Marabella. He needed to find her before Brock got them.

They watched the computers search for the GPS signal. Several red dots came to life, but only one would catch their interest. All of the sudden a red beacon appeared in a sea of black.

"There's what we're looking for and it's moving." They weren't out of the woods yet.

"Syd, bring the laptop and let's roll before we lose the signal. If Brock has a brain in his head, he'll catch on that her laptop has a GPS. He'll hope we aren't smart enough to realize that." He had hope in his heart for the first time in two days, but he needed luck to be on his side too.

"Here, take the laptop and I'll meet you down there. I've got to hit the head before we go." She dumped the computer in his hands, making a beeline for the restroom. Her bathroom break seemed odd given the gravity of the situation.

Once in the car, they followed the moving red dot as it headed straight for the abandoned buildings. They wanted to stay far enough behind so they wouldn't set off Brock's alarm.

They entered the unfinished resort complex as his car kicked up plumes of dust. Dusk was starting to settle in, giving the dust cloud an eerie bluish glow, which served as their cover. They parked inside a nearby abandoned building and decided to survey the area on foot.

Sydney took her weapons case, knowing full well she might have to use the sniper rifle concealed inside. They loaded themselves to the teeth with a variety of weapons for every situation. He handed her the communications earpiece as they surveyed the area.

Early evening approached making the shadows grow longer. It would give them the cover they needed to covertly move around. The red dot stopped moving, revealing Brock and Marabella's location. He turned toward the sound of tires crunching on gravel.

"Did you hear that? It sounded like cars approaching from the other side of that building." He didn't need a third player entering the game.

"No. I didn't hear anything. It was probably the rustling of leaves. A storm's coming in, though." She pointed to the horizon over the ocean where dark, ominous clouds suddenly appeared. The wind picked up, lifting up light objects and swirling them around.

They drew their weapons continuing to move in and out of the shadows. As they rounded the corner, he saw someone moving past a window opening on the third floor of a nearby building.

"I'm going in. I need you to set up your sniper rifle in that adjacent building. You're on standby. Avoid a shoot to kill. Got it?" His heart pounded in his chest. His target was within reach. He needed to throttle down. His biggest hurdle would be getting him to give up Marabella.

"Got it." She reached in her pocket and pulled out a cigarette.

"Is this really the time for that?" Her calm demeanor and casualness threw him off as she lit up.

"Nicotine helps keep me calm and steadies my hand." She took a couple puffs, threw it to the ground, and stubbed it out under her shoe.

"Get him in your sights if you can, but fire only on my command. I hope I can get to her before he hurts her."

They split up. She headed for the adjacent building as he strode toward the one where he hoped to find Marabella.

Protocol had her swept each floor on her way to the roof. "Hey, McClane, I found the room where they were. He found her phone. It's in a million pieces. I bet that set him off. Be careful. You might be walking into a real shit storm." In the field, she always called him McClane from *Die Hard* as a joke and a warning. He had been known to go in guns blazing. His training prepared him for all kinds of dangerous situations, just not the ones that involved the love of his life.

"Roger that," he barely breathed. Making his way up the staircase, he waited for Sydney to set up. He may have gone into some situations without backup, but not this time. This time, the woman he meant to spend the rest of his life with, needed him. All of this had to be handled by the book or things were liable to go shit up fast.

"I'm set up. I have the window opening in my sights, waiting for your go." Her voice was calmer than normal.

It was music to his ears, even if he didn't know what lay ahead. He would love to give her the go to kill Brock, but they needed that bastard for a bigger cause and a lot of unanswered questions.

Coming through the doorway, his eyes focused on the door at the end of the hall. He strained to hear anything coming from the room. There was only the sound of blood rushing in his ears. A bead of sweat slid down his spine. He stepped closer to the door, leaning his ear against it. Brock mumbled about the slowness of the computer and the shitty satellite service in the area. He didn't hear her voice. If he was still waiting for the computer to fire up, he hadn't gotten the passwords yet.

He slowly let out the breath. The show was about to start and he would be leaving with her alive. Hostage negotiations weren't his forte but he needed to talk him down, letting him think he could still get out of this unscathed.

Everything hinged on his timing. As he got ready to execute his plan, he stepped on a piece of glass, hiding in plain sight. He froze immediately as the scuffling on the other side of the door signaled his presence.

# CHAPTER 33

*H*e *heard the* glass break and lunged for Mara, yanking her up and clamping his hand over her mouth. He wasn't going down without a fight. Taking his .22 from behind his back, he held the barrel against her temple. She screamed in his hand.

He wrenched her head to the side. "Shut the fuck up or I won't have to use my gun. I'll break your rich bitch neck. Let me guess, you managed to leave a breadcrumb for lover boy. I should just kill you now because you are such a goddamn curse, but I'm too close to getting what I deserve." His teeth ground shut as the muscles twitched in his jaw.

"Who's out there? Is that you, lover boy? Because I have Mara and a bullet with her name on it." He made taunting people an art form after years of practice.

"The name is Mac. I assume you're Brock, Marabella's not-so-dead husband. Look, if you hand her over to me, you have a good chance of making it out of here alive." This is what he sounded like in action.

His voice was like a warm caramel pouring over her. The lilt of his accent calmed her, giving her strength. Her breathing started to slow as she focused on him. She wanted nothing more than to run to him, but was trapped by a demon.

"Oh, you call her Marabella, how sweet. Let me tell you how this is going to go, Mac. Mara has something of mine, and I need it. Once I'm done with her, I'll think about not killing her. So you better be on your way, or I'll put a bullet in her head right now." His voice sounded strong and sure, but the hand over her mouth was cold, clammy and trembling.

Mac came back with a few passing shots of his own. "I'm armed and not alone. You can make this a whole lot easier on yourself if you let her go. We know you have the computer. You can keep it. We understand you're a pro at hacking them." His voice was even and strong, maintaining control of the situation.

"Oh, what, you've suddenly turned into a cop who can carry a weapon across the Mexican border? Not likely." Brock called his bluff.

He turned her face to get her complete attention and lowered his voice. "Who the fuck is this guy, Mara? Why does he have a gun and backup? Or is he a really good bluffer? Either way, I give this guy credit. He's got balls." His anger raged in his hollow, bloodshot eyes.

She trembled from head to toe unable to form words. He moved his hand far enough away so she could speak. "I told you I don't know that much about him. I haven't been with him that long." She focused her eyes on his forehead to hide the lie.

He responded with a grunt, moving his hand

to cover her mouth. Beads of sweat formed on his forehead and above his upper lip. Behind him on the floor, the computer still tried to find a signal.

"Fuck all!" His frustration level started to peak. He pushed the laptop around on the floor with his foot, hoping a different location in the room might speed up finding a signal. "You know, I'm really torn between needing to stall this asshole from doing something stupid and wanting to shoot you without a second thought. But I'm too close to getting what I want so I'll keep you alive for now." The breath from his nose continued to warm her cheek.

"Tell me something, lover boy. Now that you've had my sloppy seconds, is my wife a frigid fuck or what? She's absolutely useless in bed." He threw his head back laughing, but it lacked authenticity. He played the game without knowing all the players.

She held onto his forearm, trying to pull her mouth free, begging for mercy against his muffled hand. He twisted her head back and through gritted teeth, spoke the only words that would shut her up. "Shut up or I am going to blast him to kingdom come." He raised his gun and fired off a warning shot through the door. "I hope he's idiot enough to stand in front of the door and get himself killed." The blast of the gun echoed violently in the room. She screamed into his hand.

———◆———

*The shot rang* through the earpiece. "Shit. He's

armed. What's your twenty?" Sydney asked.

Mac spoke quietly. "Syd, hold your fire. I'm outside the door." His mind calculated eighteen different scenarios on how this could go down. This stand off was about to get real for Brock, whether he was ready or not.

"I'm not a cop and yes, I can carry a weapon in Mexico." He let the sentence hang in the air, giving Brock something to think about. He wanted him put two and two together and fully understand all the players in this game. This was for keeps.

Brock knew what that meant. He was dealing with one of the big boys. CIA? He couldn't be sure because his accent would throw him off. "So, you're one of the big boys, Mac? Sometimes, you guys have to do some ugly undercover work, like fuck my wife to get to me. I'm sorry about that. Must have been the worst dry work you've ever had to do, because we both know it wasn't wet." His laughter came through the door.

The comment would spear Mara. He was a master at stabbing her where it hurt most.

"*Leannan*, please don't listen to him. He's trying to break you by upsetting you. Just stay with me. Focus." His voice was a plea rather than a command. The conversation seemed as if it were only the two of them. He needed her to remember that invisible connection that held them together. Brock was trying to make her question her tie to him. He guessed she hadn't uncovered his true line of work.

"How touching and even a pet name. I think I just threw up a little in my mouth. But I don't really care who or what you are. At the end of the day, I have something you want. So if I were you, I'd back away and leave us alone."

He gave his offer one more try, needing to take the focus off her and back on business. "We need you, Brock. You see we're very interested in all of your backroom dealings with the Russians. By now, they must also know you're alive. There's probably a contract out on you as we speak. In the end, it's either them or us. Who are you going to choose? I think the choice is obvious, don't you? You need to make a deal with us while you still can." He played his last card.

Brock yelled out, "Fucking bitch!"

He heard the commotion and kicked through the door, ready for any situation.

Everything happened in slow motion. Brock gripped her wrist as she stood beside him when a crack pierced the air and then another. He fell face-first on the concrete floor as she jumped out of the way, wrenching her wrist out of his grasp. Her eyes went wide.

Pain burned across his upper left arm without fazing him. His sole focus was Marabella. All he could hear were her screams as she slid down the wall, her eyes fixed on Brock's head. He barely recognized her in the blonde wig and heavy makeup, but he knew those blue eyes.

Pulling his stare away, he looked down at blood red fingers growing from Brock's head across the gray floor. Bending closer, he found the hole in the back of his head. He recognized the shot as through-and-through. There was no need to check for a pulse.

"Syd, what the hell? I told you on my command. Fuck. Brock's dead." His words punctured the air as they echoed in the concrete cell.

"I didn't fire." She didn't even finish her thought before he registered what happened, his body already in motion.

A third party had made themselves known in this hunt. He dove toward Marabella, pushing her flat to the floor. "Syd, get out of there, now. I'll meet you at the car. I think they got what they wanted," his voice muffled as he covered her body with his own. Sydney knew him well enough to realize things had just gone south in a whole other way, but she also knew he wasn't in danger.

Marabella shook and cried uncontrollably. He stood hunched over her. She started to move toward him as he pulled her up by her arms, pushing her into the hallway. He went back in the room to grab the laptop and noticed the red dragon had gotten crushed in the scuffle.

It took gunshots to make kitten move toward him instead of away from him. God help him. She'd be the death of him yet, but what a sweet death it would be.

"Are you all right? Did you get hit?" He was all business as his eyes did a quick scan of her body, searching for any blood. His only concern was her safety.

She squeaked, "I'm fine." Her face drained of all color as shock took over.

The storm had come ashore, beating the land with sheets of rain. The rain relentlessly pounded the roof. He half-dragged her through a maze of stairwells into the storm to the waiting car. Sydney sat in the driver's seat with the engine running. The blood streamed down from his left arm. She nodded acknowledging his superficial wound.

Marabella was tucked into the right side of his body as he opened the back door, pushing her across the seat, following her in. "Go." He hit the front seat with his hand.

Rain beat down on the car as soft whimpers came from her. They were all soaked to the bone as a chill hung in the humid air. He didn't feel cold sinking into the warmth of her as she clung to the front of his shirt. He wrapped her in his arms while stroking her head as though he were petting a kitten—*his* kitten.

"Shhhhh. You're safe, *leannan*," he whispered in her ear. He breathed hard, holding her like a life raft. The adrenaline coursed through his veins, not from the physical exertion but the reality of having her back.

As his words seeped into her, she gulped in some air and continued to sob. Overwhelmed by the turn of events, she let herself go.

As they got closer to the resort, her tears started to dissipate. She seemed to gain some control over her shaking body. She peered up at him. Her eyes washed with pain, sorrow, happiness and passion. He didn't know which one to choose. They didn't need words. In those perfect blue eyes, he saw what love looked like from an incredible woman.

He continued to reassure her as his deep voice carried through his chest curling around her body. "He didn't hurt you, did he?" His body tensed afraid of the answer to the question.

She read between the lines. "No. He wanted

his money, but I guess he's not going to get that either." Relief came out on an exhale. He smiled for the first time since she had been taken. She couldn't take her eyes off him. She stroked his jaw and the scruffy two-day-old beard. There was nothing sexier. He let out the heavy sigh he had been holding in for the last two days. Bringing her hand to his lips, he gently kissed her palm, sending a jolt into her body. Apparently, lightning strikes many times.

"What did you do to him in there to make him scream?" Curiosity nagged at him to know her bravery.

"I bit his hand." She smiled weakly. His lioness had made an appearance.

"That's my girl. By the way, I really don't care for blondes, so I hope you don't plan on keeping the wig." His humor came back, bringing some levity to their life-or-death situation.

With a huge smile, she whipped off the wig, letting it drop to the floor. Her hair tumbled out, falling to her shoulders. "One of the first things I'm going to do when I get back is scrub my mask off, forever." She held her chin up with a sly smile on her lips.

He slid his fingers through her hair and quipped, "I always had a thing for Italian brunettes with big, blue eyes." He hummed as they laughed together, welcome relief to an insane forty-eight hours.

"I'm going to guess the Russians are here and prevented Brock from talking. Any thoughts?" He said as Sydney caught his eye in the rearview mirror.

"We'll discuss it later." She looked over at Marabella. She didn't want her to know anything more.

"So you're Sydney. It's nice to meet you. Thank you for all your help."

"How did you know?" She scrutinized her through the mirror with raised suspicion.

"Long story. I'll explain later." She played with his fingers.

He lowered his head to brush his lips lightly against her forehead, running his thumb along her cheek and jawline. She laid her head on his shoulder for the rest of the ride.

The rain continued to drench the land. He led her out of the car as she stumbled on her foot, falling into him. "*Leannan*, what's wrong?" The rage set back in as he imagined Brock had physically harmed her.

"It's my foot. It got cut on some glass. It's still throbbing and bleeding." She leaned into his body for support.

"I noticed you made very good use of that foot. I'm proud of you. You used your head," he commended her as he held her closer. He cocooned her in his protection.

His blood-soaked shirt caught her attention. "My God, what happened to your arm?" She reached out to touch him but stopped short.

"It looks worse than it is, love. I'm not fragile. It's just a flesh wound, but this scar will have your name on it." He winked at her, like this was any other day on the job.

Utter exhaustion set in as she made her way to her sisters, who he imagined waited anxiously in the suite. As she came through the door, they flung themselves at her in a vise-grip hug. They cried and slumped to the floor in one huge heap. He and Sydney stood off to the side, watching the reunion with their own want of belonging.

"I gotta roll. We'll debrief tomorrow. It's been a long day, and I need to eat and sleep." For Sydney, this was another day at the office, and certainly not the worst of them.

"Hey, I'm sorry I accused you of taking the shot. I should have known better, but things weren't adding up in the moment." His sincere apology showed he was man enough to know when he was wrong. He also knew she always had his back.

"I probably would have thought the same thing under the circumstances. No worries. Hey, swing by my room so I can stitch you up." Giving him a tight smile, she turned to leave. She caught Leigha's eye, giving her an unspoken thank-you and a flirty smile.

When Marabella was finally released from her sisters' grip, she picked herself up off the floor. She turned to him and wiped her eyes. "Thank you. I was a dead woman if you hadn't come searching for me. I owe you my life." She reached up to give him a hug as her arms wound tightly around his neck. A hum came from her as she pressed into his hard body under soaked clothes. The electricity was there, stronger than ever.

He bent down to bury his face in her damp locks, whispering in her ear, "I'll be back tonight, *leannan*, and we'll talk then. I'm coming to collect." He gave her his cheeky grin. That look made her shiver with anticipation.

She smiled back at him and whispered, "I'm not

sure talking is the only thing I want to do with you, repo man."

With another stress-relieving sigh, he held her beautiful face in his hands. "I'm so glad I found you. You have no idea." He stared at her, knowing she was the other half of his soul. When he kissed her it was a different kiss than any before, a kiss of possession, passion, forgiveness and love all rolled into one. The kiss that said, "You belong to me and only me."

Her eyes fluttered open and she became breathless. He had already shown her how much she meant to him by almost taking a bullet for her. Actions always spoke louder than words. "I'll see you later then." She whispered as a sparkle lit her eyes.

# CHAPTER 34

*Night fell as* Mara shared her story of desperation and near heartbreak. Touching each other often, they wanted to make sure the others were real. Raquelle ordered many bottles of wine with the food order. Mara gave Leigha a knowing look that this might be the only way they muddle through the rawness of their emotions. They agreed it shouldn't have taken a kidnapping to realize how much they meant to each other, exposing the invisible silk web that binds sisters.

"I have never been so lost and full of heartbreak in my life as when I walked in your bedroom. I swear I could feel you had been there before I saw the room. I guess you never lose that connection to your sister." Raquelle, near tears again, her mind revisiting the scene that took place only a few short hours before.

"Leigha was her stoic self until Mac told us you might be here at the resort. It was only then that I saw a slight crack in the veneer." Raquelle grabbed Leigha's hand, letting her know she could see through her tough exterior.

She shared the events of her kidnapping and her revelations about the real Brock. His comments were vile and he was next in line to be Satan's son. She realized she had some work to do in the people awareness department. Leigha acted surprised.

Raquelle just sighed, "That rat bastard. I knew there was more to him than met the eye, but I couldn't put my finger on it. I always felt uneasy around him. I certainly never trusted him." She rolled her eyes.

Mara continued, "All I kept thinking about was how close we've become on this trip. Sharing my story of Brock's abuse was a turning point for me. You both accepted it without judgment. You have no idea what that means to me. It's such a relief. God knows I've been judged by Papa enough to last me a lifetime. You gave me the strength I needed to tell Mac. When I shared it with him, I didn't know what to expect but if he walked away from me, I would've been okay. But he didn't." She stopped not sure she wanted to go on. "When we were finally together, he made sure I was okay with what we were doing every step of the way. When I was in my concrete cell I couldn't stop thinking about him and how if I ever made it back, I would fix things with him." She choked on a sob speaking from a place deep within her heart she had never visited before.

Raquelle glanced between Leigha and her. "I think we need a rule of full disclosure when it comes to one another. We need to share everything so we always have each other's backs. Deal?"

Leigha nodded in agreement then looked down. When she finally met their gaze, a storm brewed in her bright, hazel eyes.

Mara reached over and covered Leigha's hand.

"What's wrong?" She spoke softly, hoping Leigha would share the turmoil so clearly written on her face.

"It's nothing. I don't know. Maybe there's something. Things aren't right with Tom. Something's missing. I can't put my finger on it. It's been nagging me for a while. I guess time will tell." She looked at her sisters dismissively. Raquelle gave her a knowing look. That was only part of the story, but she didn't push her. They had shared enough for one evening.

Talking for a while longer, Mara suggested they go to bed. The events of the last couple of days plus the wine had equaled pure exhaustion for her.

She sent Mac a text telling him she was headed to bed. He wrote back that he would be there shortly and not to wait up for him. Oh, yeah, and he had a key, followed by a wink. She loved at his freshness even in a text.

"Since I have the king-size bed, I suggest we all have a sleepover in my room. I definitely don't want to sleep alone tonight. Speaking of sleeping alone, what are you going to do about Mac? That man was beside himself trying to find you. He never gave up, even when things seemed bleak." She had grown accustomed to Raquelle's ADD-type conversations.

They confirmed what she already knew about him. She could feel his intensity during the search. "I think I'm going to cross that bridge with Mac later tonight, so I'll be sleeping in my own bed. I can't even think straight anymore." Her body had succumbed to the intense events of the day, sagging under the weight of it.

She went to the bathroom to wash off the mask she would never wear again. Splashing her face with water, she watched as the light-colored makeup made streams down her face, revealing her bronzed complexion underneath. Examining herself in the mirror, she was at peace with her reflection, from her big grey-blue eyes to her clear, olive skin and full lips. Next on her agenda was a hot shower. She needed to wash away the smell, energy and words of her former abuser.

A sigh of contentment came over her as the stress of the day left her body. She slipped into a lace camisole and cuddled under the cold sheets. Hoping he didn't take too long, she needed to be near him, craving the energy his body always seemed to gift her. But the minute her head hit the pillow, she was out like a light.

———◆———

*Mac's bare feet* were silent against the wood floors. The dark room was filtered with the cool light of the full moon. He chuckled to himself that things always seemed to go sideways on the night of a full moon. The day could have ended much differently.

To say McFadden wasn't pleased to hear the news of Brock's death was an understatement. Truth be told, he couldn't be happier. It meant one less person in the world who could hurt his *leannan*. He wanted nothing more than to keep her safe from everything and everyone.

Standing over her, he was captivated by the iri-

descent light that blanketed the love of his life. He
would have fought to the bitter end for her. Her
face wiped clean without any trace of that hideous
makeup, the mask that hid her true beauty. Long,
dark lashes fanned across the tops of her cheeks.
Her lips were full, rose-colored and kissable. He
reached down to move a wave of rich, dark brown
hair that lay on her cheek. She looked angelic,
even after the hell she had endured with Brock.

Keeping his eyes on her, he stripped down, leaving his clothes in a heap. There didn't need to be
anything between them. Skin to skin, breath to
breath, heart to heart. He pulled the sheets back
to see her body covered in lace and her gorgeous
legs tucked up close to her. His body responded
immediately. He had to find restraint not to wake
her and take her right then.

Her eyes fluttered open. She peeked up at him
as her lips turned into a soft smile. "You came.
I missed you." Her eyes lazily roamed his body
from head to toe. This time, no soft blush stained
her cheeks. She knew what she wanted from him.

"I will always come for you. I missed you, too."
Those words held so much more meaning.

"Can you just hold me tonight and we'll talk
tomorrow? I promise," she sighed.

"It's going to be hard to just hold you, but I'll
give it a try." He gave an exaggerated sigh with a
shrug.

She smiled and rolled over. He spooned in
behind her, laying his arm around her waist as she
gave a contented hum.

"MacGregor?"

"Yes, Marabella."

"I don't need Eros. I need you."

Her words hit his chest as he let out a small gasp. He was her Eros, just not the dragon variety, protecting her forever. Sleep took them over as their breathing fell into a rhythm.

The next morning his body rejoiced at the first full night's sleep he'd had in two days. Being wrapped up with her all night felt like home. If he had his way, it would always be this way.

He glanced over to find her fast asleep. Quietly climbing out of bed, he headed for the shower. Possibly a cold one to hold him back from ravaging her. He wanted her to know, without any reservation, that he was all in.

# CHAPTER 35

*Mara lay in* a cold bed, missing her lover's heat. Stretching like a cat to get out all the kinks, she could hear the sound of running water. What she needed was in the bathroom. Her body and mind were well rested and ready. Her heart was content and the thought of him in the shower made her body hum with desire. She wanted to give in to her new hunger, braving to have him inside her again. She stroked her foot where it was beginning to heal again. All things heal eventually.

Standing at the glass door of the shower, she shed her lace camisole. She boldly wore nothing but her newfound self-confidence. The last time she fantasized about him, she was in the shower thinking about what he would do to her. The reality of him was so much better than her fantasy. Some wishes do come true.

His arms were stretched over his head as he braced the wall. The rain-shower water streamed down his back, curving over his very fine ass. Playing in the background was Ciara's song 'Body Party'. Its sexy beat filled the space. The song had always been one of her favorites, but she never related to it until that moment.

———◆———

*Mac heard her* enter the large marble stall/soon-to-be playroom. He didn't miss the subtle shift in energy she always brought with her. Gone was the shy woman he met only days before. His woman had transformed into a boldly colored dragonfly, emerging from her cocoon.

She wrapped her arms around his waist from behind as she laid her head on his back. Her nipples hardening as her breasts pressed against him. Her hands started to roam over his tight six-pack. She followed the ridges of his abs down to his already-hard cock.

Letting out a groan he said, "God, what you do to me, woman." He closed his eyes as she continued to stroke him up and down, tightening her hands and squeezing with the right amount of pressure. He took in a sharp breath and grabbed her wrist as he turned to face her.

He pulled her to him as their bodies came into full contact from head to toe. His cock pushed into her belly. She ran her fingers up and down his back, never losing eye contact. Her talented hands lovingly had recorded every inch of his scarred body.

"I love all your imperfections." She smiled up at him.

He leaned down and pressed his forehead to hers. At that angle, the water sluiced his back, protecting her from the spray. They stood there touching and stroking one another in a moment of utter tenderness.

He leaned back, cupping her face in his hands as he admired her naked beauty. "Listen to me, *leannan*. You have my heart and soul. I was so scared I had lost you forever. That was the most scared I've ever been and I've been in a lot of tight, life-threatening situations. Nothing took my breath away like being separated from you, not knowing if I would ever be with you again. I don't know if I would have survived that. It would have changed me forever."

Her eyes brimmed with tears. He wanted his words to wrap around her heart like a soft vine, holding it tight. "I'm so sorry I doubted you before I left. I know why you didn't tell me about your job right away. I was in a very different place than where I am now. I kept feeling your pull on me. You were always with me. My mind kept going over everything, but it's my heart that had the louder voice. It knows you and recognizes you. I misjudged you and the entire situation. But I know for sure I don't want to be without you." She was devoted to him. Her eyes were wide open this time.

"I don't think I will last long, but I need to be inside you. It feels like it's been forever." He started to lose himself. They had come full circle, exactly where they needed to be.

His lips crashed down on her, spearing, possessing, and owning her as his tongue invaded every part of her mouth. She wanted some of the control, though, and began sucking on his tongue. He let out a low moan, showing his appreciation for her effort. She broke the kiss, rising up on tiptoe, peppered his jaw with soft nips leading up to his ear. With her hand on his heart, she smiled. "I have your heart in my hand."

"Aye," was the only word he could utter.

Continuing down his neck, she bit where it met his shoulder as he groaned his satisfaction. Her tongue journeyed down to his nipple where she licked and sucked. Her hands grabbed his tight ass, pulling his cock between her breasts.

He couldn't keep his eyes off the woman in total control of his body. This was the woman he would surrender to. The assault continued as she licked her way down the channel of his abs to his waiting rock-hard cock. Her tongue did one swirl around its proud crown before he grabbed her arms and pulled her up.

"You make me lose my self-control, *leannan*," he growled looking at her lust-filled eyes.

"Oh, I'm just getting started in showing my appreciation, my wild Highlander." She gave him the sly grin he always gave her. Turnabout was fair play.

———◆———

*Mara turned deadly* serious when she asked the only question she needed an answer to. "I want to give you all of me. But can you take the good with the damaged?" She held her breath, wondering if he would truly accept her.

"Aren't we all damaged or marred in some way? Can you take all of me, the good, the bad and the ugly? We can work on it together because we're both worth it and love's what binds us." The questions hung in the air between them as the sound of falling water filling the void.

"Yes. Always."

"Forever." Fell from his lips in a whisper, making his intentions clear.

Her steel encasement fell away, shattering as if it had been doused with liquid nitrogen. None of the pieces could ever be put back together. He did that for her. He revealed her essence to her, the true her, and she was stronger than she ever thought possible. Wasn't that what real love did—made you stronger, not weaker; lighter, not heavier; happy, not sad. She would never get her fill of this man. She would continue to grow with him.

Holding onto those thoughts, she opened herself to him completely—mind, body, and her true soul. She had let go of her past self as those shattered pieces evaporated into mist.

He felt her release and smiled. "I will finally claim you."

He nudged her back to sit on the bench in the shower, pulling her knees apart. "Show me. I want to see how you pleasure yourself." He wanted her to bare herself to him in every way. He wanted all her truths.

Holding her heels, he put them up on the edge of the bench, totally exposing her. Using her fingers, she began to stroke herself up and down. She swirled around the nub that peeked out begging for attention. His eyes riveted to her, as he became unhinged with every touch.

She saw nothing but sheer love and acceptance

in his face. She never thought she would have that from a man looking at this part of her anatomy. The real Mara had emerged, a confident beautiful creature who shone in his eyes.

"That's it, my girl. Your pleasure is my pleasure." He ran his hands down her body, tweaking her nipples only to be laved by his tongue, showing her the fine line between pain and pleasure. He trailed a path of fire on her skin down her stomach. Lifting her fingers away, he replaced them with his tongue as the strokes turned into licks and swirls.

"So fucking incredible," he murmured.

He easily slipped in two fingers, hooking them up to tease her sweet spot. She let her feet drop to the shower floor and ground down on his hand, wanting her release, supporting herself on his broad shoulders. As he sucked on her clit, his beard brushed the inside of her thighs, stoking the intense flame. She panted as she began to swell, tightening around his fingers. He made her so wet, as she threw her head back, free-floating on the high.

"Please. Please, Mac. I can't hold out any longer. I need you inside me," she managed to say in-between breathes. She moved her hips forward grabbing his hair.

He chuckled between her breasts. "Patience, my love. I'll make it worth the wait."

She called out the name of her savior, her protector, and her love: Mac. Her body began to tighten then she was empty as his fingers slipped out of her. "Don't come yet, *leannan*. I want to be inside you when we come together." His voice was tight like a man holding on by a thread.

The warm rays of morning light had broken through the clouds, casting a warm sheen on the marble that surrounded them. Drops of water covered his tan skin as he stood like a warrior before her. His stance spoke of a claiming coming that required all or nothing. His eyes so dilated there was only a hint of green.

He gathered her in his arms, knowing she was ready for him in every way. She wouldn't be able to hide. Her heart begged her to give him everything. He would claim her. She needed to trust him completely. "Mac says. Put your hands above your head and hold to the shelf. Don't move them until I tell you to." The command sent a shiver down her spine, her body instantly complying. She would have done anything he told her to do. Totally at his mercy, she found strength and peace in her surrender to him.

In one swift motion, he hoisted her up to his hips as he thrust into her. She gave out a small cry of pain mixed with pleasure but moved with him. His eyes focused on the point where they connected, becoming one. He pushed upward as she gripped his shoulders with her head resting against his cheek.

"I need to touch you, hold you," she whispered.

Balls-deep inside of her, they both felt something snap as his control vanished. He unleashed himself. "Always eyes on me, beautiful." His eyes filled with the intensity of love, lust and loyalty.

He began to move in and out of her, pinning her body against the wall. She followed her instincts, bringing her knees up, giving him greater access

to her body. She was full with him. Feeling fulfilled, neither was sure where one began and the
other ended. They panted in unison. She began to
tip over the edge as he thrust into her, looking for
his release. His eyes never strayed.

She cried out his name as white lights exploded
behind her eyes and electricity shot to every part
of her body.

It's all he needed and with three more thrusts,
he followed her. She felt him swell inside of her
and then let go as he moaned into her shoulder
and whispered, "*Leannan.*"

He took away all the hurt Brock had inflicted
over the years. She didn't feel used and abused.
She felt loved, cared for and claimed by her Eros.

They held on to each other, as they floated back
down to earth. He slowly slipped from her as he
released her to stand. The emptiness shocked her
after such an intense moment, wishing he could
stay inside forever. "I didn't know my body was
capable of that," she said between pants.

"That's what your body does when you finally
let your mind go. You trusted me to take care of
you, and you let go." His voice full of tenderness
as his thumb caressed her cheek. "Now, let's wash
up."

He spent considerable time washing her hair
and soaping up her body with gentle strokes. He
made her feel cherished. She returned the favor
by cleaning him from head to toe, something she
could get used to on a daily basis. As she dried
him, she paid close attention to the stitches in his
arm.

"Who stitched you?" She gently patted the

wound dry.

"Sydney. She's a jack-of-all-trades and an expert out in the field. In case you're wondering, and I know you are, I've never slept with her. She prefers women," he smirked, anticipating her train of thought. "You were jealous, weren't you?"

"Maybe. A little."

"I like your possessive side." He smiled.

She ran her finger along the outside edge of the wound. "What did you mean when you said it has my name on it?"

"I'm thinking about getting my first ink. Across the top will say *Leannan* and along the bottom will say *My Eros*. What do you think?" He waited for something clever to come from her.

"Here I thought you already had that written across your heart." She peered up at him with one raised eyebrow as they laughed together.

"Oh, I do. I want a reminder that light can come from darkness." Those words seeped into their small dark hollow spaces, filling them completely. Two souls found each other to complete the puzzle. He brushed his lips across hers. "Now, woman, you've made me hungry burning all those calories. Let's get some food. Then I'll make sure to ravage you again before the day is over. Oh, and Marabella, no more running away from me, *capisci*?"

"*Capisco*. I didn't realize you were versed in Italian."

"I wouldn't say versed. I wanted to make sure you understood me." He pulled her in for one more kiss as he seductively sucked on her lips. His excitement poked into her belly again. Giving him one stroke, she heard him groan at her touch. "If you keep that up, we're going to starve to death, my greedy girl. I'll be expecting some of that great Italian cooking."

Her stomach dropped. How this was all going to work after Cancun?

# CHAPTER 36

*They joined* Leigha and Raquelle in the living room. Mara's body hummed with satisfaction.

"From the look on your faces, I guess I don't need to ask how things are going with you two." Raquelle's smart mouth was welcomed back by everyone as a sign that things had returned to normal.

Leigha got up from the table. "I'm going to call Sydney to invite her for brunch." She stepped into her bedroom leaving the door open a crack.

They stopped their conversation to listen to the laughter coming from the next room.

Mara commented, "If they didn't know better, I would think she was talking to her boyfriend. Come to think of it, she hasn't talked to or mentioned Tom for the entire vacation." She stared at Raquelle waiting for a response. "What? No response? Okay, what do you know?" Placing her elbows on the table, she leaned in.

Before Raquelle got a chance to answer, Leigha sauntered back into the room, staring lovingly at the phone in her hand. Her cheeks flushed like she was embarrassed about something.

"What's going on, Leigha?" Mara said.

"Nothing. Sydney's just very funny." She laughed at some unknown secret between them.

Twenty minutes later the food arrived with Sydney. She greeted everyone with hugs and kisses, with special attention to Leigha.

Mac was quiet and glanced at Mara often. He squirmed around in his seat.

After brunch, he pulled her out to the balcony. He couldn't seem to keep his hands off her. As she passed one of the end tables, she glanced at something on his phone. "What's this?" She questioned with a tone of 'guilty before proven innocent'.

"Your gorgeous legs. I took it while you were dancing at the club. I couldn't help myself. I had fantasies about those legs wrapped around my waist for a while now." He had the smile of a cat who caught the canary.

She laughed and followed behind him, her heart raced at his touch. He would always have this affect on her. He spun her around to face him and pulled her body flush with his. Gently grabbing the back of her hair, he held her head in his hand. He had a slight smile as questions swam in his eyes. Tilting her face up to him, he leaned in and gave her a gentle kiss.

"Come sit with me. There's something I need to tell you." He sat in a lounger facing the ocean, settling her between his legs with her back to his chest. He buried his nose in her hair, breathing in the scent that would always remind him of his new home, her. They sat in silence for a while as a light warm breeze came off the ocean brushing their skin.

"I'm disappointed I missed the sunrise here in

Cancun," she said. She heard a low chuckle coming from his chest.

"Oh, *leannan*, I saw the sun rise this morning. It was the most beautiful sunrise I've ever seen."

She lightly smacked his thigh. "Oh, I see someone's feisty side is finally coming out. I like 'em feisty." He grabbed her hand and kissed it.

"What did you want to tell me?" She peered over her shoulder nervously as his green eyes sharpen on her.

He looked away, his eyes uneasy about telling her his news. Hearing the words would make it all too real. "Let me start off by saying, I know what I want and I'm not going to let you wiggle out of anything. I'm leaving the British Intelligence Agency." Her body tensed. "This is something I've wanted to do for a while. I'm burned out. I had a great career with them, but I need to move on with my life. This is the first time in a long time I took a holiday, and then I met you." Her shoulders relaxed. She turned her body to face him. Weariness consumed his face, as if his job had finally caught up with him. "I applied for a job in New York City with McKenzie, Bryan, and Knight, MBK Global Security. They need an international guy and they want me to start right away." He held his breath, waiting for her reaction.

She could imagine the questions going through his head. "I was wondering how we were going to make this work. It seems like fate might be on our side, twice." She held her hand to his clean-shaven jaw. "Well, it just so happens I'm in the city quite a bit. Maybe we could get together sometime."

She couldn't help but smile at her own freshness.

He lifted her up as she straddled his thighs. "I want to be crystal clear, *leannan*. I'm in love with you, and when a Scotsman falls in love, it's forever. Mac says...you're mine."

Tears came to the edges of her eyes as the passion emanated from her soul. Her eyes were always the windows to her truth. She would be his forever.

Without warning, his mouth came down on hers, nipping her full lower lip as he pushed his tongue into her mouth. She was unprepared for the upwelling of emotions that came with this kiss, but if the last couple days taught her anything, it was to live life to the fullest. Her tears stopped as passion took over. She answered his need with her own and pushed her tongue forward, swirling around his while nipping at his lips, wanting full access to everything he offered. She took control of the kiss and began to slowly move on his hardening cock.

He wrapped his hand in her hair and pulled her back with appreciation of his new creature. She looked at him shyly with flushed cheeks. When he laughed, her hands felt the vibrations of life and love. With a glimmer of mischief in his eye, he carefully rested her cheek in one hand as if he held a fragile piece of Venetian glass. "I always knew you had a *bite* to you. I like *Mara the Fierce*. Oh, the things I'm going to do to my kitten." He lightly smacked her ass.

His words with his smack shot right through her body. Words had never affected her like that before, but this man locked her heart and held the only key. She retorted, "Just remember, kittens have claws." Her smile faded as it gave way to the intensity of the moment. "I'm falling in love with you, too. It's real this time, full of light and hope. You make me stronger and better at being me. I need some time though. This is all so new to me. Mara says, Mac wins."

"You'll get some time, love, but this man is getting old and wants some beautiful Scot babies. We're going to have to make them boys because if the girls are anything like you, they'll have me wrapped around their little fingers in no time." His eyes became glassy.

She threw her head back and laughed until tears ran down her face. It occurred to her that she and Brock never talked about having children. She felt her younger self making a return to her body after a long time away.

She poked him in the chest. "Well, you're the one with control over our Italian boys, buddy."

"Yes, let's not forget who's in control." He winked at her as she laid her head on his chest to listen to his heartbeat, the heart that belonged to her.

She was still curious about one more thing. "Do you mind if I ask you a money question?"

"Sure."

"You're staying in a very expensive suite, and the dinner under the tent was extravagant. Does British Intelligence pay you that well?"

"Actually, I inherited money from my uncle, who was an engineer for the government. He didn't have any children, so my brothers and I are set for life. But that's not my style. I take pride in my work and I believe in what I do for my country."

"Well, that seems to be one more thing we have in common." She nuzzled her head into his neck and breathed him in.

"I have some things to wrap up today. We'll talk later about our trip to Scotland."

She jerked her head up in surprise. "You're taking me home with you?"

"To know the man is to know the land he comes from. My family will be thrilled to meet the woman who has captured me, heart and soul." He winked at her, lifting her off his lap.

Kissing her on the forehead, he turned to leave, not that she minded the view from the back. His ass was glorious. God, she had turned into an insatiable vixen. It must've been in the genes. Now there were two Luccenzo women who were vixens. It made her wonder about Leigha.

She spent the rest of the day with her sisters and Sydney, hanging out poolside. She filled them in on all her plans with Mac. Both Leigha and Raquelle commented on how happy she seemed and how they noticed major changes in her. Then, like it always did, the conversation turned to their latest projects. The sisters never let a day go by without talking about ideas for their works of art.

Leigha and Sydney went for a dip in the pool and splashed around when Raquelle turned to her. She kept her eyes on the two women as she leaned over. "Do you notice something going on between them? I know flirting when I see it."

"I've been kind of wrapped up in my own world, but now that you mention it, they're definitely flirting. What's going on with Leigha? I feel like she's changed somehow. Do you think she's interested in Sydney?"

"Well, whatever it is, it brings a smile to her face that I haven't seen in years. I guess only time will tell." Raquelle gave her best kitty cat smile as she bit down on her straw and wiggled her brows.

———◆———

*Mac took a* call from McFadden in the privacy of his suite.

"We sent our cleaners to the scene. It has Russian mob written all over it. Needless to say, it was already cleaned. My question is how the fuck did they know so quickly what was going on in Mexico? We barely had a chance to get in on it ourselves." Anger speared McFadden's words at being outdone by anyone, let alone the Russians.

"I don't really know. They have a lot of surveillance and contacts all over the world." He took a breath to ready himself for what he wanted to say to him. "By the way, Neil, I'm leaving MI6. I'm taking a job with the security firm MBK Global Security." He braced himself for the fallout.

"Congratulations, old man. Doing a lifetime in MI6 isn't for everyone. You'll be working for one of the top security firms in the world. I may be calling on you to help me with this Russian problem, though. It's still open. I'll need your expertise for the case. Good luck, Mac."

"Thanks, mate." He clicked off the phone with him. Something wasn't sitting right with him. It had been nagging at him as it sat just underneath the surface. Something felt off about Brock's death.

In the meantime, he would be focusing on his new life with Marabella. Hopefully, it would go smoother than their vacation. It seemed Eros was in the air, ready for his next target.

# EDGES

## *Art of Eros Series*
Book 2

Leigha Luccenzo is a strong confident woman who has her life under control. Her nightmares have returned. They haven't resurfaced since her days as a model. Her armor hides them keeping her restrained. She comes home to find her apartment in shambles, the possible doing of her ex-lover, the beautiful Sydney. As things begin to unravel, layers of lies start to peel away.

Dean is a hard edge man who has an appetite for beautiful women, fast bikes and shattered souls. His secrets bind him, keeping him from any real relationship. They latch onto him like heavy chains keeping him from his beloved Australia. He sees behind Leigha's armor, convincing her he can help becomes his mission. He hopes she's strong enough to handle what lies beneath. Has he found a woman strong enough to with stand his harbored pain?

Through events out of her control, Leigha's forced to face her demons head-on. As other people's secrets get entangled in her own, she struggles

to find her own identity. Can Dean be the man
to help her uncover the truth behind all the lies?

# ACKNOWLEDGMENTS

There are so many people to thank because you never write a book alone. Eventually it has to be shared, taken apart and put back together.

I want to thank my husband who didn't see me for many hours on end and still gives me his unwavering support. You're wonderful!

My mother, the actress and writer and who was brave enough to read this and give me feedback. Writing runs in the family as my brother was the first to publish a book on Miles Davis. I hope you're up there somewhere smiling down on me.

Elbow, friend and sister from another lifetime, fellow writer, write on.

Nikko, my muse, who was by my side each time I sat down to write. May he rest in peace with Koda Bear.

Thank you to my beta readers who weren't afraid to 'get real' with it. Your input was invaluable.

I want to thank anyone and everyone who read my book and took the time to leave a review.

# ABOUT THE AUTHOR

Kenzie lives with her husband in New England. She has been fortunate enough to travel all over the world to places like Africa, Greece, Switzerland, Holland, France, England and, of course, Scotland. Edinburgh is one of her favorite places. Creativity seems to be part of her soul as she paints portraits, takes photographs, and bakes. They have all added to her overactive imagination especially writing about strong women and alpha men. She looks forward to adding to her adventures and yours.

She loves to hear from her fans.
You can find her on:
Website: www.kenziemacallan.com
Sign up for her newsletter for cover reveals, news and giveaways
Facebook: www.facebook.com/kenziemacallan
Instagram: www.instagram.com/kenziemacallan
Twitter: www.twitter.com/kenzie_macallan
Email: kenziemacallan@gmail.com.